That Guy

By Belle Brooks

ISBN 9780648377009

That Guy
©2018 by Belle Brooks

Published by
Obie Books Po Box 2302
Yeppoon Qld 4701
AUSTRALIA

Edited: Lauren Clark
Proofread: Jenny Sims
Cover: Emma Wicker
Formatter: Jaye Cox

A NOTE TO THE READER

This book has been written using UK English and contains euphemisms and slang words that form part of the Australian spoken word, which is the basis of this book's writing style. Please remember that the words are not misspelled. They are slang terms and form part of everyday Australian vernacular.

Dedication

For Chris
You're imaginary.
You crashed into my mind like a wrecking ball.
I MUST find you so I can tell you I've dedicated this book to you.
Everybody needs a Chris in their life because with Chris, life would be so much better.

Chapter One

For the past five years, I've been on a diet. I like to refer to it as my 'train wreck' diet. Why? Well, that's because it always ends up derailing within a few weeks.

I have successfully gained five kilos during my latest attempt at weight loss, so I'd say I'm failing at this point. But I solemnly swear, I'll never give up because I'm a go-getter and giving up on my train wrecks is not in my nature.

Tomorrow, I'm sure I'll contemplate some miracle pill seen on an infomercial or even another fad liquid shake. Who knows? But right now, at this very minute, I must try to get through the delightful challenge of my weekly food shopping adventure.

Every time I set foot into the local grocery store, I hear soft whispering, whispers promising me a never-ending supply of sweet nothings. I'd be lying if I didn't admit I love to loathe such taunts. Today is no different.

Hey, Mindy, a six-pack of glazed doughnuts is on special. You've been such a good girl. A treat is in order. Mindy, there's a bonus! You can eat them all at once because there's a one-day only expiry date. The challenge is yours.

My mind is such a temptress with an alluring and seductive voice. Every time she corners me, I scream, *Yes! Yes! Put all of it in my mouth. I can take it. I can take it.*

I swallow hard and frantically hum as I try to drone out the promises of another happy sugar-filled ending. Sadly, it doesn't work. After taking only a few short steps into the complex, my eyes glue to one of the most beautiful creations I've ever seen. Gasping, I place my hand on my chest and breathe, "Oh, hell no. You're glorious."

Staring at the delicious red velvet cake, with the extra tiers of cream and freshly chopped strawberries placed symmetrically on top, I can already feel its rich sugar sparking my taste buds to life.

I must have it.

Do it, Mindy. You know you want to. You like it sweet and extra moist, now, don't you?

"Shut the heck up," I scold myself under my breath while trying to drown my mind's taunts. "Steamed vegetables and brown rice. Not cake."

But no matter how many times I think about

alternative healthier options, I can't divert my thoughts. I twist my lips to the side and press my teeth together as firmly as my chunky thighs currently are.

Having an internal battle with myself over this halo-lit red velvet cake has my head twitching and my eyes narrowing with every passing second. *You can do this, Mindy. Walk away! Walk away!*

I can't. Instead, I bend down and place my fingers against the container. A long arm reaches in front of me to claim the delicious treat. I smack the hand encroaching my vision, the one attached to a very hairy arm, and scoff loudly before proclaiming, "Mine," in a possessive growl.

I'm such a mess.

A man with greying hair scowls at me when I come to stand. He suddenly huffs in an over exaggerated manner, then stomps away.

How rude!

Placing the container encasing the rich treasure I won into the seat of my shopping trolley beside my handbag, I proudly bustle past the remainder of the long wooden table—the table filled with every imaginable decadent dessert.

Just this one cake can come home today, I promise myself. *Just this one.*

I've almost made it out of the danger zone when a silhouette catches the corner of my eye. I'm drawn to this figure instantly. I know I'm gawking with my mouth wide open, yet I can't seem to stop. *Mindy, cut it out. You look ridiculous.*

I draw in a large breath. I close my eyes before confirming I need to get the hell out of here and fast. But when my eyelashes flicker open, I'm greeted by the kindest smile I've ever seen beaming in my direction. This isn't a delicious dessert holding my attention. More like a tempting hunk of man meat.

"Hi," he speaks hesitantly.

Me? He's speaking to me? How can a man like that be addressing me in conversation? He's so perfect, like the ultimate macaroon, and I'm so … I'm a cream bun. A gooey white mess.

He's looking at me, waiting for a response. *Shoot!*

I blurt out the first thing that comes to mind. "Yeah, so … cake … eat … gotta go."

What the hell was that? I'm not two or four; I'm a grown-arse woman, for goodness' sake.

Moving like a gust of wind, I turn and stumble out of the bakery section, entering the fruit and vegetable aisle. Once the coast seems clear and Mr Too Hot to Trot, with his perfect charcoal hair and pale baby blue eyes, no longer fills my view, I applaud myself for having the stamina to move in such a way.

The elation I experience is short-lived because once a cob of corn is in my grip, I reprimand myself for acting like a complete and utter idiot in the first place.

Men and Mindy don't seem to mix.

It's not that I'm for the pink lady taco. I'm not. I

think lady's private parts are appalling to look at. But every time I'm in the company of a man, I blurt out stupid shit and run like a criminal in escape mode. I can't seem to be around the opposite sex in a romantic way, and sadly, this might explain the fact I'm twenty-nine years old and have never had a boyfriend.

Don't get me wrong. I've rolled around in the hay with a few gentleman suitors in my time. Oh yes, the Min-Star has had her fill of the *'D'*, but nothing more has ever eventuated. This might be because those romps only ever came after I'd danced the mambo with a bottle of liquor.

Every miserable foot placement I take has my heart heavy and my mind sombre. Right now, my life isn't exactly impressive in any way, shape, or form. I'm single, living in a tiny one-bedroom apartment with my furry feline friend, Fletcher, and I work in a horrible job as a receptionist for an escort service.

My best friend, Chris, is so gay that when he walks, glitter sprinkles from his arse, and my family lives kilometres away with no desire to ever set foot in a big capital city like Melbourne.

You seriously cannot make this shit up.

Turning into aisle three has my hands clammy and my bottom lip clamped between my teeth. Mr Too Hot to Trot is back. Oh damn, he's all sorts of fine wrapped in a pretty bow with a tag that says, *Mindy, care to own me?*

I do, I really do. Right now, I'm admiring his

backside. It appears he must have been at the gym prior to coming here; his loose muscle top and gym shorts spell this out. Every defined muscle from his neck down to his ankles screams, *Just look at my body. Go on—look at my body. I work out.* Boy, is he as mouthwatering from behind as he was from the front.

Mindy likey. Mindy likey a lot.

And there goes my immature brain, melting at the sight of a man.

Chapter Two

Beep. Beep. Beep.

The sound of my groceries scanning is the only noise I hear as I examine a poster pinned to the wall in front of me.

Do you want to win an exotic holiday for two?

I do, but I never win anything, not even a simple bingo game or raffle drawing, so there's no point in entering. But that doesn't stop my mind from drifting off into a daydream that has soft sand parting under my feet in a place where I'm completely relaxed, shaking my booty as I dance along the shore, free from all the worries of life. A canary yellow cocktail fills a tall glass wrapped securely in my hand. I throw my head back and smell the salty sea air. The breeze, so refreshing. The beach, alight with warm sunrays. The water, complete with crystal patterns, which sparkle like diamonds.

I need a holiday. I need a holiday with the man I've just stalked for nine aisles.

That guy was everywhere I was until I raced to the checkouts to escape from the perv mode I found myself permanently homed in. I checked him out in the same way I took to the freaking cake on entry. I had no shame. I had no morals. I stared and gawked. I devoured him in my mind. Oh, boy was he hot. But a man like him would never think twice about a woman like me. He's Hercules, and I'm Plain Jane.

The story of my life: Wanting things which are well and truly out of my league.

Biting down on my lip, I replay every step this mystery man took. The way the black tribal tattoo danced on his tight perfectly sculpted calf. His arse … I want to bounce a quarter off his arse. He was indeed an image of beauty, and now I'll have no choice but to bank his muscular frame into my memory and bring forth these images on cold and lonely nights when I wish for the company of a man's touch.

"Miss, do you want me to bag this toilet paper up for you? Or are you happy to take it as is?"

Toilet paper? I didn't buy any toilet paper. "Pardon, what did you say?"

She waves the pack of forty-eight rolls in the air as if she's auctioning it off to the highest bidder.

My face instantly heats. "I don't need that," I rush in saying.

"O-kay then."

She's young, so young, in fact, I think her mum still buys her toilet paper supply. Her glossed lips stretch wide as I find myself scowling in her direction. Her heavily blushed cheeks expose the most perfectly formed bone structure I've ever seen, and in a moment of pure jealousness, I decide I dislike her youthful appearance.

Where did my time go?

Where did my life go?

Did I miss the bus that rolls down the gloomy street of Single Town, the one transporting you to Happily-Ever-After Couple Land?

I wasted my youth in medical school with constant study. I forgot to stop, smell the roses, be young, and party. I hid away in libraries, lecture theatres, and study halls.

In three weeks, I'll be thirty. Thirty! And I'm still single.

There's a clearing of a throat followed by laughter, deep, from-the-stomach laughter. I twist my neck in his direction. Oh, good Lord. It's him. He's at checkout seven, right next to eight where I've loaded all my stuff onto the conveyor belt mindlessly.

"Hi." A twinge of humour lines his voice.

"Hi," I say, looking away as fast as I would when faced with a blood-covered mask worn on Halloween. Those things scare the crap out of me. His straight sparkling white teeth scare me just the same.

More laughter.

What's so goddamn funny?

I shift uncomfortably from one foot to the other. I brush my hand over my bottom, worried maybe my dress has caught in my knickers and I have an arse cheek poking out for the world to see. Swiftly, I relocate that same hand to my nose once I realise my derrière is protected and wipe at my nostrils hoping there's no boogers hanging out. I'm self-conscious as I sense his eyes violating the side of my head.

"Big weekend planned, hey?" I can hear the amusement in his tone.

"Pardon?" It's a croak of the word. Did my voice crack? When did I become a pubescent boy?

I glimpse in his direction and notice he's pointing at my checkout. I shift my eyes, following his elongated finger, and gasp. Not a small-sounding gasp. Not a medium level of noise either. But a noisy suck of air producing a choke-like sound.

What in the ever-loving fuck?

"Um. They're not mine," I spew out, racing to the moving conveyor belt, fumbling with the boxes—trying to make them disappear—and holding two against my chest. I've no frickin' idea how these boxes of condoms got there in the first place.

He laughs once more.

My palms are sweaty. My heart races as my mind forms visions of a pyramid designed out of inflated condoms. I think I'm having a stroke from the sudden rise in my blood pressure.

The man closes the gap between us. His breath rushes past my ear and down my neck. I immediately stand frozen in response. He's close to me. Too close.

"Wow. You have been busy while grocery shopping, haven't you?" There's no mistaking his humour.

I can't formulate a word or thought. I flick my eyes left, then right, up, then down. Flashes of products, ones I've never purchased in my life are waiting to be scanned by the pretty attendant.

I'm dreaming. I'm asleep. *Wake up. WAKE UP!* I scream internally.

"Men's deodorant. Lubricant. What's that? Seven, eight, nine boxes of frangers, and you have a lot of toilet paper. You must live in a share house like me by the looks of your items. Come to think of it, your shopping looks identical to mine. Funny, isn't it?"

Oh shit! Was I so focused on checking this man out as I shopped that I mimicked his movements and selected the same products he did?

"You should be mindful when shopping, you know. Concentration is an important part of selecting your essentials."

I did. I bought the things he did, and now I look like a total sex-obsessed weirdo who might be prone to a case of the runs. I want to die. Please God, strike me down with a bolt of electricity to the head. I could do with the experience of a heart attack right about now.

"These are for my boyfriend." It flies out of my

mouth. I lie. I lie with an unconvincing rattle enlaced with my mousey tone.

"He's a stallion, that boyfriend of yours then?"

"Um—"

"You're a lucky woman." His hand brushes my arm. "Or he's a lucky man."

I can't breathe. The two boxes of condoms I managed to grab and hold against my chest drop to the ground when my arms go limp.

"It was fun shopping with you. We should do it again sometime. Anyway, have a good night." He steps back and away from me. The suffocation stifling me dissipates.

I clutch the handle of my handbag still resting in the seat of my shopping cart with embarrassment spreading through my veins like wildfire. I scoop up the cake, and I walk. I keep walking. I don't look back.

"Miss! Hey, miss, you didn't pay. You didn't pay for the cake," the sweet young voice of the attendant calls after me.

I don't stop walking. I can't glance back.

I'm keeping this damn cake.

Chapter Three

I'm home. Safe. I'm more damaged than I was before I stole this dessert, and I'm miserable.

Why me? I find myself asking this question a lot, mainly because I'm the biggest screw-up ever to walk the earth.

Fletcher runs his long tail up the back of my leg, causing an itch from the tickle it creates.

"Hello, kitty." My tone is irritated as I bend suddenly to scrape my nails over my skin to alleviate the irritation at my calf.

Bang!

"Motherfffff—" I growl as my head collides with the bench I was hovering over. There's an instant ache. Clumsiness is my specialty, and it most certainly wasn't a good quality for a trainee doctor to possess, so when it came to choosing a career specialty, surgery was off the list of possibilities for me lickety-split.

Being the responsible party for the flying needle embedded into a hefty nurse's arse was not a great start to my second week of rotation either. I think our professors and the other students knew immediately that a scalpel and Melinda Grant should never be allowed in the same room together.

The upside: Karma made sure that flying prick found the butt of the meanest nurse to walk the halls of the Presbyterian University Hospital. And for this, I was grateful.

With two paracetamols sliding down my throat and an ice pack on my head, I fetch Fletcher, the neediest cat I've ever known, some tuna in spring water for his dinner. I tip it into his bowl. His tongue laps in mid-air as he attempts to catch tuna flakes in free fall.

"Chew your food. Fletcher, chew."

He hoovers his meal down like he hasn't eaten in more than a week.

"Or don't chew. Do what you want, Fletch. You do anyway."

I shift in the small space of the kitchen until I'm facing the sink. I rinse the empty tin, and as I do, I can't shake the feeling of being a fry fish swimming hopelessly in the vast sea we call life.

When will things change?

I press my palms against the bench I not long ago bashed my head on and scan the unit. Plain white walls I've yet to decorate even though I've been in this apartment for two years now. There are no photos displayed, only quaint furnishings placed around the rainbow rug Nana Violet left me in her will. I never liked that rug. In fact, I used to roll it up and stuff it under her couch when I visited her as a child. It's hideous and faded, but I can't seem to part with it, because every time I look down, it reminds me how much I loved my nana. How easy my youth and my life were before tweenhood and young adultness snuck up on me. Nana's rug is the part of her she left behind for me, and it's a piece of my life and history at a time I felt free.

The matte grey recliner pushed up against the rug's frayed edges calls my name when I come to shift my eyes. The book on its armrest only intensifies this summoning. I drag my feet the short distance until I drop exhausted in the chair and curl up into a ball, instantly grabbing the paperback and flicking through page after page.

Romance novels—how I love them. I wish I could fold myself into a small piece of origami sometimes and slip into the pages where I could live the lives of the characters filling them.

If only.

Click, click.

The lock on the front door turns over. I flash my vision towards the sound for a second, then dismiss the need to wait for his entry, focusing my attention back to the fight occurring between Delilah and Hugh in this addictive read.

"Hello, sugar dumplings. Daddy's home," Chris calls out with the most feminine tone a male can possess. The door slams shut.

"You know you don't live here." I'm all attitude in my welcoming. "One bedroom and all." I point at the wall behind me when Chris comes into view, the wall which separates the bathroom and the bedroom from the remainder of the place.

I lay the novel down onto the small circular table beside my recliner, the recliner situated by the only window I have in this entire unit. Well, the single window apart from the box fan-sized one residing in the bedroom and the bathroom.

Chris suddenly giggles.

No man should giggle, but Chris does. And it sounds like a hyena on crack. He says his many lovers find this to be an endearing quality, but for me, it's plain annoying.

Sexcapades and Chris: He juggles multiple suitors at once, and he's laid more men in the past year than I have in my entire sexual life. Chris's giggle brings all the dicks to the yard, as he often says. It seems mine makes them turn and run away from the milk bar.

How does he do it? Churn out man after man? Give his entire heart to someone he's just met only to allow it to be crushed over and over? He won't admit it, but

Chris loses in love all the time even though he's convinced himself love is not something anyone should want to attain.

"What ya doing, sugar?" he says with a Southern drawl.

I wish he would drop these short-spurt accents he adopts. "I was reading."

"Oh." A hint of a smile touches his lips. "So I bought you a little something to cheer up your sad-as-fuck face." He holds a pink gift bag in front of his chest with one hand while his other hand is placed on his hip at the same time as his head tilts to the side.

I can't see through the bag. Initially, I've no idea what could be inside since no store label is displayed. But then I have a feeling, this realisation, that this gift being delivered by Mr Fairy, Fuck All the Men in Australia has something to do with a conversation we shared about a week ago. My suspicion grows even more firm when his manicured eyebrows suddenly sit a few centimetres from my face. They wiggle up and down over the top of his enormous Bambi sized green eyes.

"Are you wearing mascara again?" I mumble.

"No, doll face, I've had my eyelashes tinted. You should try it." He pecks my cheek with his sticky glossed lips as he drops the bag onto my lap. "Open, open. I think you're going to love." His voice reaches an impressive Oprah giveaway pitch on the word *love*. "Why are you so glum all the time? You sure know how to take the sparkle out of the world, Miss Sad, Hasn't Had the '*D*' in a Millennium."

I sigh right as Chris shuffles his bony butt down beside mine in the chair. He wraps his long scrawny arm around my shoulders. His blond Justin Bieber hair brushes against my cheek. "I love you, Minty Mindy. It will all be okay if you open the bag."

"Fine." I smile, peeling back the straw like handles. I already know a new friend is waiting inside for me. One which probably requires batteries and slips between one's legs.

I wasn't wrong. I'm never wrong when it comes to gifts from Chris.

"Isn't he won-der-ful?" Chris draws out every syllable as though this is the most beautiful piece of machinery he's ever laid eyes on. In all seriousness, it's probably the only piece of machinery he knows the ins and outs of. "Um, the rainbow colouration was necessary because he's a dream. A fantasy. Eight speeds of pure delight."

"Chris, you can't buy me a vibrator."

"I can, and I did. What are friends for if they don't help their besties find their happy places somehow? Now maybe you'll smile, and these frown lines currently growing deeper and deeper right here ..." He runs his finger around my lips. I smack his hand away. "... these might disappear." My left eye spreads wide due to his fingers parting it. "Girl! You need to use the moisturisers and cleansers I buy for you." He sighs. "You could not survive without me."

Chris is right about one thing: I couldn't survive without him.

"Get your hands off my frown wrinkles, you crazy man." I bat his hand away again and stand. "Thank you for your generous gift. I'll add it to the other purchases you supply me with, shall I?"

"Use it," he growls as he wiggles into the centre of the chair before crossing one leg over the other. "Trust me, babe, it's so good."

"You bought one of these for yourself, didn't you?"

"Oh, hon. Oh, sugar tits. Oh, Minnie Moo. I have six. In six different colours." His hands frame his face in the perfect *Vogue* pose. "Look at me. I know my products. I ain't no amateur when it comes to bedroom playtime."

I can't help but giggle. There's one thing I can say about Chris: he's pure entertainment.

"Of course, you do." My smile broadens.

"So tell me." His tone fills with curiosity. "Did you sign up for the online dating site I was telling you about?"

"Um ... so ... no."

He chuckles. "I thought not. I took the liberty of doing it for you."

My jaw drops. Chris didn't. He wouldn't.

Yes, he would. It's Chris. Chris knows no boundaries.

"Run along. Get your laptop. I think you're going to

be chuffed with my creation." He flutters his eyelashes. "You already have two spankings, a kiss, and a lick of the lips."

"A spanking? A kiss? A what? Are you speaking English?"

"Oh, you'll see." He wiggles his eyebrows, then uncrosses his legs before standing. "Give me a minute." He disappears as quickly as he spoke. I can only assume he's raced off to get my laptop.

I slump my shoulders. My head follows suit. Today has not been a good day for me. First, there was my shopping trip debacle with the hottest guy I've ever laid eyes on, and the shoplifter status that came with the stolen cake still resting on my bench. Then a gift of a rainbow-coloured vibrator to rid me of my apparent misery. Now, this. Can today finally wrap me up in a large quilt and smother me to death?

There's a flash of pink, the pink colouration of Chris's T-shirt whizzing by me. "Sit, sit." He pats the fabric pillowtop of the chair he's pulled out from under the two-seater dining table. "Come see what I've done." My assumption was correct. The screen on my laptop goes from black to lit in seconds.

I don't move. Instead, I take a long inhale and let out an even longer exhale.

"Holy crap. You have even more spankings. Oh, that guy is nice-looking. I can see it. I can see it." Chris suddenly holds his hands out in front of his face, moving them like a picture frame he's trying to capture me in. "Yes, I think this will be a good match."

"Stop." I shake my head. "I don't want to do online dating."

"Mush phush. You don't know what's good for you. I do. Come now, and sit."

Reluctant, I drag my feet towards him. *Oh, boy!*

Chris's arm wraps around my shoulder when I sit. He moves the laptop a fraction until I see the full screen. He scrolls the arrow, clicking away until a picture of me fills my vision.

I'm wearing a lot of make-up, more than I usually would. My blue eyes are bright and alive, my blonde hair falls over my shoulder, and I'm smiling. I'm actually smiling.

My lips lift.

"You're such a beauty," he whispers.

"Where did you get this photo?"

"My birthday bash last year. Look at your tits in this picture. They're busting out of your top. I've heard straight men love the boobs, so I found the bustiest picture I had of you. Voila." He flicks his hands to the side, as one would when on a diet infomercial showcasing a new health product. *Have I just become an online product for the opposite sex?*

"It's a good picture of me." I'm surprised I like it. I'm not usually a fan of photographs of myself.

"Girl!" Chris's lips purse. "You're all types of fine."

"Pffft." I've never seen myself as attractive, but in this photograph, with all my happiness displayed, I don't look half bad.

"Okay, so, this is your description. Give it a read and tell me what you think," he says, clapping.

Name: Melinda Renee Grant
Born: October 2nd, 1988
Age: Twenty-nine
Hair: Blonde
Eye Colour: Blue
Height: 165 cm
Occupation: Doctor

I stop reading and twist my head until I'm staring at Chris. "I'm not a doctor anymore."

"You're still qualified. You're still Dr Grant."

"It's lying. I don't want to lie."

"You're still a doctor—you're just not a practicing doctor."

"And we both know why." I hitch my eyebrows high on my forehead.

"Stop." He places his hand on my arm. "Just keep reading."

I take a long inhale and turn my vision back to the screen.

Hobbies: Reading, dancing, and meditation.
Likes: Cold, rainy afternoons curled up with a book. Picnics. Dancing on the beach. Romance films. Go-carts. Pool. Barbecues, and the stars.
Dislikes: Smoking and almost all physical

activities.

I laugh. It's true. I'm not one for hiking, fishing, camping, exploring, or exercise.

Admires: Christopher Joseph Grandy. My best friend.

I flick my vision in Chris's direction. "Really? You? You couldn't put Audrey Hepburn, Jane Austen, or Oprah Winfrey? It's gotta be you?"

His smile touches his eyes. "I'm way better than those people."

"And you have many tickets on yourself."

"If you don't love yourself, then who will?"

I smack his chest.

"What? I'm honest."

I shake my head, turning my attention back to the screen.

About: I'm quiet, shy, and well-educated. I like the subtle and small things in life. I'm easily pleased, low-maintenance, and looking for love. I'm not interested in casual hook-ups or one-night stands.

"That's it? This is all you put about me? I'm more than these things Chris. Aren't I?" I look at Chris, deflated and unsure of my own attributes. Am I more than what he's detailed on this site?

"Of course, you're more than this. Stop with the sad eyes already. Mindy, nobody's going to read a long-winded spiel, mm-kay? Trust me. It's going to bring all the men to your milk bar."

"Chris!"

"What? It will. Straight men love the milk bar."

I roll my eyes. "So what now?" I twist a strand of my hair around my finger as nervousness bubbles away in the pit of my stomach.

"Now we look through all these gentlemen, and the one lady who sent you a big smooch. I guess I should add you're not a lesbian in there somewhere." He giggles, seemingly to himself. "We check out who's responded, then I'll teach you how to use the site."

This site. I shift my vision to the headline at the top of the screen.

Romance Gold.
The perfect way to find the one you've been searching for!

"I'm not so sure," I remark, continuously reading the name of the site and its tagline.

"You're going to love it."

Love finding love? I highly doubt it. I can't talk to men, and men don't talk to me. Well, except for the piece of eye candy at the grocery store earlier tonight. Something about that guy was different to most of the men I've met, yet I can't quite put my finger on what. Who was he? Will I ever see him again? I bite my lip. Hopefully not. The last thing I need is a reminder that people like me want things they can't have.

Chapter Four

Nightshift. How I hate working nights. I'd much prefer to work throughout the day, but my workplace operates twenty-four hours, and nights are when most of the action happens ... when most of our bookings for following days, weeks, and months are confirmed.

My job: To pencil in appointments for our many escorts. To make sure all bookings are entered, and instructions for the meetings are communicated to the employees.

Our cliental: Wealthy, high-end, straightforward, money-making businessmen and women.

There's no love involved in these appointed hook-ups. There's no illusion of a future revolving around two-point-five children, a dog, and a little girl's dream house. It's piles upon piles of hundred-dollar bills and bustling schedules. Being perfectly presentable, showing up on time, and giving the client *all* he desires is a must. I guess it's like online dating, but a millionaire's version, for hook-ups and see-ya-laters.

Working here at Kit on High fascinates me even though I can't say I enjoy it in any way, shape, or form. I stumbled into the job after replying to an online ad. It had little information about the actual profession I'd be walking into, just a request for a receptionist. I still, after answering these phones for the past two years, can't fathom how two people can put on a show of attraction and fondness when they barely know each other. It's even harder to comprehend when you consider most of these meetings take place in luxurious venues in rooms packed full of people and always end in a sexual encounter.

Ring, ring, ring.

I shift the microphone attached to my headset in front of my mouth before pressing the accept button on the console situated beside the computer. "Welcome to Kit on High, you're speaking with Mindy. How can I be of service?"

"Good evening, Mindy, it's Matthew Muller. How are you, sweetie?"

"I'm great, Mr Muller. Another booking?"

"Please. You have such a beautiful voice. I wish I knew what you looked like."

I roll my eyes. Matthew says these exact words to me every time he calls to make a booking. He'd be less than impressed if he saw what I looked like, though. "Mr Muller, you're very kind. Now, your booking, how can I help?"

"I'd like Callie for an event at the end of October. Is she free?"

"Date and time please, Mr Muller?" I click the mouse now cupped under my hand, bringing up Callie's calendar.

"Yes. I need Callie from five p.m., Friday, the twenty-ninth, until ten a.m., Sunday, the thirty-first. Can this be arranged?"

"I will check. Please give me a moment." I scroll down the page to find Callie's slot for the requested dates only to spy the weekend highlighted in orange, which means a tentative booking has already been placed. I read the name: Matthew Muller. Callie would have created this booking herself because the only person who can add a tentative booking is an escort herself. It's lucky for Matthew that Callie did because every other day up until the end of December in her schedule has already been allocated to a client. "Callie will attend, Mr Muller."

"Perfect." He sounds relieved, which is strange because I'd not noticed his tone was tense prior to him saying this.

"What requirements would you like me to note for your appointment?"

There's a long pause.

"It will be a weekend on the water. Many string

bikinis are a must. And an evening gown for a function on the yacht Saturday night. I'll supply the necessary lingerie and jewellery." He pauses. "I want Callie to wear red. Red looks so radiant against her pale skin."

I type the details into the notes section as Matthew rattles them off. "Yes, sir," I say once completed.

"You don't fancy some time out to sea do you, Mindy?"

I fake a giggle. "Water and I don't mix, Mr Muller."

"You say this every time I ask you to come out on my boat." I can hear his amusement.

I giggle again.

"Okay, beautiful, you have yourself a good night. My assistant will send you the address details, and if I think of anything else, I'll pick up the phone and call you."

"Thank you for using Kit on High. Have a lovely evening, Mr Muller."

"Goodbye, Mindy."

The line goes dead.

Pressing the end button on the console has me leaning back in my leather chair. If only making dates for myself was as easy as making these appointments for our escorts. How am I so confident in my job on the phone with the opposite sex, but in everyday life, I'm a bumbling mess?

Beep, beep, beep, beep, beep, beep.

You have to press six numbers into a keypad outside my door to gain access not only to the room I work out of but to the entire floor.

I sit stiff and upright in my chair at the sound, placing my palms on the glass table in front of me. I turn my eyes towards the blacked-out door panels, awaiting the entry of who I believe will be my boss, Ms Kathleen High. Usually I'd know beforehand who's entering, but since the security camera's outside the door are currently on the blink, I'm left blinded.

The door opens. Platinum blonde hair and blue eyes fill the gap between the door and its frame, causing me to relax my posture.

"Hey, hey, gorgeous. Is Kathleen around?" Callie's voice is soft, smooth, and sweet like honey. Her toothy smile reminds me of the same one Julia Roberts flashes in many a movie. The door closes.

"No, she's not in yet." I smile.

"Shoot," Callie tsks.

"I expect she should be arriving any minute, though." I peek at my watch. "It's one forty-five a.m."

"Okay, I'll wait. She's never later than two." As she sits, Callie's long legs seem to stretch on forever until they disappear under her small black leather mini-skirt. There's no doubting she's in immaculate shape with a body created for the catwalk. She has toned arms, a tiny waist, and a large bust currently spilling out of a corset top now sitting an inch from my face.

"How're my appointments looking?" She's bent at her midsection, sliding my mouse under her hand and tapping the glass over the top of it with one of her long black-painted nails. "Booked until December. Oh, and Matty did take that weekend. Good."

"I just took the booking."

"Fantastic."

"Why does he always book in the early hours of morning?"

"Um." Callie stops speaking. Her chin tilts slightly, in a way I assume she's thinking about or searching for a reply. "Let's just say he has a mind that never stops processing. He doesn't sleep much, and he's always working on something." She stands, towering over me. "Oh, I love your dress." Her instant change in tone, from monotone to chirpy, implies the conversation change. Callie's always so lovely and complimentary, and she's also incredibly smart from what I've gathered from our often-brief conversations. Out of all the escorts, Callie's the one who most has her finger on the pulse. She doesn't wait for her calendar to fill up; she takes the initiative and ensures her clients are rebooking her before she's even left her appointment with them. Maybe it's why she's the most sought-after escort here. Perhaps I could learn a lot from Callie on how to sort through the plethora of men I might possibly find myself facing thanks to this new online dating world I'm currently entering. I'd like to find the right guy for me in a very short timeframe.

"Where did you get it from? I love those red roses against the black. What material is this dress made from?" Her blue eyes sparkle when I gaze up at her, and I'm not sure if she does like my flowy dress or if she's just being nice.

"I actually can't remember."

"Well, it suits you."

"Thank you."

Ring, ring, ring.

"Welcome to Kit on High, you're speaking with Mindy. How can I be of service?"

"Melinda, it's Kathleen, and we have a big problem. Is Callie with you?"

"Yes."

"Put her on."

"Okay, doing it now."

I pull the headset from my head and hold it in Callie's direction. "It's Kitty, and she said there's a problem, and she doesn't sound happy."

Callie's red-stained lips tug upwards. "I'm sure she's acting dramatic. She's often dramatic." Callie slips the headpiece into her hair. "Hey, boss, what's wrong?"

Callie's face is mute of expression. "What happened?" Her eyes go bug wide. "Oh no. Is she okay?" There's a long pause. "It was bound to happen. She doesn't eat enough, and she probably got dizzy and passed out. I've been warning Alice that eating properly was essential." Callie shakes her head. "Yeah, I can manage it, but I want your cut as well as mine." She purses her lips. "It's called business, Kitty

Fingerlings, and my fingerlings want all the dollars." She laughs. "Don't you hate it when we repeat your catchphrases back to you?" Callie tips her head to the side. "Right-o, I'll be there, and I'll charge my phone so you can get a hold of me. But tomorrow, I need to talk to you. It's important, and why I came in," she says, laughing once more before hanging up and passing me the headset. "Got to fly, beautiful. I'll see you tomorrow morning?"

"I'm not on the night shift tomorrow. I have the weekend off."

"Well, enjoy your weekend, sugar." A quick turn on her six-inch heel has her hips swaying in the direction of the door. I really need to learn how to sway my hips like Callie does. It's sexy—guys find it hot. I need to go from floppy sausage to sexy diva. I'm going to appoint Chris to help me with mastering the seductive saunter. I'm sure there's a course on how to be alluring yet graceful. There's a course for everything these days.

I open my internet browser.

Courses on how to be a sexy woman.
Search.

I sit scrolling down the page, wondering how many of these will open to porn. I take a risk and click on one, reading, *learn to be as sexy and sultry as our women.*

The alarm at the door beeps. My computer speakers fill with the sound of a woman who is either having the world's most magical orgasm or she's dying. I don't look. Instead, I click my mouse frantically. "Close, no close. CLOSE!" I say in a panic.

"Coffee. Black. Strong. Now!" Kathleen stomps through the door, wearing a hoodie covering her natural tan and usually made-up face. "Watch porn on your own time, Melinda. Not at work."

Oh, thank fuck! The screams of delight suddenly cease.

"I wasn't …You see, it was …" *Just let it go. She won't believe you.* "No porn. Okay, sorry." I already know from this point to keep my head down and to be as quiet as humanly possible. When Kitty gets in a mood, all hell can break loose over even a minor situation. And I wouldn't think using the work equipment to view porn is a minor issue. When Kitty thinks you're doing personal stuff on company time, she gives you the stink eye and lets you know how pissed she is at you at every given opportunity.

"I'm not paying you to get your rocks off."

"Yes, Kathleen. I understand. It won't happen again," I reply quickly.

I don't breathe until she makes her way into her office. As soon as she's gone, I drop my head and mutter, "Seriously, why me?"

Kathleen stays in her office and barely says two words to me after her arrival. I deliver her coffee, keeping my eyes turned downward and my lips zipped. She's in full dramatics tonight, so much so that

I begin to worry about how pent up she seems. I sit, listening, extending my neck in the direction of her closed door, trying to decipher the words she's suddenly screeching down what I know to be the work phone because one of the many lines out is lit red, and I'm the only other person here.

There are bumps and banging, even a moment when she roars, then everything goes quiet again.

What's going on?

Beep, beep, beep, beep, beep, beep.

"Morning," Indie chimes, walking towards the desk.

"Morning," I answer, distracted. *Maybe Kathleen's had some plastic surgery gone wrong.*

"Busy night?" Indie puts her handbag on the table beside mine.

"Yes. Alice passed out. Kitty's in the worst mood I've ever seen her in. Be warned, there's been banging and lots of shouting coming from out of there." I point in the direction of Kathleen's office.

"Really? Oh crap! Well, this shift is going to suck."

I offer Indie a sympathetic smile.

"I'll call Alice and make sure she's okay. I love her; we've become friends, you know?"

I nod.

"You're good to leave when you're ready." Indie runs her fingers through her long, straight purple hair.

"Is it six already?"

"Five minutes to, yes."

I shake my head before throwing my arms into the air and pulling my shoulders back in a stretch.

"You look beat."

"I am. I'll see you on Monday?"

"Sounds good."

I scoop my bag against my chest and shuffle my weary feet across the floor.

"Oh, by the way, nice dating profile you have on Romancing Gold, Mindy."

I swallow hard. I know I've turned the colour of a rose from my sudden embarrassment.

I don't turn around. Instead, I hang my head in shame.

I need to delete my account. How mortifying.

Chapter Five

My mint green Barina hatchback stands out like a sore thumb in the public parking lot as I walk towards it. I take a moment to remember the day I picked up this somewhat unusual coloured car. It was right after I'd moved here. It was the day I told myself my life would change forever, and my many problems and mistakes would remain buried far away back home in Queensland where they couldn't haunt me anymore.

I ran away from home. What twenty-seven-year-old woman finds herself running away like a confused teenager? Me, that's who. But I had a choice to make, and the one I made ensured I stood on my own two feet after such a colossal downfall.

Coming to Melbourne was my fresh start. The place I would find the new and improved version of myself. I knew I'd have to figure out how to fit in with society and not hide away from all the things happening around me, and I believed, at the time, Melbourne would be the perfect destination to accomplish such a task. That and to find the love of my life. It appears I was wrong.

Finding the love of my life: IMPOSSIBLE. He's not out there anywhere. Perhaps I wasn't created in a pairing of one soul split into two. Maybe I have been doomed to walk this Earth solo from the very beginning of my creation.

Climbing into the car, I turn the ignition over. The automatic windshield wipers swish back and forth without hesitation. I sit, waiting for the misty fog to be wiped from the glass. It doesn't take long, and as I pull out from my parking space, I have only one destination in mind: The Quarter.

The Quarter is my favourite café. It's the place I met Chris not long after I arrived in Melbourne, and it continues to be the spot where we catch up after each one of my shifts, be it early morning or late afternoon.

The streets are quiet as I commute into the city. The traffic lights shine green the entire way down the main drag, and before I know it, I round the final turn and pull into a car park right out in front of the café. I leap from the car and dart through the empty tables filling the sidewalk. I don't stop until I've charged through the front glass doors and marched to the usual booth Chris and I have claimed as our own.

Chris is seated, tapping away on the keys of his laptop when I reach the padded cream seat with the well-placed buttons that don't end until halfway up the chocolate-painted wall.

Chris doesn't look up or even acknowledge my arrival.

"Indie knows," I blurt out, bypassing any polite greeting.

"Hello to you too." Chris flicks his eyes in my direction.

"Hello. Indie knows."

"Knows what exactly?"

"She knows I have an online dating profile. I'm deleting mine as soon as I get home. I shouldn't let you talk me into these things. What must she think of me?"

Chris shakes his head. "You won't delete it."

"Morning, Mindy. How are you this morning?"

I swivel my head and spy an outstretched hand holding a mug of coffee beside me. "Morning, Annie." I force a smile.

"You look like you need this. What's up, buttercup?"

"Arrrgh. You don't want to know."

Annie blows her brown fringe off her eyebrows before sitting down beside me. "That bad, hey?"

"She's dramatic. And here I thought I was supposed to act the queen." Chris giggles

Annie giggles.

I do not.

"I set Mindy up with an online dating account, and it seems her co-worker has found out. She's having a fit about nothing. If she took a moment to think about it, her co-worker only knows she's on there because she too must have an account."

My shoulders suddenly drop. I hadn't even thought about such a scenario.

"Everyone's doing it, boo-boo, so chillax and drink your coffee," Chris instructs calmly.

"I have an account," Annie admits.

"You do?" I'm surprised by this because Annie's beautiful, young, and has flawless brown skin. Her dark eyes, long, slender face, and well-kept physique complete her impressive package. She has no reason to need an online dating account, so why does she? "Good for you."

Why did I say that?

Annie places her hand on my arm. "There's nothing to be embarrassed about for either of us, Mindy."

"Annie, table six," a man's voice I don't recognise shouts.

"Gotta run. New duty manager. He's not with our program yet. He's all like 'I'm the boss, bark, bark, bark'. He'll learn, though. Drink your coffee and let it go." Annie turns on her heel and scoots across the room.

"See? Told you." Chris drops his chin and turns his eyes back to the screen of his laptop.

I take three deep breaths and tell myself to release the tension I carried in here with me as I close my eyes.

CLANG!

I open my eyes swiftly, swivelling my head until I see Annie bent down picking something I can't quite make out up from off the floor.

"I don't know why you care so much about what people think. I thought by now I'd have talked this out of you. It turns out you're a stubborn project," Chris interjects.

I point at my chest. "Project, huh?"

"A very difficult one. I've met politicians more relaxed than you."

I laugh.

"Drink your coffee."

"Yes, boss."

The sweet aroma of the coffee Annie delivered takes over my senses. I sigh, then immediately relax back into the soft backing of the booth. I bring the mug to my lips. The tip of my nose separates the artistic foam, and the first sip of my daily ritual slides down my throat like silk. I hope when I die, heaven is like The Quarter: posh, full of elegant furnishings and coffee, and lots of coffee in every variety. Life isn't worth living without coffee, especially the ones The Quarter serves.

"Really, Frothelupagus?" Chris throws a black napkin at my face. "You're such a messy drinker and eater, by the way. You have foam on your nose again."

"I know." I take the napkin, dabbing it gently against my skin. "Some guy might find this to be an endearing quality one day, you know. Like your giggles."

"I think not. Your oink-like eating style has nothing on my giggles." Chris rolls his eyes.

"Shut up. Tell me, what's the special today?" I peek over the rim of the coffee mug which I again cup in my hands.

"Caramel tart with fresh whipped cream and strawberry ganache."

I swear I'm instantly drooling, but I should say no to the tart. New diet, new willpower needed. "I might pass on the tart," I confess. "I'm starting my diet again."

"It shouldn't be too far away." Chris ignores my confession the same way he always does when I speak of dieting. "I ordered about five minutes before you stomped in here all worked up and seething." Chris taps away on his keyboard.

"Did you hear what I said?"

Chris bobs his head. "Yep."

"Well, you should know I'm serious this ..."

"You're not fat. You're always announcing your diet status. You'll eat the tart because it brings you happiness, and because life is way too short to deny yourself such pleasures, so give up while you're ahead and save your energy for shoving your crusted shell with caramel lathered inside it down your throat."

"I'm serious, Chris!"

"Okay," he scoffs. "The lemon meringue we got

yesterday was not my cup of tea, but caramel tart ... hell, anything ending in tart ... yes please." Chris licks his lips.

"Yeah, because you're a tart. It's why you're all excited—"

"Born and bred, sweetheart," he declares.

"—And I'm going to pass on dessert today," I finish.

"Sure, whatever. You'll eat it."

"I might ask for an apple. I can't keep eating special mystery desserts every day with you. I can't even keep asking you what they are when I arrive. Maybe I need to look for a new venue, a healthier alternative to our daily catch-up."

"Said ya mum."

"What does that even mean?"

"Just that. You're acting like a mum—quit it. Dessert is an important part of happiness."

"Whatever," I say, shifting my attention towards Annie, who gives me a subtle wave from a few tables over. "How's your *Twilight*-inspired, male-on-male vampire novel coming along?" I shift my attention back to Chris with full interest in knowing the answer, and not just because I want to change the direction of our conversation.

"Yeah, so I'm not doing that anymore. Yesterday's news. It turns out vampire books need lots of blood in them, and I am not a fan of blood. I seriously get queasy to the point where I think I'll pass out, even writing it." Chris pokes out his tongue. "It's yuck."

I laugh.

"I'm currently writing a romance about a fab and a drab guy who meet. The fab guy makes the drab guy completely fab. They fight for gay rights on a picket line, fall madly in love, and become the first gay couple to wed on the day marital equality passes through parliament. Perfection!"

"But gay rights have already passed through parliament."

"I know, but this novel is set before that."

"Oh."

"So what do you think?"

"Bestseller right there, Chris. Soon, you won't even have to be a personal shopper to the rich and snobby to earn your keep."

"I know," he chimes, so matter-of-factly. "One day I'm going to be a world-renowned author, and you're going to be my busty sidekick-slash-PA-slash-manager-slash-bestie until the day we die. Oh, and don't forget my drug-delivering doctor, because something tells me to be such an author, you have to reach a level of insanity which requires a lot of prescription drugs." His lips part as he portrays an exaggerated expression of shock. "Did I say the drug thing out loud?" He presses his fingertips against his mouth. "Our little secret, right?"

"You're a clown."

"Whatevs, girl! You're goin' to wanna go everywhere I am. You know ya will." And there's his fake Southern accent coming out to play once more.

"I'll be at your beck and call, don't you worry." I roam my vision across the restaurant. I take a rather ambitious mouthful of coffee while observing each new face popping up. I scan the service counter.

The moment my eyes connect with his, I choke out, "Oh shit!" before gulping heavily and sliding down the soft material of the chair until my butt cheeks connect with the carpet flooring. With one quick flick of my wrist, I pull the white linen tablecloth, the one hanging over the sides of the table, across my head and use it as a shield. "Son of a bitch," I curse between clenched teeth.

"Mindy, what are you doing?" Chris's large eyes suddenly appear upside down in front of me. "Get yourself off the ground and out from under there."

"I can't." It's a hushed deliverance. "Vamoose. I'll explain later. Act normal."

"Normal? Because what you're doing is soooo normal." I hear Chris say as he disappears, lowering my tablecloth hideaway.

"She's under the table, isn't she?" It's a deep voice that causes my heart to thump wildly.

Oh, crap. He saw me. Not only did he see me, but he also came over here. What's wrong with this guy? Why would he do such a thing?

"And you would be?" Chris says. I picture one of his eyebrows cocked high on his forehead as he pistol grips his chin.

"I would be Arlie. And you would be?"

"Chris, the under-table escapee's best friend."

Arlie—what an uncommon name. I've never met anyone called Arlie. It's not like he gave me his name at the grocery store when he was making me squirm with embarrassment.

"So, she's under the table, Chris?"

There's silence.

"I'm guessing you know why she's under the table, Arlie?"

"I have a few ideas."

"Well, I'll be a monkey's behind. How have I not heard about you, Mr Tall, Dark, and Handsome?"

Chris, now is not the time to be hitting on the poor man. Just tell him to go. I telepathically try to send Chris this critical message.

There's a long pause.

"Would you like to join me? I'm sure Mindy would prefer you'd leave, considering she's hiding like an outlaw. But hon with the buns, I sure would like to get to know you better," Chris says in his fake Southern drawl. "Take a seat. Relax your bulging muscles, or don't—I'm good either way."

Oh, not today, Chris. You'll not take this man home, turn him gay, or do whatever it is you do to make men fall in love with you.

"I'm here," I yell like a deranged woman while crawling out from my shelter, only to be stopped when I reach a pair of white sneakers. I tilt my chin up and stare into narrow eyes.

"So, it's Mindy? Nice name."

"Melinda." My voice is barely audible.

"Sorry, what did you say?" Arlie asks.

"Melinda." I speak louder.

"Melinda. Even prettier." He grins. "Arlie." He reaches out his hand.

"I heard." His warm fingers wrap around my wrist, and with one quick pull, I'm standing. His lips stretch across his face. "I'm guessing you dropped something under the table and you were down there looking for it?"

I rip my hand from his and nod. I don't know what else to do.

"I'm going to use the gentlemen's room and leave you two to get introduced, or whatever's happening here. Mindy, you owe me one hell of a story later," Chris says.

I swallow hard, not taking my eyes away from Arlie's to look for Chris.

"Hi." Arlie's tone is soft.

"I-I-you know—" My tongue ties.

"I wouldn't have come over if you hadn't dropped to the floor so quickly." He folds his top lip under his bottom as if stifling laughter. "So what were you looking for?"

"You know, just things."

"Things?"

"Yeah, things." I rock on my heels, pretending to

place my hands into imaginary pockets at the front of my dress.

"Like a lost earring?"

I look at the floor.

"Did you lose an earring?"

"Well—" I turn my eyes back to his. "No! Not an earring."

Arlie wears his smirk like some smirk-trained professional. I run my fingers over the hoops dangling from each of my earlobes.

"A fork maybe?"

"Possibly," I mumble, knowing full well that no matter what I say, he'll be able to tell I'm lying.

"Whatever you've lost, I hope you find it."

I sigh a breath of relief. He's letting this awkward situation die. "Oh, me too," I say, way too enthusiastically. *What am I doing?* "Hi, bye. Have a good breakfast."

"Hi," he says as if we had just bumped into each other and the previous conversation hadn't even taken place.

"I was just leaving." It flies from my tongue like verbal diarrhoea.

"Okay. Hi. Bye. Have a good day then."

"You too." Without thinking, I grab my handbag and walk back out the glass doors of The Quarter as tense as I was when I entered through them.

Arlie, what's your deal?

Five minutes later, Chris stands in front of the car

outside the café with his bright multi-coloured laptop bag slung over his shoulder. A crowd forms behind him as he waves what I believe to be a receipt in front of his forehead. His nose crinkles. His mouth opens wide. His lips move. I can't hear what he's saying, but I believe he's shouting, *"What gives?"*

Chris's stance becomes rigid. His eyes dip down until he's scowling, and I know he's pissed at me. I can always tell when Chris is not happy because he takes the same stance and demeanour every time.

Beeeep!

I hold my hand hard against the horn for a moment, hoping Chris will hop out of the way and take the train home today instead of relying on a lift back to his place from me. The engine of my car idles, and as it does, I sit, staring at Chris through the windshield. I take long, deep breaths to lessen a sense of stupidity currently steamrolling my guts. *Not today, Chris. I would like to leave now. Let me go. Everybody from inside the café is looking at us, Arlie included.*

"Move," I shout.

Chris shakes his head.

"Move."

Chris shakes his head again.

"Bloody move."

Chris doesn't move. Instead, he takes a step closer to the bonnet, which annoys me. I'm beyond tired. I want to go home. I wish Chris would piss off. I want Arlie, who is now standing on the footpath, and the other people outside the cafe to go away and stop staring at me in my car. I'm sick of the direction my life is taking. I'm sick of everything. I wanted a speedy getaway, and Chris is preventing such a getaway.

"What's your problem?" I don't hear Chris say this, but the sudden movement of his lips implies his words.

"Do you want to know what gives, Chris?" I flip both my arms into the air, knowing full well Chris can't hear me. "I'll tell you what gives. I'm not a functioning, mature twenty-nine, almost-thirty-year-old. I'm an immature, confused runaway with the invisible word 'coward' permanently inked to my forehead." I drop my arms and tap two fingers above my eyebrow. "I'm tired of my low self-esteem. I'm wavering on the edge of a profound and deep sadness because I thought, in life, I wanted success, to help people, to make a difference, to contribute to society, to feel important, and to be looked up to and respected in my chosen career path by both my peers and my patients." I inhale a needy breath. "But what I've come to realise is all I ever really wanted was to fall madly, deeply, insanely in love. To be held by a man who gets me and all my little quirks, and who cherishes me for who I am. He embraces my weaknesses and harnesses every one of my strengths. I'm his, he's mine, and no matter what happens around our happy little life bubble, it won't matter because we have each other, and life is outstanding.

I've also realised while I've worked my bum off to get a medical degree only to stuff it up, all I wanted was to settle down and be someone's mum. What I wouldn't give to have a bunch of kids running around my ankles, almost tripping me over, demanding my help. How ironic. How very fucking ironic!"

I drop my head onto the steering wheel and moan before repositioning until I'm staring deep into Chris's eyes. "I chose the wrong path. I followed my nattering brain over my needy heart, and now I'm struggling to find my way in life. Where's the street sign, Chris, that leads me to the life I want?" I say, turning my palms upwards and holding my arms out to my sides in question. "What corner do I have to turn to find it? Do I take a left? Or would it be better to go right? Where is it, Chris?" I drop my arms and slump my shoulders. "WHERE IS IT?" I shout.

"I can't understand what you're saying. You look crazy, by the way. Open the door. Seriously, what are you doing?" This time, I faintly hear Chris.

I shrug.

He shakes his head.

I roll my eyes.

He flips me the bird.

I flip him the bird back.

Chris laughs.

I laugh …

And, as my shoulders shake from my laughter, I realise that wishing for a different life and losing my mind in a car in front of a café with a gay dude stopping me from leaving and a hot dude watching on won't change my past.

What will? Finding a different way to direct my future.

But where do I start? What dotted line do I sign on to say today is the beginning of the new me? Because this life, the one I'm currently drowning in, isn't working.

"Mindy, can I get in the car?"

"Fine," I yell flailing my arms about wildly while sitting in the seat.

Chris rushes to the passenger side and opens the door. "Mindy, you are losing your goddamn mind," he says as he ducks his head and climbs in. "God, you're one of a kind."

I am one of a kind. One of a kind who's going to work as damn hard as I did to become a doctor, only this time the work will be to find my Mr Perfect. I'll get my dream home, and those needy kids I crave, and I'll live happily ever after even if it kills me.

"He exists, Chris," I mumble staring out the windshield.

"Who?"

"My Mr Perfect. He must exist. He's out there somewhere, wandering lost. I need to locate him. I need to pull up the granny panties I slipped on last night and grow the hell up."

"How about you drive, and I'll look out the window

for him as we go, because I'm not sure if you know this, but a bunch of people are looking at us, you crazy lady."

Fuck!

Chapter Six

Four days have passed since I ran out of the café and found myself having a breakdown in my car. Perhaps blurting out all the crap I've been holding on to was all the medicine I needed, because since then things have seemed brighter ... more positive.

In two hours, I'm going on the first and only date I've been on since I was sixteen years old. The horror of that evening, the one my teenage self had to endure, replays over and over in my mind as I pack away my make-up brushes.

My first date was a disaster. One I wish I could erase from my memory. One that if I could do all over again, I wouldn't even show up for.

Walking into the bedroom has doubt strangling my airways.

"Don't let him deter you or hurt you. Not now, not ever," I breathe as I stop, still wrapped in a towel, smack bang in front of my closet. Fletcher grooms his thick grey locks. I catch it in the closet's mirror. "I can do this dating thing, can't I, Fletch?"

His ears point, his head lifts, and his narrow emerald eyes focus on me.

Meow, meow, meow.

Hmm. Not exactly encouraging. "Well, I can. I can do it, right?" I stare at Fletcher in the same way he's staring at me—suddenly with big eyes. "No reply this time, huh?"

He cocks his head.

"Has a cat got your tongue, boy?" I stifle a snicker, because I find my question hilarious.

Fletcher's eyes return to narrow slits. He drops his head, spreads his legs wide, and licks his family jewels.

"Yeah, that seems about right. Thanks, you little turd," I mutter, amused by Fletcher's junk-maintenance timing. I slide the closet door open, and with its opening, the vision of my spread-eagled cat disappears.

I'm quick to separate each item of clothing, shifting the coat hangers across the hanging bar, trying to locate the perfect dress to wear tonight. *Boring, boring, boring.* The colour-coordinated plastic hangers clack into one another. What does one choose to wear when possibly meeting the man they're meant to spend the rest of their life with?

Closing my eyes, I try to picture a sublime outfit.

One which is not too busty, busy, tight-fitting, bright, or outlandish.

What will help me catch the eye of my lifelong companion? What will make him all googly-eyed and ooh, la, la, over me?

My date tonight sent me lip-puckerings, kisses, and love emojis through a computer screen. Now, I need him to love me in real life. What dress says, *Love me. Love me like you'd die without me*?

Nothing. Nothing in my closet says anything apart from, *I'm single, and I'm aging into a boring cat lady.*

I drop my chin to my chest. My shoulders slump. I exhale for what seems like forever. Damn, I'm nervous. I haven't felt like this since—Not since Alec. Alec, the douchebag, the popular boy, and clean-skinned teenager who started it all and ended it all in one night. You never forget your first crush, and your first date. I can't forget even though I'd give everything I have to do precisely that: forget him. My stomach roils, and my hands shake. I need to think of anything but Alec, but no matter how hard I try, he's right there, reminding me of the events which unfolded.

"You look beautiful, Melinda." Alec smiled, squishing *his plump cheeks under his dark brown eyes.*

I blushed immediately. The warmth spreading across my face was stifling. "Thank you," I replied shyly.

"I'm so glad you said you'd go out with me."

"I couldn't believe you'd even ask."

Fletcher meows, causing me to snap out of my unbidden thoughts. I shift my attention to him, but he doesn't give me a look in. Instead, he curls himself into a ball and purrs.

"For now, Fletcher, you're my needy brat child. If tonight doesn't go well, it won't be the end of the world. I have you and Chris. I'm going to be okay," I breathe before turning my eyes back to the wardrobe and resuming the search for something to match the smoky eyeshadow I applied.

I stand, staring, and as I do, I'm left wondering why I've always been so shy around the opposite sex. Was it because of my first date? Is it just who I am? With these questions, my mind again wanders back to the red and white booth at our high school hangout where I showed up eager and full of dreams about how the night would go. Alec would like me, I'd like him, and then he'd end the night with a life-changing kiss. We'd return to school on the Monday. I'd be popular, and my life would be perfect. But it wasn't to be, and my mind is hell-bent on reminding me of this.

It was a humid summer night. The air-conditioning in the diner seemed to struggle with providing relief from the heatwave our town was experiencing.

Alec Kennar, the most popular boy in school, was on a date with me. These things never happened to me. My sister? Yes. Me? No. I'd wanted to pinch myself, but I didn't. I grabbed my long locks and laid them over one shoulder to try to reduce the heat I was experiencing across the back of my neck.

"It's hot in here tonight, don't you think?" Alec's voice was freshly deepened, having broken only the term before.

"It's warm, yes." I smiled.

A table was all that separated me from Alec. I tried not to gawk at how hot he was, but I was failing. Alec was a boy who could make you miss an entire algebra class just by ogling him.

"Are you liking your milkshake?"

I didn't respond. I didn't know what to say. I had not even taken a sip of the milkshake he'd ordered for me because I was too busy focusing on perfecting the pose my older sister, Bridey, had taught me the day prior.

"Elbow on the table. Head tilted. Cheek rested into your palm and flutter your eyelashes. Now, don't forget to giggle at everything Alec says, even if you don't find it funny." *Bridey knew how to keep guys interested. Every boy at school wanted to date Bridey.*

I placed my elbow on the table even though condensation formed a water puddle from my milkshake around my limb. I was determined to follow my sister's wisdom to the letter of the law. I wanted Alec to be my guy. I wanted to be the popular girl if only for this one night.

I tilted my head, laid my cheek into my palm, and tried hard to look cute. I fluttered my eyelashes to the point Alec was hard to see.

"Oh, I see how you're lookin' my way, girl." Alec had swagger even in the way he spoke.

I giggled. My giggle grew out of control, then I heard a loud WHACK! The sound present before I'd even felt it.

"Oh shit! Damn!" I could hear the humour in his tone, and then his rumbling laughter filled the diner, followed by more laughter coming from all around me.

I lifted my head, my hair now covered in thick chocolatey liquid, only to find all Alec's friends surrounding him, us. They laughed and pointed.

"You're a loser, Melinda." Lakey, Alec's best mate, heckled me. "She made it so easy for us, too. I guess our plan to get a picture of her dress around her head wasn't needed after all. This was far better."

The sound of the camera firing had tears welling in my eyes.

"You're a train wreck, Melinda Grant." Alec only brought me here to make me a laughing stock, and he succeed without having to try at all.

"Train wreck, train wreck, train wreck," they chanted in unison.

"Why would you do this to me?" I was in pain and dizzy when I stood. I cried as I ran out the doors, never waiting for him to reply to my question of why. Why he would go to so much trouble just to humiliate me? That day, I vowed I'd never date again.

"You're not going to be deliberately embarrassed, Min-Star," Chris says, startling me.

"How did you know—"

"I know you. I knew you'd be freaking out. Plus, I live inside your head. Nobody knows you better than me, and after you told me this morning you had a date tonight, I knew you'd have worked yourself up. I know you think you're going to embarrass yourself, but you're not. You need to be you. Be you, and Mediamogul_234, also known as Graham Semi-Good Looking Gruff, will be eating out of your hands." Chris places his hands on each of my upper arms. "And he'll love you, and you'll get married and have two-point-five kids and a house with a white picket fence and a dog, because Fletcher needs to not rule this roost. You'll be happy, and you'll get the 'D' whenever you want it, and you'll go on family holidays, and I'll come with a new man attached to my arm each time because, let's face it, settling down gives me the creeps." Chris takes a gasping breath.

"You know you can pause for air when talking, right?"

He grins. "You know how I get when I'm on my encouragement rants, girl."

I nod "Okay, so what do I wear, Mr Personal Shopper for all the Rich and Hoity-Toity people?"

"Shove over." Chris bumps my hip with his. "Let's see. What to wear, what to wear," he sings.

I can't help but to fold my arms around his slender frame. "I love you."

"Girl, I've got you. You're going to be okay. I love

59

you." He kisses my hair. "Now, move. I'm going to make you dazzle."

"Oh, dazzle. Now dazzle I want."

I listen to the sound of clothing item after clothing item being shuffled along.

"Bingo! We have a winner." Chris removes my knee-length black halter dress, the one I bought when in the US last summer. "Definitely this. And we'll need some black heels and a pair of gold earrings. You go and sit on the bed and let me work my magic."

I take three long strides backwards until the back of my legs meets the wood of the bedframe, then plonk down in a heap.

"Not these shoes. My grandma wouldn't be seen dead wearing those. They need to be dumped at the tip." Chris is bent down into the bottom of the cupboard with his bum in the air, muttering loudly. "Those are … dear God, do you have taste coming out of your arse? These need to be engulfed in flames and turned to ashes." Chris shakes his head. "Ewww. No. They're hideous." A shoe goes flying over his shoulder, and I duck because I'm certain it will connect with my face. "Where are the hooker heels? We need hooker heels, damn it." Chris sounds flustered. The more he says, the more I lose hope this evening will go well at all. "Yes. These. They aren't exactly hooker heels, but they're a cute peep-toe. Actually …" Chris turns to face me "What's the state of your toenails right now?"

I tuck my toenails against the fine carpeting.

"That bad?" Chris sighs. "I'll paint them for you." He stops speaking. He stares. "Please tell me you still have the nail polish kit I bought you?"

I nod.

Chris circles his lips in a tight *'O'* shape and exhales a forced breath. "Right, we're all set. Stockings. Do you have tan stockings?" He doesn't give me a chance to reply. "Your legs are too pasty white. Oh, and do you have stockings I can cut the toe part completely off because I'll have to alter them to sit right with your shoes?"

"Yes." I bite my nail.

"Stop doing that," Chris scolds.

What?"

"Biting your nail. Stop being nervous, because there's nothing to be nervous about. I've got you, babe. I'm always going to have your back."

I drop my hand into my lap. "I'll get the stockings then."

"No. Stay there. Where are they?"

"Top drawer. Bedside cupboard. Use an older pair, please."

"Okay."

As Chris circles the bed, I say a silent prayer.

Please, God, don't let me mess up this date. I don't have to fall in love with this guy or get married or have two-point-five kids right away. I just want to get through one adult conversation with a man, on a date, without making a fool of myself. Capisce?

"Bathroom cupboard for the nail polish kit?"

"Yes."

"Be right back."

As Chris shimmies past me, I take a moment to thank God for him too.

Every stroke of bright red polish Chris applies to my now groomed toenails is made with concentration. He's a man on a mission, and I'm under strict instructions not to move a muscle.

"Don't move. Your nails are drying, and while they dry, we should go over our flight plan for tonight."

"Flight plan?"

"Yes. It's the foolproof analogy for what's about to go down."

"Okay. If you say so." I drop my head to peek at my toes.

"What part of 'don't move a muscle' are you not getting, little lady?"

"Sorry." I grin and meet his gaze.

"Okay. Firstly, I'll call you ten minutes into the date. It might sound like a long time, but it's not; this is the greeting stage, and it gives you ample time to get through the hi and bye to work out if he's a douche canoe or not. I'll say, 'Hey love, what ya up to?' If he doesn't look like his profile picture or the photos we've stalked on his social media account, his eyes are yelling 'serial killer', and his mouth is all twitchy like he plans to stab you in the face and eat your flesh, you'll answer with ... 'I'm out. Where are you?' This will be my cue to call back in five minutes and give you an urgent 'your dog is dying, come home now' emergency."

"I don't have a dog."

"I know, but he won't, and we don't want to say your mum because if she died as a result of our lie, you'd never forgive yourself."

"I'm sure it will all be—"

"Now, if you say, 'I'm out on a date at the moment. Can I call you back later?' This'll be my cue to know your life isn't in danger."

I nod. "Great plan." There's no point in saying anything else.

"I'm no amateur. Now, after an hour, I'll call back. I'll say, 'Can you tell me where you put my bottle of scotch when you came over last?'"

"I see."

"And if you say 'I drank it all', this will mean you're in dire need of me to get you the hell out of there. Now if you say, 'In the top cupboard above the fridge', I'll know you're contented and happy." Chris dips his head and blows over my nails. "Did you get all that?"

"Yes." I smile even though his ramblings went in one ear and out the other.

"Good. Alright, you're all dry. Go get dressed."

"My stomach feels sick."

"It's called nerves, and they're normal for people like you. Embrace the nerves and get your pretty on already."

You're safe. You're in a familiar place surrounded by people you know. You're in your happy place where you have dessert with Chris every day. Nothing bad can happen.

My mind refuses to stop racing even though I'm chanting this stupid speech Chris gave me before I left the apartment in my head.

"Mindy! Hey, babe." Jersey's red curls bounce as she rushes by me holding a tray of drinks. "I'll be right back," she calls as her back becomes my view.

You're safe. You're in a familiar place surrounded by people you know. You're in your happy place where you have dessert with Chris every day. Nothing bad can happen. I stand at the bar, shifting my sight between different-shaped bottles of liquor lined up like soldiers on the top shelf. I need a stiff drink, like right freaking now.

Jersey races in front of me, this time holding an empty tray. Her hand extends towards a stool at the bar. "Sit. Chat. What are you doing here all dressed up and fancy?" Her red-stained lips purse.

"Date," I mumble.

"DATE!" Her eyes light up. "Cool. Who is he? How did you meet?"

"Well, yeah. So—" I cup my face in my palms.

"You don't have to tell me, babe. We're good."

When I drop my arms, a silver cup goes flying in the air, causing me to jolt as it flashes past my eyes and nearly clips my nose.

"Oh, sorry, hon, I didn't mean for it to come so close to you. I'm having a little too much fun making cocktails tonight." Jersey bites her lip between her teeth. "I think your date might be here."

"What?" My body stiffens. My heart pounds frantically in my chest. "How do you know what he even—"

"I'm playing with you." She taps my hand playfully. "But good lord, did your arsehole just pucker tight."

I sigh, leaning back, then remember the chair doesn't have back support. I swing my arms to prevent myself from falling.

"It's going to be fine. Relax, okay? You look super stressed."

"I'm not good at this dating thing."

Jersey pops the lid on the silver canister she not long ago threw in the air. She pours pink liquid into a tall glass before placing a strawberry on its edge and a straw in its centre. "Honey." She leans into me. "None of us are good at this dating thing. Just have fun with it." She points at the glass. "I recommend you drink this down real fast to curb those nerves. Doctor's orders." She winks. "Gotta run. Be back soon."

I do just that. I tuck the straw behind my teeth and slurp the liquid, which is stronger than I thought it would be.

"Melinda." It's a deep yet oddly hoarse, throaty tone.

I swivel on my seat.

"Hello. I'm Graham. You weren't hard to find in the crowd. You look just like your picture."

I gulp hard. I stare into grass green eyes. I bite my lip to prevent myself from saying, *you don't look anything like your pictures at all.*

Graham's partly bald even though in his photos he has a full head of thinning brown hair. He looks much older than what was described online, by at least ten years, and he has little scars all over his face, which again were absent from his photographs. He's also much skinnier than his portrait displayed.

"Hi." I speak softly.

"Hi." He smiles revealing yellow-stained teeth, not the bright whites he has on his profile. "Would you like to go to the table or sit and have a drink here?"

"A drink here is okay." I breathe. I'm doing it. I'm talking to a man. Admittedly, not the man I was expecting, but still, I'm not acting a fool.

Graham tugs at the cuffs on the long white business shirt he's wearing when he comes to sit. He clears his throat as he twists in my direction. "This is a nice spot. I've never been here before."

"It's lovely, and the food's good too."

"Hey, I'm sorry I was a little late. I ran over a cat on the way here."

I place my hand on my chest. "Oh no! Is the cat okay?"

He jerks his head back. "Who cares? I can't stand cats. I didn't even stop. I was late because I needed to wash its guts from my car."

My stomach sinks. Visions of Graham skinning me alive enter my mind in the most dramatic of ways, and I tense.

"I'm not much of an animal lover. Bloody pests, if you ask me. We can't all love those freaky furry critters."

"Hmm," I say, shifting uncomfortably on my seat.

"Wow!" Graham's eyes leave mine, and without any hesitation, he rakes them over my body. "Has anyone ever told you that you have the body of Marilyn Monroe? Because damn, you do. You're curvy and beautiful. I didn't think you'd be this pretty. You know, photoshopped pictures and all."

A compliment. He's complimenting me in the rudest of ways. I tense even more.

"I can only imagine how good you look under that dress of yours." He winks.

I jerk my head to the bar where I find Jersey's thick lashes blinking right in front of me. "What can I get you to drink?" she says mechanically. Jersey's tone implies the same shock I'm feeling. She must have been eavesdropping.

"I'm—"

"I'll have a beer, love. A light beer because I better not get myself blotto, you know."

I rotate my head slow, real slow, only to find him pointing at me. "I'll be needing to keep my eyes on this prize, so she doesn't get away."

I cringe. I stare gobsmacked at this stranger named Graham beside me. *Who the hell is this man?*

"One beer. Not a problem. Mindy, do you want another?" Jersey's voice sounds distant as I slowly shake my head.

I'm in shock. "I need to go."

"Go? What do you mean, go? I just got here," Graham says with a heightened pitch.

"My dog died. My mum died too, and I drank an entire bottle of scotch, which is missing. My face. My poor faceless face." I stand abruptly and turn in the same way. "I'm sorry. Have a good night."

I don't walk towards the doors or even march. I run, but this time, I'm not fleeing from embarrassment with tears pouring from my eyes. This time, I'm fleeing because that man might kill me and boil my body parts for his supper.

What the hell just happened?

I wonder how many duds it will take until I meet my stud?

Chapter Seven

The red traffic light glows brightly against the night sky as I wait to take the exit leading to my estate. The sound of my blinker clicking to its programmed musical tune has me clacking my tongue to its beat. I wasn't supposed to meet the cat killer who turned up tonight. I was supposed to meet a guy with a kind smile. I want a guy like that. I want a guy like Arlie.

Who is Arlie? Why have we crossed paths twice in such a short period? Is it fate? Is he my guy?

Loud booming laughter forces its way through my lips all the way from deep down in my stomach. Arlie looks like a god sculpted by the heavens. Arlie is not my guy. But maybe someone's out there who has the same smile as him, only who's more in my league.

Ring, ring. Ring, ring.

I shake my head, and as the sound of ringing continues to vibrate through the car speakers, I realise I've been finding my way back to safety in complete silence wrapped up in thoughts of a man I'm never going to have.

I always want things I can't have. I'm drawn to the things I'm undeserving of receiving. I cock block myself from the get-go.

Maybe this is why I'm so ridiculous around the opposite sex. Perhaps, it's because I find every single man out there—well, every single decent man—out of my league. I don't want to settle for any guy. I want a good, decent guy.

I reach out my hand and accept the call.

"Hey love, what ya up to?" Chris says.

"Driving home. Mediamogul Graham was a face-eater."

There's no reply.

"He killed a cat on the way to our date and didn't even care, Chris. He stopped to wash the guts from his car."

Chris gasps in the most overdramatic way.

"It was a bust."

"Are you okay?" His tone is unsteady.

"I am, surprisingly. I did run out of there, but this time, it was different, and I know I'm ready for this to happen for me now. I need to find the right fit. He can't be a cat killer, though."

"No! He can't, because Fletcher would have no hope."

Fletcher would have no hope. "Where are you?" I

mumble, hoping Chris can catch up for a laugh and a drink back at my apartment.

"Don't get mad."

"What have you done?"

"Nothing."

"Why would I get mad then?"

"Because you're often cranky."

"I am not," I scoff. "Where are you?"

"I'm sitting on your couch stroking your furry friend while watching *The Bachelor*. It's getting so juicy."

I laugh. Because Chris is right where I hoped he would be, and because his addiction to *The Bachelor* is on a level of obsessive. If that show were a sermon, Chris wouldn't miss a single day in church.

"Anyway, I'll be here when you get back. Unless you want me to leave?"

"No. Stay. I'm glad you're there."

"I thought if things didn't go well, you'd probably need a friend, and since I don't drive, and the train takes so long to get to your place, it was better to sneak back in once you'd left."

"I love you."

"Aww! Right back at you, babe. Would you like me to make you some hot cocoa?"

"Yes, please."

"Are you hungry?"

"Starved."

"Why don't you grab some Chinese on the way

home? I'm famished and could go for some honey chicken."

"Could you now?"

"Pleeease. My stomach is growling. It's crying, 'feed me'."

"Okay. I'll turn around and get you some dinner."

"Thank you, pretty lady," Chris says in a Southern accent.

"Why, you're welcome, bestie." I attempt the same accent back.

"Don't ever do that again. Appalling. Like, were you going for American-Irish-Scottish? If so, you nailed it."

"Shut up."

"Drive safe and I'll see you soon."

"Okay."

The line goes dead as the traffic light turns green. I don't hesitate in completing an illegal U-turn and head in the direction I travelled from.

Shania Twain's "Man! I Feel Like A Woman" booms through the speakers as I end my second illegal U-turn for the evening and reverse park right into the only vacant spot outside the Chinese shop.

Before hopping out, I take a moment to dance in my seat, belting out the remaining lyrics of a song which has always made me feel empowered. Singing like I'm on stage at *Australia's Got Talent*—loud, proud, and in control—makes me feel free. When I was a teenager, my mum always told me the best way to relieve any frustrating or unsettling situation or emotion was to sing. To sing loud and proud until your throat burned and you were exhausted of all feelings. It truly helps me when trying to work through moments of utter shit in my life.

I turn the volume control down before the next song on the CD plays, then open the car door, being careful not to scrape the metal at the bottom of the door against the heightened footpath. I brush my hand over my arse on a very awkward exit to ensure my dress is where it's supposed to be. For some reason, my clothing likes to tuck itself up, and as a result, my arse plays peek-a-boo with unsuspecting bystanders. *Not tonight, arse. Not tonight.*

"Do you feel like a woman? Really like a woman? Because I promise you, you look like one tonight. Damn!"

"What the hell, man?" I say, whipping my body in the direction of the deep voice behind me.

"Hi." Arlie's smiling while wiggling his eyebrows up and down.

"Oh ... it's ... hi."

"How loud do you play your music? Your car was jumping on its wheels."

I gently secure my tongue between my teeth to prevent myself from saying anything stupid.

"You're quite the little groover, too. You do a much better job singing and dancing than you do shopping. Oh, and hiding under tables."

My face fills with warmth. My heart kicks into a

faster rhythm.

"Don't be embarrassed. I find you endearing, slightly insane, and incredibly funny."

Arlie finds me funny. Nobody finds me funny because I'm not funny. Hang on, did he also say insane? I think he said insane. What a bitch.

"Are you stalking me?" I blurt this out like verbal diarrhoea.

He deadpans. "Stalking is a severe crime. It's not something to be joked about."

My mouth forms a flawless 'O'. *Way to blow that, Mindy.*

"I'm joking." His big white teeth are on display.

Without thought, I smack my hand against his chest, only to leave it to rest against his pale green T-shirt for much too long.

He clears his throat.

I snatch my hand back.

"It's you who's stalking me." He cocks his thick dark eyebrows.

I giggle loudly, much too loudly, and then I realise this is the part where I'm supposed to put my elbow on the table, rest my head into my palm, and flutter my eyelashes. Only there's no table in front of me.

What am I doing? Abort. Abort, Mindy.

I drop my arms to my sides and become stiff as a board. Did he see that? Of course, he saw it; he's not blind.

Do not joke about blindness. Do not ask him if he's

blind.

"So you wouldn't happen to be blind, would you?"
Why? Why did I say what I told myself not too?

Arlie throws his head back and laughs.

I'm frozen to the spot, unable to move, horrified. Yep, he's right. I'm fucking insane.

"I'm not blind, but I assure you I didn't see anything. I didn't see you do some bizarre thing with your arm and face."

"Okay! So ... I gotta ... you know ... go now. It was nice bumping into you again."

"You too. I'm sure I'll see you around, Melinda."

"It seems I will. It appears I'm hell-bent on humiliating myself in front of you."

I turn on my heel and slowly walk towards a wooden door with a red sign. The word *OPEN* is written in big white lettering hung inside the small glass panels of the door.

Don't fall. Walk like a lady. He's probably still watching you, waiting for the big finale to your train wreck life.

"Have a good night then," he calls out.

He's still there. Maybe I should turn around and ask for his number. Ask him if he's hungry. Something. Anything. Perhaps I'm supposed to get to know Arlie. Maybe the universe wants us to be friends.

Without another thought, I turn sharply. My cheek smashes against a hard, muscular surface. My body fills with warmth. My hands and feet tingle when I hear a heart beating against my ear. Strong arms hold me in an embrace. Either I've hit an invisible brick wall, I've died and angels are holding me, or I'm being held by a man who smells like a mixture of sweat and ginger biscuits; a man who makes me feel safe, secure, and like I'm coming home for the very first time in a long time.

"I'm sorry. Are you okay?"

I tilt my chin and turn my sight upwards only to find familiar eyes looking back at me. "You smell like ginger. Why do you smell like ginger?"

The warmth from his body disappears, as do his eyes. He steps away from me. The bright streetlight takes my vision until I shift my eyes to again find Arlie. I want so badly to skirt my fingertips over his beautiful face. He's gorgeous to look at, and I'd love to wake up next to him every day, that's for sure.

"Are you, okay? I shouldn't have snuck up on you like that," he says again.

"I should have looked before I turned. I didn't realise you were getting Chinese too."

He runs his hand through his hair. "Do I really smell like ginger?"

I nod.

"I was making gingerbread cookies with my niece earlier."

"Oh."

"Are you sure you're okay?"

I haven't answered his previous question. If I had,

I would've responded with 'sure', but the truth would have been I'm not okay because he no longer has his arms around me, and his heart's no longer beating against my ear, and those things made me feel more than okay. They made me feel wonderful.

"Melinda?"

"Sure," I say abruptly. "I'm fine. I can be a tad clumsy."

"Okay."

"Anyway, after you." I gesture for him to take the lead and enter the establishment.

He follows my outstretched hand but stops once he's opened the door and steps backwards. "After you. I'm a gentleman, you know."

"Thank you."

The wait in line is more than awkward because I have a tall, dark, and handsome stallion standing behind me, one whose breath I swear I can feel rushing over the back of my neck. I shudder from the goosebumps riding the length of my spine, and then I find myself shifting from one foot to the other. *Relax*, I tell myself, which only makes me move faster.

"Do you come here often?" Arlie says over my shoulder. This guy has no boundaries when it comes to personal space. If his head were to drop an inch, his chin would rest on my shoulder.

"Not very. You?" I say, slowly rotating my body as he backs away, giving me some space.

"I do. It's the best Chinese takeout in town."

"You actually eat takeout?" I cock my eyebrows. Is he really here for the food? Or is this where he comes to hit on and stand too close to women?

"Why wouldn't I eat takeout?"

"Have you seen yourself? Like, do you own a mirror? You're in shape, dude. Like, really in shape." I use my hands to demonstrate the extent of his physique.

"Do you think people who work out don't eat Chinese, takeaway, and rubbish food? That's very single-minded. Are you single-minded, Melinda?"

I take a moment to think about his question. No, I'm not.

Holy shit.

I am.

"No," I groan, feeling even more uncomfortable than before. I swiftly turn until I'm facing forwards, only to clap eyes on a butterfly tattoo on the neck of the lady standing in front of me. 'No regrets' is inscribed below it. *No regrets.* I need to face life never thinking of the future regrets I'll have because of my actions.

I hesitate in turning back to apologise to Arlie for my stereotypical comment, but I eventually do, and when I peek over my shoulder, I spy a smile much too broad for his face. "I'm sorry. I shouldn't have said that," I say.

"All good." His smile fades rapidly, like a nearing sunset. "I'm just feeling a little—you know, today I've felt …" He stops speaking.

"You felt?"

"Never mind. It was nothing."

Do men really feel, though? Do they have feelings?

There I go again. Why do I think like this? What the hell is wrong with me?

"I'm good." Arlie closes his eyes briefly.

"Hey. Do you want to like, you know, dine in here with me? Like, at a table over there, and talk about things?" I point in the direction of the attached restaurant. "Instead of doing the takeout thing?"

"I wouldn't want to impose on your evening."

"You wouldn't be," I rush in saying.

"Your boyfriend isn't waiting on you."

Oh shit! Boyfriend. I forgot about that. "Um. No. Not tonight. I'm eating alone."

"Okay, sure. I'd like to."

Butterflies flutter in my gut. My heart races as if I've run for the first time in a long time. Arlie wants to have dinner with me. What about Chris? He's waiting for me and his dinner. Would Chris be okay with me ditching him for a meal with Arlie?

Maybe I should make this eating out thing for another time. Chris needs me, and I should get home.

Chapter Eight

Do not make a fool of yourself. Listen and try not to talk too much. Also, don't do the elbow on table thing again. It doesn't work. Why did I ask this man to dine with me? Why am I sitting here in this restaurant?

What have I done?

The table is placed near a large windowpane overlooking the shopfront's footpath. A crystal vase with a single yellow daisy sits beside oversized salt and pepper shakers on top of a crisp white tablecloth. My hands shake as I lift my phone from the table and open the messenger app.

Shuffling in my seat—trying to alleviate my nerves—only makes my shaking hands tremble worse. *Pull it together, will you? This isn't a date. It's dinner with a friend. It's no different than dinner with Chris.*

Shit, you need to message Chris.

I roam my vision past the people standing in the pick-up line until I find Arlie. He's standing side on, and I forget about messaging Chris for the second time. Arlie is hot from every. Single. Angle.

He suddenly snaps around until he's facing me.

"Do clue bout any toy cause?" Arlie mouths.

I hitch my top lip upwards. "Huh?"

"Do clue bout any toy cause?" he mouths again.

"What?"

"Do you want any soy sauce?" he yells with a smile.

"No, thank you," I mouth. "Did you get that?" I yell.

"Yes," he mouths dramatically before turning his back to me.

I'm giggling when I relax and shift my attention back to my phone. Oh shit, I still need to message Chris and tell him what's happened. Holy hell, how did all this happen? What spurred courage to spark through my veins until it found its way to my mouth?

Me: CHRIS!! I'm at the Chinese place. You're not going to believe who's here.

I keep my vision planted on the screen, hoping for an immediate reply.

I don't wait long.

Chris: OMG! Who is it? Chris Hemsworth? Please say it's him. I'm grabbing my coat. Hang on, I don't have a coat. I'm clutching my crotch, and I'm on my way.

Me: Bahaha. No! It's not Chris Hemsworth. You can unhand your genitals. It's Arlie. That guy from the cafe. You know, the one I darted under the table to escape?

Chris: Get the farq out. Well, say hello or something! Fake fall into him if you need to. GET HIS ATTENTION NOW! Don't hide under any tables. DO NOT RUN!

Me: Lol. I didn't hide. I did fall into Arlie, but it wasn't faked for attention, I swear. However, I've somehow managed to ask him to eat with me.

Chris: OMG! OMG! Did you? That's my girl. Awesome. What did he say?

Me: Yes! He's collecting our food right now. I'll bring something back for you to eat, I swear.

Chris: I think I've fainted. I've never been as proud of you as I am right now. Food? Don't be silly. Go enjoy yourself. Fletcher and I'll eat tuna. We like tuna. Plus, you're already dressed to impress.

Chris: Hey! Off topic, but the book on your recliner. I started reading it after *The Bachelor* finished. GIRL!!!! THIS SHIT IS STEAMY AS FUCK!! I'm thoroughly entertained, and a tad shocked you own a book like this.

Me: Is it *Secrets in the Night*? If so, you bought me the book.

Chris: Yes! Well, this makes more sense then. Ha ha.

Me: I love you. I'm sorry I'm not coming straight back.

Chris: You wash your mouth out. You're in a restaurant with a MEGA-HOT guy. If it were me, I'd be ditching you without a second thought. There is no 'bros before hoes' code in our friendship. Go get him, tiger.

Me: OMG! Wish me luck?

Chris: You don't need it. Baby bird, I've taught you well. Trust me, this fluffy pink chicken thinks you're ready to fly the nest. Relax, fly free, and most of all, have fun.

Me: Chickens don't fly.

Chris: Why? Why you gotta mess with my spectacular euphemism? This chicken flies, and since you're my baby bird, so do you.

Me: Lol. Love you.

Chris: Shh! I'm reading. Go away already. These two are about to get it on. I don't want your face to be the one I'm left to imagine. Chris Hemsworth is the face I need to be visualising. Scat!

I snicker before placing my phone screen down against the tablecloth. I rotate my head towards the collection counter and admire Arlie's back. I can see every muscle outlined thanks to his tight T-shirt. His boardshorts sag just enough off his butt, but not so much that he looks like he's packing a major turd in his pants. Oh, the surfer chic look—he does it so well.

Slowly, he turns, and as he does, all I'm thinking is, *turn for me, baby. Show me all of you, every single bit.* That is, until I see the two plates in his grip and the wicker basket filled with prawn chips tucked under his chin. I leap upwards and dart towards him.

"Here, let me help you." I take the plates from his hands.

"I would have been fine."

"I'm sure you would have, Hercules, but you know I have two hands, you have two hands, and more hands make for light work and stuff."

He grins.

We sit on either side of the squared table. Arlie takes a cream cloth napkin and tucks it into the top of his shirt before we again make eye contact. "I can get a little messy when eating." He shrugs.

"Me too," I say, reaching for my napkin, opening it out, and laying it against my lap.

"I'm so hungry," he groans as he licks his lips.

I squeeze my thighs together as fast as Usain Bolt sprints the one hundred metres, at lightning speed, because the way Arlie licked his lips was sensual, too sensual, and it's making me tingle in places I don't need to be tingling right now. "Me too," I manage to choke out with a gentle clearing of my throat.

"Dig in."

I pick up the set of chopsticks laid against the plate and glare at the wood skewers, trying to remember the last time I ate with this type of utensil. It's been a while, and honestly, I've never been good at using them. I fiddle, trying to place them between my fingers correctly, and I know I'm making a fool of myself with my clumsy manoeuvring, but I keep trying in the hope I'll sort it out.

I don't. I tilt my chin back and close my eyes in prayer. *Please, can you do your thing and make me look like a Chinese chopstick ninja in front of this hot guy? I'll be more than thankful if you can, big man.* Not a usual dinner prayer, probably not even an appropriate one, but one I had to make.

I slowly part my eyelids and lower my chin, only to find Arlie holding a fork. I clear my throat as he shovels a large forkful of pork into his mouth. "Oh, thank God." My tone is filled with relief. "I can't use chopsticks well."

Arlie chews quickly before swallowing. "I've never bothered to try hard enough. I'm no chopstick ninja. I'm Aussie, not Chinese, and if I'm honest, I'd prefer to eat my food with these utensils." He moves his fingers like a hand puppet. "But I'm in the company of a lady, so I'll use a fork for you." He tips his chin knowingly.

I feel my lips stretch across my face until they burn.

"This makes you happy?"

"You just said chopstick ninja."

He nods.

"I internally willed my chopsticks to help me perform like I was a Chinese chopstick ninja only like a second ago."

A small laugh passes his lips. "Great minds think alike, hey?"

"I guess so." Nothing's going to wipe this smile off my face. Nothing.

"Eat up before your chicken goes cold. I love this place. Their food is delicious, even more so when enjoyed hot."

"It is." I snatch a prawn chip from the cane basket. "Now, these little pink suckers are my favourite. Who doesn't love a good prawn cracker?"

Arlie opens his mouth and leaves it open as though he's a seal waiting for a fish treat. After a few seconds pass, he smacks his lips together and narrows his eyes. I'm not sure what's happening.

"Go on. Put one of those in my pie hole, would ya?"

I steady my hand when he dips his chin again and opens his mouth.

"Don't bite my fingers, you hear?" I edge in closer to his big white teeth, and he smiles right before he uses his lips to pull the prawn cracker from my fingertips.

I giggle in response.

"Best prawn chip ever. I'll have another, thank you."

I bat my hand into the air. "Get it yourself."

He leans in, taking a chip from the basket. "Open up. I'll repay the favour."

I gulp. It's not a soft-sounding gulp. It's hard and easy to hear the noise.

"Relax," he says, breathy.

I follow his request and part my teeth. I close my eyes. His finger skims my bottom lip, causing a tickling sensation which makes me shiver. I bite down softly and claim the cracker for myself. "Yum," I moan as I spring my eyes open.

"Right? Best Chinese in town."

I nod, flustered, flushed, but oh-so satisfied.

The chatter of those ordering at the counter fills the quiet between us as we eat. It's not an uncomfortable silence. It's very mellow and homey. I've only ever known this feeling with Chris, a few of my closest friends from back home in Queensland, and my family.

I relax into my seat opposite a man I don't know with no fear of saying anything dumb anymore. There are no nerves steamrolling my gut or tying it in knots, and I've no sirens wailing in my head telling me to boycott immediately. I'm dressed to impress in a place where nobody goes to such effort with their appearance, but with Arlie, I feel like I'm in the company of a trusted and old friend.

"So, tell me something, Melinda. What do you do? Work? Daily stuff? Something?" Arlie takes the napkin tucked into his shirt and dabs the corners of his lips before scrunching it up and dumping it on his empty plate.

"I'm a folder, not a scruncher." I tilt my head to the side and bat my eyelashes melodramatically as I take the napkin from my lap, dab the corners of my lips, and neatly fold it into four before resting it on my plate.

He stifles a laugh as he again narrows his eyes, only this time in a way that makes him appear more serious. "Well, that's something we don't have in common then, because I scrunch everything. I'm a born and bred scruncher. I love to scrunch."

"Good to know. Folding is my jam." I smile.

Arlie laughs. His laugh is the sexiest laugh I've ever heard.

"So, tell me something, Arlie, what do you do? Work? Daily stuff? Anything you want to share?"

"Nice. I see what you did there. It takes some real talent to flip the questioning. Bravo."

I cross one arm in front of my body and bow my head to my impressed audience of one.

"Is this your talent?"

I shrug. "Maybe. I don't know."

"Sure, sure. You're the master of conversation flipping."

"Arlie, are you now trying to divert the conversation so you can flip the question back to me?"

He pinches the material of his shirt just under each collarbone and pretends to straighten it at the same time as he lengthens his posture. "Not at all. Here goes: so, I'm a gym owner. I have a younger sister I call Boo because I used to scare the crap out of her as a child, all the flipping time, and she would scream BOO instead of screaming in horror like a normal person." He tilts his head to the side and smirks as if he's thinking of a time this happened. "My sister, Hazel, has a four-year-old daughter who is my most favourite, and may I mention the only niece I have in the entire world. Her name is Agatha, and yes, she was named after Agatha Christie because my sister had her when she was only seventeen. You see, throughout her pregnancy, she would hide in her room and read mystery and crime novels to pass the time. The name suits her, though, Agatha. She's a miniature crime-solving detective if I've ever seen one. Smart little brat." Arlie twitches his nose and turns his eyes upwards for a moment before rebounding his sight to mine. "My mother passed away when I was ten. My father is still alive, though. He raised Hazel and me alone for a long time until he met Tillie. Tillie's nice, and we like her. My dad is a bloody brilliant dad." Arlie twists his lips. "Okay. One more thing, I drive a truck, she's my baby, my pride and joy, and together we go on many outdoorsy adventures." There's a long pause. "That's about me. You?"

"Oh, okay. We're both doing this. I see."

He nods.

"One moment." I take a mouthful of water and try to buy some time until I know what to say. "Okay, so, I'm a receptionist." *Do not tell him it's for an escort service.* "I've lived in Melbourne for just over two years, I think. Yeah, that's about right. I'm originally from Queensland. I have one sister … older. Her name is Bridey. She's not had any children yet, but she recently got married. Well, about four years ago now, actually, but she's married, and I know she wants kids so maybe one day soon." I cross my fingers. "My mother and father are both living. They were and are good to us. I have a best friend, Chris, who you met."

"He's a character that lad, yeah?"

"Oh, isn't he ever? He'll crack onto any guy who has 'a good booty and all the looks', as he puts it. I'm sorry he hit on you."

"Nah, don't be. I was flattered." He pauses. "So, you think I have a good arse and some looks, hey?"

"I didn't say that." *But hell, am I thinking it.*

"I see. Keep going."

"Umm. Chris is great to me. I don't know what I'd do without him." I rack my brain for other things to say. I bite down on my lip and then it hits me. The cat killer from tonight. What if Arlie hates cats too? Worse still, what if he mows them down? "I have a cat named Fletcher. He's a needy old cat." I wait with bated breath.

"There's no way he's needier than Baskins. That cat runs our shared house."

"You like cats?"

"I love all animals. I have a dog, a dachshund, as well. His name is Miscuit, like biscuit, but with an M. They're both my animals, but the three guys I live with treat them like they belong to them too."

"Shared house?" I cock my eyebrows.

"Yeah. I like it. We're training buddies. Football. Play on the same team. It's what we've done since after we finished school. The company is amazing, and we have enough space to be really comfortable."

"That's pretty sweet."

"I wouldn't say sweet. Maybe manly." A soft line forms in the centre of his forehead.

I laugh.

"So you live with your boyfriend and a cat. You've not mentioned the guy you're with."

I shift uncomfortably in my chair. I'm going to have to tell Arlie I lied, but then what does that say about my character? Maybe I can tell him he died? No, that would look even worse, considering the timeframe. Plus, saying something of that nature in general is a bad thing to do. Karma—she's a controlling bitch I need to avoid. Maybe I can tell him we broke up, but then he'll think I know how to be in a relationship, which I don't. Oh, what a mess.

"I don't have a boyfriend. I lied." Like ripping off a fucking Band-Aid. Fast. Get it off, and hope for the best for whatever lay underneath.

"I knew already. You're not a convincing liar."

I drop my chin and mumble, "I know."

"So, you live with Chris?"

"No. It's only me and Fletcher, my cat, in an apartment together."

"Cool. What's with the frock and look you've got going on tonight?" He waves his hand up and down in front of his chest.

"Oh, this little old thing? I wear clothes like this all the time."

"Are you doing that lying thing again?"

"Yep!"

Arlie shakes his head. "So what were you up to, if you don't mind me asking?"

"I had a blind date. It didn't go very well."

"Too bad."

"It's okay."

"Sounds like the guy was an idiot, if you ask me."

I know I'm blushing. I don't need any mirrors to inspect my now flushed cheeks.

"Melinda, do you think it would be okay if I asked you for your number? I have to go in a minute." Arlie glances at the watch wrapped to his wrist. "But I'd like to see you again. Maybe we can catch up sometime?"

Oh, my GOD! My mind's screaming, bum dancing, and hyperventilating all at the same time. "Yeah. Cool. Whatevs."

Why did I just speak like a punk teen?

Arlie laughs as he grabs his mobile phone from the table. "Do you want to punch the numbers in or should I?"

"I'll do it," I reply very quickly, probably too quickly.

When Arlie's fingertips touch mine, I feel an instant connection. It's not like sparks of electricity shoot through my body or fireworks explode in front of my eyes, like I read in books. It's a calm, contented connection ... a homey feeling.

I type my details into Arlie's phone, taking a moment to stop and catch a glimpse of this god-like man who sits across from me. I need to know what his expression currently projects. Body language means so much more than words, and I'm hoping his body language can tell me where I stand right now.

Why has he asked for my number? Is it out of kindness, now that he knows I've had a lousy date, but he'll never call and I'll never see him again? Or is he being sincere?

Arlie's eyes target his phone. His face speaks novels. He's eager, maybe even a tad excited, and this sets an air of exhilaration to blossom within me.

"All done," I say, passing his phone back.

"Thanks. I'll give you a call sometime."

"That'd be nice."

"But I do need to go."

"Okay."

"Have a good night." He stands.

"You too." I watch his tattoo on his calf as he walks away. I hope him leaving isn't the end of this because being around Arlie is like walking through a freshly mowed park on a warm summer afternoon after it's rained: refreshing, comforting, fresh.

I've been on a date with a man who was all types of crazy only to end up on another date, not even an hour later, with a man who sets me at ease.

Fate had a plan for me tonight, and I witnessed it firsthand. Talk about a serendipitous moment when I needed one the most, and a chance of maybe finding my happily ever after.

Is Arlie going to be my happily ever after? I sure hope so.

Please, God, let him be mine. Please.

Chapter Nine

It's been one week since I sat across from a guy in a Chinese restaurant and thought for one moment that there was a possibility, a chance, I'd found someone who liked me in the same way I liked him ... romantically. I mean, what's not to like about Arlie? He's handsome, incredibly chilled, and socially adept. He seemed a little one-footed when asking for my number, but he asked, and as soon as the words left his mouth, I accepted his request as fast as lightning could obliviate the healthiest of trees. And maybe that is where I went wrong. Too eager and too desperate. I've not heard a peep from Arlie. There have been no texts, no phone calls—nada. Seven long days and nights have passed, and he hasn't bothered to reach out in any way. I thought we had a connection, but maybe he was only being a gentleman, like I thought, and offering sympathy after an already botched blind date.

Chris and I've searched social media for the last week trying to find anyone who resembles the man who's now plaguing my mind. At first, I didn't think it would be hard to locate someone with such a name, but to my surprise, there are many Arlies out there in the big wide world. The only account which could be his is locked down tighter than Fort Knox. A profile picture of a dog, a dachshund, made me believe it must be his. The picture could have been of Miscuit, but then again, what does Miscuit even look like? Why didn't I ask more questions? Like his last name, where he lives, where he hangs out, or who his friends are? Why didn't I go super stalkerish and ask for his tax file number, bank account details, and credit card information? *What gym do you own, Arlie?* The gym thing should've been up there on the list of shit to discuss.

Blight, Arlie Blight, is the owner of the super-secure social media account. Could it be him?

What I should be asking myself now is how long does it take until you let someone go after you've enjoyed a lovely meal together and gotten your hopes up?

Ring, ring, ring.

"Welcome to Kit on High, you're speaking with Mindy. How can I be of service?"

"Morning! Matthew Muller here. How are you, sweetie?"

I'm confused is what I want to say. "Very well, Mr Muller. Another booking?"

"Please! Oh, Mindy, I can't get enough of your voice. Do you know how very sexy you sound?"

"Mr Muller, you're always so sweet to me." I pause. "Now, your booking, how can I help?" I need to steer this conversation back to business so I can go back to beating myself up.

"I'd like to see if I can book you. Are you interested?"

My head jerks back so far I almost lose the headset tucked behind my ears.

"Mindy. Are you there?"

"Um ... yes, I am."

"Well, how about a date? All expenses paid."

"I'm sorry, but—" I stop speaking. Maybe I should consider a night as an escort with a successful and wealthy businessman who thinks my voice is super sexy. Sure, he hires escorts. It's not the best quality to have, and I'm pretty sure no woman has such a quality listed on their picture-perfect man list, but Matthew Muller is a man who knows what he wants, and he goes after it. There'll be no pussyfooting around with a man like him. Today, he wants me.

Live a little, Mindy. Walk on the wild side.

"Mindy, hello, can you hear me?"

Oh lord, what am I thinking? No, Mindy, you can't accept his invitation of a date.

"Hello?" he says.

Beep. Beep. Beep.

He hung up. The sound of a disconnected call beats through my head.

Slowly, I remove the headset. I throw it on the desk, leaning as far back into the chair as I can.

"Melinda, what happened?" Indie's dark chocolate eyes zoom towards my face.

"You know what? Life. Life happened."

"Yeah, life's a bitch, and then you kick the bucket. We've all been there. What happened with the call?"

"Matthew Muller happened."

"Lordy, have you seen that guy?"

I shake my head.

"Talk about a tall, dark, and handsome brew of deliciousness." Indie sucks back pretend drool, then moans.

"You've seen him?"

"I have. You can easily look him up online, you know." Indie pauses. "I would screw Matthew all day and night, and every day and every night for the rest of my life if given a chance."

"Settle down there, horn dog."

"Hang on. Let me show you. I have a picture of him in the flesh. There was a night about two months ago where Alice asked me to come out for drinks," Indie says, sitting back at her desk. "We ran into Callie and Matthew at the casino. I about fell off my chair when I realised who he was." She tugs her tote bag up on her lap before hanging her head between its handles, digging through her possessions. "Got it." She waves her mobile phone in the air. "I tell you, trying to find my phone in this thing is hard, but I love that it can carry everything I like to keep on my person at all times, including my kitchen sink." She giggles.

Indie's bag falls to the floor. She holds her phone in both hands right in front of her face. "Oh," she moans. "Matthew's so smoking hot." She's practically drooling again when she holds her mobile out for me to take. "Panty-soaking hot. I almost need to rub one out just looking at his picture again."

"He can't be that good looking." I take the phone from her grip and glue my eyes to the screen. "Holy fuck!" I squeal like a piglet whose tail got stomped on. "Jesus, God, and the Mother Mary."

"See? Told you."

"And he hires escorts? Why? Why the hell does he do such a thing?"

"No. Matthew hires Callie and only Callie. He's never hired any other escort, ever."

"Really?"

"Alice tells me he has very particular tastes when it comes to what he likes in the bedroom." Indie stands, dragging her chair close to mine. "We don't want Kitty to overhear us." She leans into me. "I'm not exactly sure what his bedroom needs are, but Alice told me if she could get one night with him under the covers she would die from the number of orgasms he'd be able to deliver her."

I gulp at the same time as I squeeze my thighs together.

Indie laughs. "I saw that. Seriously, though, your bud is pulsating, isn't it?"

I stifle an embarrassed giggle, cupping my hand to my mouth.

"Look at him. He's a god. And his voice when you take his calls? Deep, smooth like melted milk chocolate."

"And his voice matches his skin colour." I never pictured him to have dark skin or to be so young.

"Right? And the manscaped five o'clock stubble on his chin gets the juices flowing even more."

My eyes are bugging out of my head as I enlarge the photo of Callie and Matthew and shift the screen so half of Callie gets cut off, and Matthew becomes my only focus.

"Mouthwatering, clit-pulsing perfection," Indie growls.

"Who has such skin, such dark hair, and such bright blue sparkling eyes? Is it even genetically possible?"

"Matthew Muller does. It appears it is." Indie sighs. "I think I need to use the restroom," she says, shifting uncomfortably in her chair before rising. I reach out my arm, grab her hand, and pull her back into a seated position.

"He asked me out," I blurt out.

"Who?"

"Matthew. On the phone just now. The call I took."

"Get. The. Fuck. Out. Of. Here." She pronounces each word singularly and with purpose.

"He did. I swear he did."

"Why?" Indie dips her eyebrows, causing my heart to grow heavy.

I'm not pretty enough. Skinny enough. Good enough for a guy like Matthew Muller. Go on, say it. I turn away and focus my attention back on the computer monitor. "Don't worry about it."

Indie leaps upright and throws her arm around my throat, hugging me from behind. "I'm sorry. I shouldn't have said what I did. It wasn't meant to come out like ... I didn't mean to say it in such a way."

"What did you mean?"

"As far as I know, and don't quote me on this, but apart from Callie, Matthew Muller does not see any other woman. You know Callie sees him off the books too. A lot. The only reason he books her in the first place is to keep her business going, and Kathleen's pockets full. Matthew and Kathleen are good friends."

"Does he love Callie?"

Indie's lips are so close to the tip of my ear it makes me feel uncomfortable. "Alice says he doesn't. Alice says he's never been in love. Never."

Matthew has never been in love. I've never been in love, but then again, I've never dated either.

"Indiana, shouldn't you have left?" Kathleen's voice booms from behind me.

Indie plucks her phone from my hand, and after

she does, my neck and shoulders become absent of her weight. "Yes, ma'am. I was catching up on some files I fell behind on." She takes a shaky breath. "On my own time, of course."

"It doesn't look like you were doing much filing—more so gossiping. I don't like such chatter in this office. I only need one of you working in here at a time."

"Understood. I'll go. See you tonight."

"I won't be in. I'm going to be away for a few days. Callie will run the place in my absence." Kathleen looks wrecked and not her usual put-together self.

"Are you okay, Kitty?" I ask softly.

"Yes. Why wouldn't I be?" she snaps.

"No reason." I turn back to face my computer before Indie and I look at each other at the same time. Without a word spoken between us, I know we're subconsciously sending a message to each other. A message saying *Kitty's never taken a day off*. What the hell is going on here? Why does she look so worn down?

"Have a great break." Indie slings her tote bag over her shoulder. She pulls her long, deep purple locks across her lips. *"I'll message you,"* she mouths from behind the strands of hair.

I nod.

As Indie walks around the opposite side of her desk, she glances at Kathleen and says, "I'll see you when you get back." She then offers me a subtle wave, and she's out the door.

Great! Now I'm left to deal with the Kitty monster and my Matthew Muller situation on my own.

Ring, ring, ring.

I stare at the headset and freeze.

Ring, ring, ring.

"Answer the phone, Melinda," Kitty snips.

I pick up the headset and put it in place.

"What has gotten into you lately?" Kathleen tuts before I hear her stomp away.

"Welcome to Kit on High, you're speaking with Mindy. How can I be of service?"

"You could go on a date with me. What do you say?"

My heart stops beating. My palms become clammy. Matthew Muller. Oh, dear God. He called back.

Chapter Ten

Fletcher's tail flicks from left to right in a timed beat as he curls into a tighter ball against my lap. He purrs excessively, which I find soothing.

I stroke my hand down his back to meet the rhythm of his tail swishes as I hold the novel I'm dying to know the ending of in front of my face. I'm focused. I'm following the words of chapter twenty-three as they bleed across cream-coloured pages, and for the first time since I returned home, my mind is quiet.

It doesn't take long, half a page to be exact, until I find myself distracted and my mind filled with excessive chatter once more.

A wealthy, handsome man who has complimented my voice many times asked me out today. That happened, and I turned him down. *Idiot.*

My boss, the woman who's as straight as an arrow, committed, and always in charge, showed a side of herself I've never seen before: vulnerability.

The guy I thought I made a connection with in a serendipitous moment is somewhere out there flying under the radar, floating, drifting far, far away from me, never to be heard from again.

I'm unsettled, confused, and lost.

I close my eyes. "Please stop racing, brain. I don't want to think. I need the quiet again. I need to concentrate on this book," I mutter.

Fletcher wiggles until he's tucked up against my lower stomach instead of my upper legs, and I feel the sudden cold where he once was before I'm gifted his warmth again, only now it's splayed across my gut.

"Who needs a hot water bottle when I've got you?" I stroke Fletcher's fur and look out the window. "Rainy, cold weather—it's a relief from the heat I guess."

Fletcher purrs harder as I tell myself to focus and allow myself to be captivated by a tale of two entirely fictional people created by an author whose words have so far brought me hope in my search for love.

I push my shoulders back to relieve the twinge of heat I'm experiencing down my neck due to my rigid posture. Finally, I'm relaxing and drawn back to the words filling the pages.

"Don't do it," I murmur through a tensed jaw, turning the page. Are you kidding me with this shit? *Delilah wants you, Hugh. So what if you're damaged? She'll love all your parts, every one of them, because they belong to you. Will you let her make up her own fucking mind and not tell her what she should want?* I growl as my teeth grind together, and I continue reading.

"You son of a bitch." I hurl the book across the room, and Fletcher jumps. His claws sink through the material of my skirt and into my skin. "It's okay, boy." I run one hand up and down his back rapidly while I use my other hand to wipe away my falling tears.

Click, click.

I hear the lock turn on the door. I pick Fletcher up and stand.

"Daddy's home, sugar dumplings. How was your—" Chris stops speaking. "Oh, crap. Well, I guessed you'd be here doing something of this nature after I receive your text message and you stood me up at the cafe. It was apple crumble with some really sweet nectar poured on top, if you were wondering." Chris doesn't look mad at me for standing him up. His expression is more of concern. "Come here, honey." Chris marches towards me.

I put one hand up like a stop sign. "Don't."

Chris lifts his arms into the air. Two bags dangling from each of his wrists. "I've come prepared. I knew everything would've finally consumed you. I wish I got here sooner. I hate seeing you cry."

"You can't swoop in and be my knight in shining armour all the time, Christopher Gandy."

"Who says?" He's expressionless.

"Society. Me. My mother."

"Your mother? Pfft! Please. That bitch is batshit crazy."

I giggle and cry at the same time.

Chris takes a long stride towards me. "Mindy, let me tell you something: I may love the guys, and I do find all women sexually revolting, but honey, I can be your knight in shining armour. There are no rules to say a gay man can't love a straight woman in such a way. Plus, I'll only be filling such shoes until your forever man, the one lost, taking his sweet-arse time getting to you, who doesn't know his way around a fucking love map, gets here."

I giggle harder.

The comfort I feel as Chris wraps his arms around Fletcher and me, pulling us against his chest, is just what I need right now. A hug can take a small chunk of a burden away from a person.

"Fletcher." I wiggle myself from Chris's grip.

"Are you alive, furball? Do you need Unky Chris to give you kitty mouth-to-mouth?"

I look at Fletcher whose eyes are narrow. His ears are pointed, and he is most definitely giving Chris his famous death stare. I shift my eyes to Chris, and I find myself wishing just for a moment he was straight, and that I had unrequited love for him. Maybe I would love Chris in that way if he were straight. How am I to know I wouldn't? It would be easier for me if Chris were the possessor of my apparent love map because at least I know we'd get along great and I could talk to him about anything and everything.

"In these bags, I have everything to make you feel better. You leave it to me, okay?"

"I'm crying because of the stupid book you got me. Why is Hugh such a dick? And how the hell is Delilah ever going to survive the soul-crushing aftermath of his dickery?"

"Oh, you got to that part. Probably not the best time to get there."

"Tell me they live happily ever after."

"I can't ruin the book for you, but Mindy, they can if you believe they will. You know, you never have to pick it up and finish it. You can write your own ending to their story."

"I can write the end? Well, in that case, the scene in the restaurant never actually happened. Delilah dreamt it. Growing inside her womb is a little pea-sized Hugh. He'll get down on bended knee, confess his deep and undying love for her, and ask her to be his wife all before she even gets a chance to tell him she's carrying his child."

"Well, it's an interesting direction to take this particular story in." Chris shakes his head. "I mean, it's a beautiful and creative ending." The smirk that follows makes his words unconvincing. "Mindy, if you could write the ending of your own love story, what would it be?"

I don't answer. I picture Arlie and me dancing on a

beach in the tropics, sipping cocktails on our honeymoon.

Why the hell am I so infatuated with a man I barely know, one who apparently has no intention of ever being in the same room with me again? If he did, he would have made contact by now. I should've agreed to the date with Matthew Muller. I've probably blown my chance with him now too.

My love life: Currently messy and incredibly complex.

Does this continue to get worse after you turn thirty? I sure hope not because the big three zero is less than two weeks away, and my twenties and my youth are about to expire.

Thirty! Why do I have to turn thirty?

Chapter Eleven

I walk towards the bedroom door but stop when my mobile phone chimes. I'm hopeful it's a message from Arlie. It's not.

Mum: Are we still chatting tonight?

Me: Yes, give me a minute. I'll Skype you in five. Sorry, I'm running late.

I enter the bedroom. Chris turns away from me, stripped of the gym gear he was wearing when he arrived, now standing in his birthday suit.

"It's called my hot body, biatch, and I know you appreciate what you saw."

I shake my head and close my eyes, no longer able to see his pasty white, yet extremely toned butt cheeks. "I saw nothing."

"Sure, you didn't. I'm going for a shower. I know the

bedroom is about negative four degrees, but me turning the air conditioning down to freezing has a purpose. You'll need to wait to find out why, though."

"Okay," I say slowly. "You're so strange," I add. "I'm going to go Skype Mum, because she's waiting to hear from me, while you wash up." I open my eyes to see Chris take a step closer to the en suite. I quickly close them again.

"Perfect. Oh, and while you're out there, pick up the book you threw and put it back on your chair. You'll get back to it. Trust me, it's worth it."

"Yes, boss. Can I open my eyes now? Are you out of sight?"

"You sure can, sugar. I'm covered," he says with a Southern drawl.

"Chris!" I squeal.

"What?" He's stood posed like a model with his backside again filling my vision. "Hot damn, can I get an amen?"

"Oh my God! Go shower and put some bloody clothes on."

"Oh my God is right. I hear that line a lot."

"Chris!"

"I'm going."

The dial tone for Skype is ringing through the speakers of the laptop. I wait, and I wait until finally,

Mum accepts the call.

"Hello, sweetheart. I didn't think you were going to make contact tonight. It's nine already, and you said you'd Skype me at seven thirty."

"I got busy, Mum." Suddenly, I'm gifted a vision of her large saggy cleavage. "Mum, you need to push the screen back."

"Why? I see you fine."

"Well, I see your boobs, not your face. Every time, Mum. Every single time."

"I didn't hear you complaining when you fed off my bosoms until you were over the age of two. Most kids give up in the first year—not you, though. You refused to give up the breast, full stop. I had to force you off. It was like trying to get a drug addict to detox."

"Mum, I've heard this story more times than I care to remember. Tilt the freaking screen."

The camera's position shifts back. "Can you see me now?"

"Yep. Better."

"What's wrong?" Mum brings her face so close to the camera I have a visual of only one of her hazel brown eyes. "Your face is all puffy and blotchy. Have you been crying?"

"Allergies," I lie unconvincingly.

"You're lying. You've been crying."

"Whatever you reckon."

"Did something happen to upset you at the brothel

you work at? You really need to quit that terrible job."

"Mum, it's an escort agency."

"Same thing. I just feel your talent is wasted. Why don't you consider going back to a hospital and—"

"No." I shut her down, my voice colder than I mean it to be.

I can't think about going back.

Not after what happened.

"Well, let's talk about something else then, dear. How's the love life?"

"Is that Mel, Mum?" I hear Bridey say.

"Yes, dear, it is. Melinda's been crying. She's all blotchy."

"Scoot over and let me see," she says as Mum's face zooms out and Bridey's comes into focus. "Oh, you have been crying. What's happened?"

"Nothing." I shift uncomfortably in my chair.

"I hope it's a guy." She places her hands in prayer in front of her pointed chin, the same shaped jawline our mother has. It's no dramatization when people say Bridey is the spitting image of our mother, and I'm the girl version of our father.

"Mind your business."

"Your Mother Teresa image is getting old," Bridey says.

"What's wrong with you? Why would you call me that?" My annoyance is evident.

"Because it's true."

"Whatever."

"Now girls, stop the bickering." Mum flicks her dyed black locks.

"Yes, Mum," we say in unison.

"So what made you cry? For real?" Bridey pulls her brown locks over her shoulder, twisting the ends.

"A book, okay? It was a book I'm reading. The guy was an arsehole, and it made me cry. There. Now you know. Go on, have a good laugh at my expense."

"All men are arseholes. Lane's an arsehole often, I'll have you know."

"Your father is an absolute dipshit about eighty percent of the time."

"Mum!" I yell.

Mum picks at her nails with her eyes turned down. "It's true. Just this morning, he got me all peeved off."

"Here we go." Bridey rolls her eyes.

I giggle.

"Where do I start? He didn't make the bed. He was the last out of it. He left his jocks on the floor. Thirty-five years of marriage and I'm still picking his littered clothes up from the floor. He's no better than a teenage boy."

Bridey laughs.

"Then he slurped his cereal. You girls know how homicidal I get when people eat loudly. I wanted to stab him in his wrinkly neck with my spoon."

"Mum, stop it." I'm laughing so hard.

"Lane. Oh, my God. You know what he does?" Bridey asks.

"Do I want to know?" I reply, screwing my face up.

"He picks his toenails in the lounge." Bridey fake dry-heaves. "He leaves them in the chair, and I have to dig around, finding them."

"Eww. That's foul."

"Right? I swear some nights I want to grind them all up and put them in his food."

I'm laughing so hard now I'm crying.

"Some days, I want to poison your father. He's like a man-child who's never going to grow up. You're probably living the life right by being single, my dear daughter." Mum nods. "Toilet rolls. They never change them. Dishes. They never wash them. Towels. They leave those suckers on the floor all wet, left to get mouldy. They fart in bed. They fart through sex. They fart in the car when the windows are rolled up—"

"They fart all the time, and it stinks. It's rotten like something crawled up their hairy arses and died in there," Bridey continues.

"Don't even get me started on your father's snoring. If it were legal to suffocate him with a pillow, I'd do it tomorrow. No, I'd do it today, right now."

"Where's Dad anyway?" I say through my tears.

"Well, you won't believe me, but he's at the gym. He goes to the gym every day now. Tonight, he's gone late because Crawly—you know Crawly from down the road?"

I nod.

"He's also on a health kick, and they need to hold ..." Mum does air quotations. "... 'each other's hands' while they exercise."

"Mum, you sound bitter about your marriage. You realise this, yes?"

"I'm not bitter. It's called resentment. You stay married for thirty-five years and come tell me you don't want to go all murder on the dance floor on your husband's face with a knife."

"Mum!" Bridey and I say simultaneously.

"Thirty-five years of marriage and come talk to me then," Mums says so matter-of-factly.

Bridey snaps her neck to face Mum. "You love Dad, right? Like, we don't have to worry about being children of divorce?"

Mum softly backhands Bridey across the chest. "No. Of course not. I love him. He's just annoying, and he's driving me bonkers."

"Thank God." Bridey sighs.

There's a long silence.

"Have I cheered you up, baby girl?" Mum again moves too close to the screen. This time, her nostril is all I see.

"Yes. You have. Sit back away from the screen. I can see up your nose. You're too close."

"Good. Sometimes all we need is a laugh to get past sadness, even if it's because of a book." She slowly zooms out into a more visually rewarding position for me.

"You two are crazy. You know this, right?"

They're both nodding.

"We miss you." Mum's expression becomes sombre.

"Yeah, we do." Bridey purses her full lips.

"You could come visit me here in Melbourne."

"One day," Mum replies.

"The city isn't for me. Come back home and visit soon," Bridey says.

"Okay."

"What are you doing tonight?" Bridey says.

"Chilling at home. I better go. Chris is here; he was taking a shower, but I can't hear the water running anymore. We're going to hang out for a bit."

Mum tuts. "That Chris is a flamboyant young fellow. He's as prissy as a suckling, and you won't be getting anywhere with him."

"Mum, I know he's gay."

She places her hand on her chest. "Oh, thank the lord. I'd been worried you'd not seen."

I drop my head into my palms and laugh. How anyone could mistake Chris for straight is beyond me.

"Well, go have fun. We'll talk again on Saturday." Mum leans into the screen.

"Sounds good. Well, unless I have a date."

And before Mum or Bridey have a chance to say a single word, I end the call and shut the lid of the laptop. That'll give those two hens something to gossip and cluck about this week.

With a sigh, I walk towards my bedroom. I turn the doorknob and step right in, closing the door behind me.

The lights are dim. The television at the end of my bed is turned on, but the screen is blue, and Chris is lying on his stomach on top of the comforter with his hands under his chin and his ankles crossed behind him together in the air.

"You sounded like you were having a good laugh." He smiles.

"Bridey was over at Mum's, and they were saying silly things. Did you know Mum thought I didn't know you were gay?"

"Does the woman think you're blind?" Chris scoffs.

I nod, scanning my eyes over the outfit Chris is wearing. "What the hell is with your get-up?"

He leaps to his knees. "You know, I thought you'd never notice. This, my beautiful friend, is our attire for tonight. You've got one too."

"A bunny onesie? Why?"

"Because why the hell not? Do you love these bunny ears?"

"There's Snapchat for bunny ears. You don't need

to wear store-bought ones anymore."

Chris's eyes bug from their sockets. "You know what Snapchat is?"

I bobble my head. "I've heard of it."

"You don't have it, do you?"

"Nope."

"Thought as much." Chris turns until I'm looking at his back. "The onesie came with a bunny tail. Look. Super cute, right?"

I grin. "Very."

"Okay, well get your kit off and put your onesie on, and while you do, I'll go prepare our snacks."

"Alrighty then. I'm game."

"Oh, you're going to love it." Chris's turns and leaves the room.

Maybe I don't need to find a knight in shining armour. Perhaps I need to appreciate the people I have in my life right now—well, for as long as it takes until the slowpoke who's supposed to make me want to murder him after thirty-five years of marriage finally shows up. Who am I kidding? I need to appreciate the people in my life, for all my life, and stop taking them for granted.

I hold a mug of hot chocolate with baby marshmallows floating on top in my hands. A bunny onesie covers my skin, which is so soft and comfortable I plan to sleep in it every night with my air conditioner set to freezing. The comforter is pulled over my legs and midway up my belly. My bunny ears sit positioned on my head. *Pretty Woman* plays on the television screen, and Chris lies beside me in bed, taking care of me as he has done since we've become friends. Chris has been my rock, and as the lines of the movie play out, I think of the day I met him.

__The Quarter:__ One month after my big move to Melbourne, there was Chris. I'd stumbled upon a cute little coffee house after trotting the pavement for far too long. I was dying of thirst, starving, and sweaty. The air-conditioning was cold and inviting. I'd travelled much farther on foot than I'd planned to on my self-made tour, and if I hadn't found somewhere to stop immediately, I was bound to pass out.

I slumped into a booth towards the back. I hadn't noticed Chris sitting at a table across from me. How I hadn't seen him, I still haven't figured out—well, unless you count the fact I was beyond exhausted.

Chris was wearing fluorescent yellow. He had hot pink sweatbands around each of his wrists and an identical one around his head. He was typing away on a laptop when he said, "You have to get the daily special. It's a dessert, and it's a different one every day."

His eyes found mine. His cheeky smile said, 'I'll be your friend forever', and before I could even open my mouth and reply, Chris had shifted his stuff across the table from me and sat down. "I'm Christopher Grandy. I'm gay, and this get-up is to show people how stupid their stereotypical view of homosexuals are. Nobody dresses like this anymore because it's ridiculous. And you are?" He offered his hand.

I took it in a long handshake. "I'm Melinda Grant. I'm new to the city. I've moved from Queensland. I'm as straight as they come, so I won't be sourcing any girlfriends for the, you know ..." I leant in to shield our conversation from prying ears, "... bedroom stuff. I think your outfit suits you, so I think you should dress in such a way if I'm being honest."

Chris's smile grew, as did mine.

The rest is history.

"Wait for it. Wait for it ..." Chris's torso lengthens as he perches on his knees.

Richard Gere snaps the box closed, causing Julia Roberts to get a shock before she delivers her iconic laugh.

"Cinematic gold. Oh, I love this movie so much." Chris tips his head to the side until it's rested on my shoulder.

"I love this movie too."

We watch in silence. We drink hot chocolate, and eat sweets and way too much junk food until little piles of wrappers form across the bed.

"I'll start my diet again tomorrow. I heard the lemon detox is good for you," I mumble.

"You don't need to diet, babe. You're all curves. You should be proud of them ... of what you have. Embrace what you were born with." Chris shifts until his eyes connect with mine. "Like, you know you're not fat, and you look like a woman, yeah?"

I don't answer Chris. Instead, I break eye contact and go back to watching the love between a hooker and a millionaire play out.

"I wish you could see what I see," he mumbles before snuggling into my side.

When the credits roll, Chris and I both sigh.

"He fulfilled her fairy tale. It was the quintessential happily ever after." Chris sighs again.

"It was. I will never get sick of watching this movie or listening to you say the lines as though you were performing them yourself."

"I've talent—what can I say? But it's got me thinking."

"How so?"

"You work for an escort agency. Maybe you should become an escort and bang one of the millionaires. Then he can come climb some rusty old ladder, even though he's petrified of heights, and you'll have your own real-life *Pretty Woman* story."

I choke on my spit.

"Melinda Grant, hooker. Now, who'd play the millionaire? That is the question of the night."

Without thought, I blubber out, "Matthew Muller."

"Say what? Who's this Matthew 'Millionaire' Muller?" Chris's head rotates until our eyes meet. "Who is Matthew Muller?"

"A millionaire who is some type of super lover between the sheets. He also looks like a god carved from only the finest body parts." I've never seen Chris speechless until this moment. "It's why I didn't come to The Quarter today. It's why I curled myself up with the book. He asked me out on a date. He's a client."

Chris smacks my arm frantically. "He's a client."

I nod.

"Oh, fuckity, mcfuckity, no friggin' way. When were you going to tell me? Oh, oh, when are you two going on a date?"

"I'm not."

"Why?" His voice reaches a higher pitch.

"I said no. Matthew hires escorts—well, only one escort, Callie. He lives a life where everything he wants is right at his fingertips. It's not a life for me. I don't want a *Pretty Woman* story. I want my own story. It's why I said no."

"You're insane. Does this Matthew bend both ways? Because, honey, I'd be all over him like a horny teenager loaded up on Viagra. I live for a sugar daddy—a sweet, sweet, delicious sugar daddy."

"Chris!"

"He's my dream guy."

"Do you want to see a picture of your dream guy?"

"Do I want to see a picture? Do I want to see a picture? Do. I. Want. To. See. A. Picture?" Chris says, each time his vocal range heightening in pitch. "Yes, damn it. Where's the picture already? Why aren't you moving?"

"Indie sent it to me after she left work this morning. I could show you, but ..."

"Gimme, gimme." Chris taps his fingertips to his palm repetitively. "I want to know what my secret sexual dream guy looks like."

"Be prepared for a boner."

"Oh, this is the best night of my life."

I retrieve the phone from the bedside cupboard. I open the gallery and hand it to Chris. He instantly slides down the mattress until he's lying flat. "Yes, God! I'll have that one, please. You do incredible work. Great frickin' work. Let's face it, big man, you're brilliant."

I laugh as Chris continues to stare at the screen.

"You need to say yes to this man," he mutters.

"He's all yours," I reply before climbing off the bed, walking across the small space, then opening the door. "I'll be right back."

When I return, I'm holding my laptop in one hand, and its power cord in the other. "Do you want to stalk the internet and learn all there is to know about Matthew Muller?"

"Do you even have to ask?"

I chortle.

Every page we scroll through on the internet shows the impressive life of Matthew Muller, from his humble beginnings as a bank teller to his later success in the stock market. Chris is drooling. I'm not. Instead, I realise Matthew is just a person who started out with basically nothing and followed the life he wanted until he practically received all he desired. I was once on this same path—well, until the day I killed a patient. That day, I saw my world crumble at my feet, ripping me into a deep, dark sinkhole until I was only a shell of who I used to be. Sure, I was clumsy. Sure, I wasn't well-suited to emergency medicine or surgery of any sort, but my diagnostic abilities far outshone those of the other doctors in the hospital. I was saving lives until a fatal mistake meant I was responsible for the loss of life. A father, young, with two small children. He should be alive watching his kids grow up, but thanks to me, he's buried in a cemetery and his family live on without him. How could anyone bounce back from something like taking someone else's life?

I still can't. Guilt fills me. He never leaves me.

When I started out in the medical profession, I was warned that at some point, every doctor is responsible for a death. *"We're human, not robots. We get it wrong."* I told myself it wouldn't happen to me, but it did. Sure, the doctors around me shared their personal stories and responsibility for mistakes which led to someone's death. Sure, I wasn't the only one to make such a colossal balls-up. But no matter how hard I fight to bury my wrongdoing, I can't, because Leon Drucelli's frightened face will always pop into my mind as a reminder. He's dead, I'm alive, and I can't undo it, and due to the circumstances surrounding his death, I'll never allow myself to perform the one job I truly loved doing.

"Mindy. You've gone all spacey." I hear clicking fingers.

"Leon Drucelli." It's barely audible.

"It was a mistake," Chris says. "You need to learn how to let him go, how to stop his ghost from haunting you."

But I can't.

Chapter Twelve

It's one a.m. Crying, I pull out the storage container in the linen closet, the one with all my medical textbooks, and Leon Drucelli's medical file, which I've kept a copy of. Through my tears, I relive my mistake. I go all judge and jury on myself until I mutter the word, "Guilty."

Chris doesn't leave me to wallow in my self-pity and my incrimination. Instead, he brings me tissues, hugs me, and replenishes my water supply so I avoid dehydration. When I close the textbooks and file everything back into the storage container, Chris sighs.

"We have a number, Melinda," he says, using my full name. He never uses my full name. "When our number ticks over, that's it. It was you standing by his bed when it happened, sure, but it could have been anybody else, and still, the result would have been the same. His number ticked over; his time on Earth was done. His purpose for being here was served. You can lock yourself into eternal damnation until your number arrives, or you can grow some lady balls and do what you're supposed to be doing: saving the lives of those whose numbers aren't up yet, who need you here to help them. You're wasting your ability. You're not providing the service you were meant to, and for the love of God, will you seriously get some counselling so you can see I'm right?"

I stumble backwards with the storage container in hand. I glare at Chris in a way I've never done before. His words sting. I swivel on my bunny footed onesie and return my nightmare to the cupboard, then close the door.

For the next thirty minutes, we sit in silence, then, as if nothing has happened at all, Chris picks up my laptop and says, "Let's see who's getting all hot and heavy over you on the dating site. You don't get to give up, Mindy. Not on this."

I don't. Maybe if I'd tried harder with Leon, things would have been different.

Now I need to try hard with me. We laugh, we poke fun, and we search through pages and pages of people, who are just like me, living in a cyberspace world of dating. Until a large pop-up covers the site and claims my attention.

Are you looking for YOUR Perfect Catch? We can help you. Click 'yes' below for your chance to find

the one you've been searching for. He's right here.

I look at Chris, whose eyes are wide and filled with excitement.

"What is this?" I say.

He shrugs. "I don't know, but click yes."

I do.

The site loads a new page. A man and woman posed in the most sensual of ways fills my vision. Their lips are parted from one another a fraction, a kiss imminent. A very eye-catching opening image. Above this sexy photo, it says, *Would you like to submit your profile for the upcoming show* Perfect Catch? *If so, click the 'submit' button below.*

"This has to be spam, right?"

"I know how to clean your device if it is. I want to see. Open, open." Chris bounces on the spot.

"Me too." I click submit.

Grey Stone Productions is seeking three ladies to join three selected male counterparts on our new show, *Perfect Catch*. We're looking for ladies between the ages of twenty-five and thirty-five who are single and ready to find the love of their life.
Click 'more' to learn about the show.

"Do it. Do it now," Chris says, all deep-throated and manly, a tone I've never heard come out of his mouth in the entire time I've known him.

"Okay already." I click the 'learn more' button.

Welcome!
Our computer system has the details of three gentlemen suitors already logged. They've answered a series of random questions, as will you. (See the 'questions' button at the bottom of the page for entry.) Once all answers are submitted, our scientific computer analysis program, the Love Catcher, will pair these gentlemen with their perfect catch. Submissions will be closing tonight, so make sure to enter now.

"Do it," Chris encourages.

"I'm not going on a television show. Have you lost your marbles?"

"Do it," he says again.

"No."

"Do it," Chris demands.

"Why?"

"Because maybe your directionally unmotivated soul mate is waiting for you on this show."

"You're all unicorns, rainbows, and fucking bunny onesies, aren't you?"

"What have you got to lose?"

"My dignity. My sanity. I can barely speak to the opposite sex, let alone do it on a television show."

"There you go, putting limitations on yourself again."

"No, I'm not. I'm a go-getter in life."

"Says who?"

"Me."

"Prove it."

"Fine," I snap, scrolling past the next five paragraphs of information until I find the questionnaire link. "Here goes wasted time."

Chris doesn't reply.

Full Name: Melinda Renee Grant
Date of Birth: October 2nd, 1988
Email address: MelindaGrant@gmail.com
Occupation:

"What do I put? I can't put receptionist at an escort agency now, can I?"

"Type doctor. It's what I did on your dating profile. It's not a lie. You're still licensed."

"Okay."

I type *doctor*.

Are you single? Yes
Are you a virgin? No
Are you currently employed? Yes
Your highest level of Education: A doctorate in medicine.
Postcode: 3195
Are you religious? No
(If yes, please supply the further information below.)
Do you have any children? No

How many siblings do you have? Male or female? One. Female.

Are you parents married, divorced, living together, widowed, or deceased? Married.

Were you born in Australia? Yes.

Is there any medical reason you could not complete physical challenges or stay on a tropical island for three weeks? No.

You're now entering a series of random questions. The answers to these selected questions are relevant regarding the systematic programming we're using to create a perfect match.

Please note: There are no right or wrong answers. You need to complete each question with full honesty and to the best of your ability. Relax. Put your feet up and complete the remainder of our questionnaire. Don't forget to hit the 'submit' button when you reach the end, and write down the identification number which will appear on your screen.

What's your favourite colour? Yellow.
What's your favourite scent?

"Favourite scent?" I search for Chris's reaction. "Can I put coffee?"

"It said to be honest, and you sure love the smell of coffee."

I type coffee in the vacant spot.

If you had to choose a number between one and ten, what would you choose? Six.

"Six?" Chris's eyes connect with mine.
"I've always loved the number six."
"Fair enough. Continue. Mine's three, by the way."
"I know." I smile before reading the next question.

Beer, wine, spirits, cocktails, or I don't drink? Cocktails
Bus, plane, train, or car? Plane
Sweet, sour, or savoury? Sweet
Beach or meadows? Beach
Hot or cold? Cold
Dress, skirt, or pants and top? Dress
Flats or stilettos? Flats
Rain or sunshine? Rain
Snow or sand? Sand
Outdoors or indoors? Indoors
Reading or television? Reading
Cursive or bold text? Cursive
Cruises or destination vacations? Destination vacations
Dark or light? Light
Casual or formal settings and attire? Casual
Businessman or labourer? Labourer

"Really? I would have thought businessman."
"I get that, but there's something about a man who gets his hands dirty ..."

"Not my cuppa tea, but to each their own."

"You like them clean-shaven, rich, and with expensive taste."

"Girl, you know me so well."

"I do."

"Keep going."

"Okay."

Maths, English, science, or art? English

Hot-air balloons or speedboats? Hot-air balloons

Circus or Carnival? Carnival

Hair up or down? Down

Shave or wax? Shave

Tea or coffee? Coffee

G-string or briefs? Briefs

Vampire or werewolf? Vampire

Dice or cards? Cards

Rivers or lakes? Lakes

Grass or carpet? Grass

House or apartment? House

Car or motorbike? Car

Fine dining or barbecue? Barbecue

Café or Restaurant? Café

After another three pages and fifty thousand pointless questions later, I upload the photograph Chris used for my dating profile and hover the mouse over the 'submit' button. Chris's eyes connect with mine.

"Press submit," he whispers.

The mouse stays pointed over the big green button. My stomach roils like an ocean wave. My heart races like I'm running a marathon. My hands shake.

"You're a go-getter, remember?" Chris says.

Click!

Congratulations, and thank you for entering to be a contestant on *Perfect Catch*. You'll receive either an acceptance or denial email, or a phone call, in the next twenty-four hours. If accepted, you'll be given a location and a day and time to appear in our studio. Good luck, and we hope your ideal guy is one of the stars already selected for the show.

Make sure you've read our terms and conditions.

Your entry number is 2,000,004.

"What the hell have I just done?"

"Lived. You just lived in the fast lane, Mindy. Twenty-four hours." Chris claps his hands together. "We'll know in twenty-four hours."

I drop my head and swallow hard to avoid throwing up. Melinda Grant on a television show? No freaking way. Talk about a disaster waiting to happen.

Chapter Thirteen

Chris falls asleep curled up beside me as I try desperately to drift off myself, but my mind keeps racing with so many thoughts. Thoughts of being successful and having to go on a television show. Thoughts of Arlie, Matthew Muller, Leon Drucelli, Mum, Bridey, the cat killer, Queensland, Alec, Kitty, Callie, and for a little while, I even play out some scenes from *Pretty Woman*. But after I finish thinking about all these things, I come back to the fact I've entered a competition to be on a television show.

Why? Why did I do it? I'm not a live-in-the-fast-lane type of girl. I'm the drive-in-the-steady-slow-rule-following-lane kind.

The producers won't call, so why am I lying here thinking about all of this in the first place?

I toss. I turn. I toss some more until Chris yells, "For the love of God, are you wrestling a shark? You better be wrestling a shark, or I'm going to whip your butt."

"Sorry, go back to sleep. I'll stop moving."

Three o'clock passes, then four, and finally five. I'm still wide-awake with a racing mind and restless legs.

At six a.m., I throw back the covers and clamber from the bed, making my way to the kitchen where Fletcher waits by the refrigerator, meowing.

"Morning, my little love." I pick him up and hold him against my chest as I grab the milk from the now open fridge door. "You want your brekky bites?" Fletcher rubs his cheek against mine. "I'll take that as a yes," I say as I remove the box of cat biscuits from one cupboard, and a mug from another, before I lower Fletcher to the ground.

"Here you go, boy." I pour a large amount of food into his bowl.

The automatic machine brews my morning coffee, and before long, I'm sitting on the couch with a cup of steaming joe in hand. I'm going to need at least six cups of coffee today, if not more. I flick on the television.

Ring, ring. Ring, ring. Ring, ring. Ring, ring.

Who wants me so early in the morning?

Slowly, I make my way to the bedroom where I left my mobile phone. Chris is stirring by the time I reach it. 'Private' flashes across the screen.

"Morning, Melinda Grant speaking."

"Good morning, Melinda. I hope I didn't wake you."

"No." *Who is this?*

"I know it's early. I apologise for calling you at such a time, but I needed to get in contact with you right away. My name is Susan Rye, and I'm telephoning you on behalf of *Perfect Catch* and Grey Stone Productions. Did you sleep well?"

"Good." It's all I manage to say through my shock.

"Excellent. Well, we have good news: you've been selected as a match for one of our gentlemen suitors. We're so happy to have you come into the studio and undergo the necessary requirements to ensure you're in tip-top shape to participate. Could you arrive at the Grey Stone Productions, studio, by nine a.m. today? If so, we can get all your paperwork filled in and your medical requirements completed."

"Nine? This morning?"

"Clear your plans for today and the next three weeks, because you're off to paradise."

"What? Now?"

"Yes, now."

"It's early in the morning. Like, six. Is this a joke? Aren't entries still open? I'm confused."

"You've been selected. That's all I can tell you."

"Me?"

"Yes. I promise you this isn't a joke."

"Okay."

"Now, can you wear something comfortable? Completing a medical and stress test is one of the conditions of entering the show."

"Show?"

"Are you okay?"

"Fine."

"Great. Okay, nine a.m. I'll text the address to you, and we'll see you then. Make sure you eat a big breakfast."

"Breakfast. Yes. Eat."

She laughs. "Okay, see you then, and on behalf of *Perfect Catch*, congratulations."

"Why do you look like that? What's wrong?" Chris whispers, now standing in front of me.

"Thank you," I say with hesitation. "Goodbye."

My hand goes limp. The phone drops to the floor as I stand with my jaw hung low and my breathing unsteady. My heart beats like a drum. It's thumping so hard I can see my breast jumping.

"Mindy, what happened? Oh my God, are you okay?"

I can hear Chris speaking, but I'm finding it impossible to answer him.

Chris grabs both my arms and shakes me. "Woman, speak. What happened?"

"The show. I ... I ... I'm going on the show."

"What?" Chris's tone is high-pitched.

"I'm going to be on *Perfect Catch*."

"Holy shit. This is amazing."

"I can't breathe," I say breathlessly.

"Oh dear. I've got you." Slowly, I feel Chris moving me from where I once stood. "Here, sit on the bed. Just keep breathing. You're okay."

I cry. It's not a whimper or a sob—it's a full-force howl projecting from my lungs. I'm petrified.

"Oh, Mindy-Moo." Chris holds me tightly.

I can't do this. "Chris, who'll feed Fletcher? Take care of my apartment? Pay my bills? Get my mail." I take a shaky breath. Who'll feed the fish."

"You don't own any fish."

He's right, I don't.

"Don't worry about any of that. I'll take care of everything here. You need to do this."

"I'll have to let work know I'm taking time off. What if I get fired?"

"Would it be so bad if you did? You hate your job."

Would it? Be so bad?

I do hate my job.

The building is navy blue with the words 'Grey Stone Productions' inscribed on a huge billboard attached to the roof. Every step I take towards the front doors has my legs turning to jelly. I twist abruptly, headed for the car. Chris grabs my shoulders and shifts me back in the direction I was heading.

"You're doing this. I have an amazing feeling about this entire situation, Mindy. You need to get away. Have an amazing holiday in paradise with a hot guy— no distractions, no life interruptions. This will help you to get over your fear of men, sort your mind out, and sort your life out. And I hope to God you finally get the '*D*' because you are as pent up as a constipated arsehole."

"I'm not having sex on national television, you idiot."

"They totally won't put the sex on television. Trust me."

"Chris! Not helping."

"One foot in front of the other, you big fluffy chicken. Where's my chicken who's ready to fly?"

"She can't fly because she's a fucking chicken, and she also got shot by a hunter. I want to go home." I reach for the door handle as I gulp down my fear.

"Keep moving."

Jingle, jingle, jingle.

"Okay, I've opened the door. Now you need to walk through it. Go on, I'm right here." Chris won't let me leave. My only way to flee is to kick him in the nuts and make a break for it.

I'm standing in the doorway with a wave of heat racing through my extremities. It's like a heatwave of fear making me sweat.

"You can do this," Chris whispers against my cheek. "I'm right here with you. You're not alone."

I take one big step, followed by another, then another, until I stand at a blue marble countertop which reaches my armpits.

"Good morning. How can I assist you?" The man behind the desk has kind eyes and sun-streaked hair.

"My name's Melinda Grant. I have to meet Susan

Rye at nine."

"Oh yes, congratulations. How exciting. What I wouldn't give to go on a vacay to paradise. This show is going to be amazing. I'll be watching." He's flamboyant in his expressions, and it takes Chris all of two seconds to catch his eye like a moth to a light. "I'll take you to where you need to go," he says, smiling in Chris's direction, not mine.

"Thank you," I say quietly while rolling my eyes.

We walk down one long hallway which parts off to another, which we also travel down, until we reach a room with an open door, and before I even manage to exhale the breath I wasn't aware I was holding, I'm standing in front of a middle-aged woman dressed in a navy pantsuit.

"Susy, Melinda Grant. Melinda Grant, Susan Rye."

"Thank you, Samuel." Her smile is kind and all-knowing.

"Welcome. Have fun," Samuel says sweetly before ducking past me.

"Yeah, have fun, chica." Chris grins.

"No! Chris, you're staying." I tense my jaw.

"Girl! I'll see you when you're finished doing all you need to do. Can you show me the way back out of here, Samuel? It's like a maze."

No, it's not. It's two corridors, you flirtatious traitor.

"Of course. Not a problem." Samuel flutters his eyelashes.

Dear lord, these two are as obvious as a blood stain.

Samuel steps close to Chris, who turns and winks in my direction before giving me a thumbs-up. All I want to do is flip Chris the bird and scream 'traitor' in his face.

"Are you ready to get started?" Susan's voice is softer and more feminine than it sounded on the phone.

"Yes, I am. Sorry. I'm a little nervous."

She doesn't offer words of reassurance or comfort. She instead half smiles, then lengthens her arm. "This way. We'll do all the forms first. After, you'll spend time with Dr Lennington."

"Doctor?"

"For your medical exam. Don't worry, it should be a breeze for you."

"A breeze," I repeat nervously. I must look the picture of health.

"Yes, with your medical background and all, I'm sure you know just what to expect."

Of course. Because to Susan, I'm a doctor. "Right! Okay."

"You are nervous."

"Can you tell me anything about the guy I've been matched with?"

"Oh no, I can't." She waves a finger in the air. "What fun would it be if you knew? You'll have to wait until Saturday, if you pass the medical, when you sail ashore."

"But I'm the only girl, right? The show isn't like *The*

Bachelor, or a group of couples or anything? I read there were three guys, and you needed three girls."

"Just you. All separate islands. Did you read through all the information when applying?"

"I sure did," I lie.

"Great. Well, there are no surprises. It is what it is. Three weeks in paradise with your perfect match and the perfect catch." She laughs, and I sense her excitement immediately. "There'll be rules and tasks and ... oh, it's going to be so much fun."

"Great." I know my smile looks as fake as it feels. "Rules?" Maybe I should have read all the information and not skimmed it.

"We'll go through most of it in a moment."

"What if I don't like it, on the island, can I leave?"

Susan hitches her eyebrows high on her forehead. *I really should have read the information.*

"You can leave whenever you want. All you need to do is hold up your get-out-of-jail-free card and say, 'I'm leaving.' You get three cards. Three chances to leave. We provided this information in the submission online.

"Oh, I know." I didn't know because I didn't read it.

"Good! Well, that's all you need to do."

"Great."

"Take a seat." Susan points at a black leather chair tucked under a dark wood desk. "There's a mountain of forms to go through. It'll take a while."

"Okay." I move to the desk.

"Before we start, do you have any questions?"

Do I have any questions? I do. A lot.

"When does this show go to air?" I don't give her time to answer. "Like, does it happen as we're living there? Or after it's completed?"

"We're still confirming this, but it will be at least a couple of months after filming." Susan's chin wrinkles as she pushes thin metal-framed glasses she takes from the desk to her eyes. "Let's get started, shall we?"

"Okay," I say, puffing out my cheeks.

Forms, medical tests ... I sure as hell hope this guy—no, this show—no, this stupid situation I've found myself in turns out to be worth it. If it isn't, then this mistake is one I'm probably never going to bounce back from. I'm too fragile for the media attention.

I can't do this. What was I thinking? I can pull out before I need to sail away. I need to get a cold—no, a flu. No, a contagious vaginal disease before Saturday. Yes, I'll contract the clap. I can diagnose a fake case of the clap. I'm sure I'll have some old hospital letterhead around somewhere.

"Melinda, you look concerned. Is everything okay?"

"Sure." I gulp.

"Great. Here's form number one, oh, and a pen." She leans across the desk, and with only a second of hesitation, I claim the paperwork and begin.

I want to go home. I'm wasting Susan's time.

But something compels me to fill in those forms, to

agree to send a copy of my passport, and to let Dr Lennington stick a swab into my vagina a few hours later.

Looks like I'm in paradise.

Chapter Fourteen

Four days later

The sun shines so brightly it burns my irises. I slide the oversized designer sunglasses Chris said were a must for a luxury holiday from the top of my head and over my eyes. The wind whips my hair as I stand on the deck of a small luxury yacht, a yacht I finally boarded an hour ago.

An emotional goodbye at the airport with Chris, two plane trips later, and a ride in a limousine fit for a movie star finally led me to a marina where this yacht awaited my arrival.

Destination: Heart Key

"He's waiting for you there." It's what Conrad, the old skipper who captains this craft, said before we took to the sea.

A man scientifically matched to be my missing soul mate is growing closer and closer, and I'm not ready.

I'm fighting my hair, which thrashes my cheeks, and my flowy dress, which is taking flight from my knees to above my head. *My sanity is on the line.* I huff, then complete an untimed and awkward twist. My hands race between my head and my thighs. *Why can't I keep my bits and pieces in place?* I huff louder when I imagine the sight my flapping arms will be creating. Instant tears pool in my eyes. I'm not an outdoorsy girl. I'm not even a boat person or a camera-loving floozy either. What am I doing?

I need to get off this yacht. I want to go home.

Waves part underneath the vessel, and the farther we travel the harsher they grow. Every bump and jump has my stomach spinning on a dime. Every washing machine rotation my gut makes tells me if I can't find solid ground, and soon, I'm going to be sick. I need to get out of the sun and wind. I need to find a place to sit, and pronto. *How do I get back inside?*

I duck, slide, and manoeuvre along the side of the yacht until I see a closed door I'm sure I must've exited through. I struggle to push it open because I'm still attempting to rein in my dress before it transforms in a parachute, whisking me sky high. *Help me!*

With a throaty groan and a rumbling growl escaping my lips, I manage to heave the door sideways. I rush through its opening into a calmer environment.

I straighten my light pink dress. Chris had exclaimed it was so 'summer chic' I'd be crazy not to wear it for my first meeting at the luxury hideaway. Upon fixing the material, I notice a nipple on the run. My nipple, now poking out for all the world to see. A cameraman, dressed in all black, appears to my right. I suck back a harsh breath not expecting anyone to have seen my accidental exposure. *Where did he come from? Has he been on this boat the entire time?* "Umm. So, yeah, can you not film that."

He grins before lowering the camera and stepping away.

Why didn't I wear a bra? I know why: because Chris said bra straps look tacky and cheap under such a pretty garment. *Garment.* Who even uses such a word these days? Chris, that's who. This choice of outfit is too revealing and too tight for me. It's also very Marilyn Monroe, posh city girl, and high-end. I'm not a city girl, and I'm most definitely not high-end.

Why did I let Chris talk me into doing this stupid show? Into buying this dress? And even worse, wearing it? Why didn't I put on a tee and some capris like I wanted to? I know why: because Chris makes life sound like a rainbow-coloured dildo with eight speeds of pleasure-filled endeavours to be encountered every single day.

Every time I think I know what I want in a

situation, Chris is the one who has me rethinking it and doubting my judgment. I end up way out of my element, and this, by far, is the most colossal of them to date.

How did Chris brainwash me this time? The shopping—oh dear lord, the shopping he made me do was overwhelming, yet I enjoyed dressing my body in a way I'd never done before. The string bikini in the one suitcase I packed is still messing with my mind as I sit on a cream leather couch in front of an oak bar. I wish we'd turn around so I could flee. I'm not a bikini-wearing chick. I'm a tankini and boardshorts girl. Coming on this adventure, has been a terrible mistake. And it's all because of Chris.

"Champagne, Dr Grant?" Conrad pops out from behind a wall. He's holding a bottle of champagne in one hand and a flute in the other.

"Shouldn't you be driving the boat?" It seems like a logical question. However, Conrad mustn't feel the same way because he smirks at me in the way someone would to an inexperienced rookie.

"Everything's fine. The boat is on course. I wanted to offer you something to drink to extinguish your nerves."

"Oh, okay."

"You're nervous, aren't you?"

"Yes," I breathe.

"You're much more unsettled than the other two

ladies I've already transported over."

"I bet they were six-foot Amazonians with tan skin and beauty to match."

Conrad doesn't reply. Instead, he smirks at me in the same way he did when I questioned the operations of the yacht.

I break eye contact, and Conrad pours bubbled liquid into the glass. "Here, drink some of this. We're about to enter calming waters. It'll settle your stomach and your nerves."

"Okay."

"Would you like a hat to hold your hair out of your face?"

"Um."

"I think it's best you go back outside and enjoy the beauty. Even suck back some fresh air." He pauses and tips his head slightly to the side. "I'll get you a hat."

"Do you have Velcro to hold my dress down, too?"

He chuckles. "You won't need it. We'll be slowing now. We've not far to go at all."

"Thank you," I say, taking the drink from his rough, dirty hands.

"Give me a minute, and I'll be back."

"Okay."

Conrad turns and exists the same way he entered. I take a large mouthful of champagne and desperately try not to cough as it tingles down my throat.

"Here," he says, returning to my line of sight. "This

style should go nicely with your pretty dress." His turquoise eyes match his shirt, and they sparkle against the white of the large-brimmed floppy hat he holds out in front of him. The hat instantly reminds me of the ones worn by fancy actresses on film. "Let me take your drink for you so you can put it on."

"Thank you." I hold out the glass and retrieve the hat at the same time. Placing it to my head makes me believe I'll look as sophisticated and classy as those actresses do. *One can only hope.* I need all the class I can get right now.

"Excellent," Conrad compliments me, passing me back the drink.

"So do I go outside now?" I'm dreading it. I wonder if he can tell by my tensed limbs.

"Let me top you up first."

I wave my hand in front of him. "No, no. It's okay. I'll only have one."

"A little more won't hurt." He bobs his head just once, in an understated yet knowing manner. He takes the bottle in hand, then slowly approaches me as if I'm a fragile ornament. Every drop is more than I should consume, but I say nothing, even when the liquid meets the rim of the glass.

"I'll put the bottle here on the bar. Feel free to get more. I best be taking over the controls."

"Oh, okay, sure. I appreciate your help. Thank you again for the hat."

"No worries." Conrad steps around me and opens the sliding door halfway, gesturing for me to get back out there. His wispy grey hair is blown into a cowlick. "When you're ready. Just give me a moment to slow Magnolias down."

"Magnolias?"

"That's her name. It's the name of my yacht."

"Oh, pretty name."

"For a pretty yacht."

"Very true. It's luxurious."

"I know." Magnolias is obviously Conrad's pride and joy. "I'll come help you when we dock."

"Excellent." I stand. Conrad leaves, and I slip off my sandals, then shift until I'm positioned right by the open door.

Breathe in, then out.

Drink a mouthful of champagne.

Breath in, then out.

Drink another ten mouthfuls of champagne.

I do what my mind instructs until, as promised, we slow. In an instant, we go from bumping to gliding. I retrieve the champagne bottle and pour more bubbles into my glass before hesitantly making my way to the deck. *I'm sure I'm going to be blotto drunk before we make the island at the rate I've just knocked these drinks back.*

I tiptoe in my bare feet, and each step I take sees my mind floating, in the same way four orange buoys far out in the distance do. The champers has definitely reached my brain. There's no doubting it.

I duck under a metal awning and secure my floppy hat to prevent it from tumbling off, then resume drinking the sweetest champagne I've ever had the pleasure of enjoying.

Taking a large breath has my lungs filled with fresh sea-salted air. I'm calm, halfway to plastered drunk, out in the fresh air, on the open sea. There's ocean to the left of me, to the right, back, and front. I'm quick to note that if we were to crash right now, I'd inevitably be swallowed by this ocean and eaten by hungry sharks. I should instantly tense at this thought. That's generally how my body reacts to such a realisation, but I don't. Instead, I giggle and take another mouthful of liquid courage. It seems drinking and boating go hand in hand. Conrad was onto something with this treat.

"Mindy! Good girl. Now, do this the entire time. No more sabotaging yourself." It's Chris's voice I hear as clear as if he were standing beside me. *"Take another big breath in. Relax. You can do this. You need to do this."*

Even when Chris isn't with me, he's still in my head trying to keep me in line. Maybe this won't be as bad as I imagined it to be.

I turn to my right, with every intention of heading back inside and retrieving another drink, but before I take a single step, a large splash to my left holds my attention.

Holy crap. That was a fish. A fish leapt into the air. Is that even possible? I take one step towards the railing. Then another, and another, until I'm looking down at calm, sparkling blue waters.

"Wow," I mouth when I peek over the edge and down upon silky, crystal-clear ripples. I search beyond the surface, through the parted-curtain-shaped waves the boat creates. Below, there are fish, so many fish of differing colours, shapes, and sizes. They dance around each other playfully. I can't help but move closer to get a better seat. The railing supports my entire body weight.

An orange-and-black-striped fellow darts towards a passionate blue lady. Well, this is how I surmise their sexes when spying into their little world. They wrap around each other in a way that makes me think of comfort, kindness, and possibly humping. *Can they mate? No, surely an orange fish and a blue fish don't play sea bedroom nookie together? Do they? Do fish crossbreed?* I've no clue, but I realise I probably should have paid more attention in biology class, and taking another mouthful of champers right now is probably a good idea, so I do.

I turn my eyes back to the show below and continue watching sea creatures perform different productions. It's peaceful, natural, and beautiful, and it makes me smile in the nerdiest of ways.

"Paradise," I breathe. *I'm going to be living in paradise.* I continue to watch the ocean playground for what feels like ages. Well, until the fish suddenly disperse.

"Did you see the schools down there, Dr Grant?" Conrad asks from somewhere behind me.

"I did. The fish are stunning," I say, standing upright and planting both my feet back on deck.

"They sure are. You wait until you're snorkelling along the reefs. It'll be like nothing you've ever seen."

Snorkelling? I don't know how to snorkel. I wonder if the guy I'm set to meet likes to snorkel, knows how to snorkel ... What if he's super outdoorsy? Will I be able to handle such a man? I ponder this for a moment before my mind switches angles, and I imagine what he'll look like, then worse—what if he's somebody I already know, like the cat killer from my blind date? Please don't let it be him, because if it is, I'll be marching off the island as fast as a hippie can draw a hit from a bong.

I walk in the direction of the bar and the champagne bottle perched upon it. Will my mystery man be tall or short? Does he have tattoos, or will his skin be untouched by ink? And what if he has a beard? I'm not a fan of bearded men, and I can only hope he doesn't have a Tom-Hanks-in-*Castaway* appearance going on. That'd be a total turn-off for me.

No sooner do I find my brain tying in knots with an overload of questions does the yacht suddenly come to a halt. My heart gallops. My toes curl. My head is dizzy, but I put it down to the amount of alcohol I've consumed.

"Dr Grant?" The voice comes from inside.

"Yes, I'm here. I'm coming in to grab another drink."

"We've reached our destination, and we're going to disembark now," Conrad says, still out of sight.

"Sure. Give me one minute." I rush through the cabin door. *One more drink. I need at least one more glass to help aid me in being the bravest I can be.*

"You don't have time for another drink. Are you ready?" Conrad suddenly appears to my left.

"I feel buzzed, so the answer to your question would be 'after one more drink I'll be ready'."

He laughs. "No more alcohol." He walks past me and opens a rectangular door I didn't even see at the other end of the room.

I turn my vision to my one suitcase sitting by the chair. With hesitation, I put down my glass and retrieve my luggage, gripping it by its handle. "Here goes nothing," I mutter, taking the same exit Conrad did a few moments ago.

I still, looking out over the white sand. *White sand!* It's just like I've seen in magazines. I honestly didn't believe sand like this existed. It does—I see it now with my own two eyes.

Coconut trees, so many coconut trees stretch from the ground up into the baby blue sky. I bet I could climb one of those suckers, I think, before realising that'll be an impossibility, and currently my booze-soaked brain thinks I'm Fletcher, and I've built-in claws. I don't. I don't even have any fingernails left because I've chewed those down to the wick over last week's stress-a-thon.

Conrad stands at the side of the boat waiting. He reaches out his hand for me to take. "Welcome to Heart Key, the most exquisite island on the Great Barrier Reef."

My chin drops. My legs become as heavy as stone. "Arrrr ..." My mouth opens so wide it could catch flies; I know this because a fly French kisses me before taking a hike off my tongue. I snap my jaws closed and don't make another sound.

A man in boardshorts appears, walks towards me, holding a camera. *Shoot.*

He saw that.

And that means so did the entire world.

"Dr Grant?" Conrad says. "It's time to get off the boat now."

"More cameras," I whisper to avoid prying ears.

"Yes, there are going to be plenty of those." He pauses. "It's a television show."

"Hmmm," I moan, keeping my lips together like a

vise.

Conrad snatches my hand and leads me down a small ramp onto the sand below.

"Let me take your luggage."

I nod.

The sand is fine and warm beneath my feet. Tall grass-covered dunes meet a glassy sea. This is the beach from my dreams. The breeze caresses my exposed skin as sunrays bounce against my naked back, causing a tingling and burning sensation. I take a deep breath as I stare down the biggest lens I've ever seen.

One step, two steps, three steps has the cameraman travelling backwards with my forward momentum. I stop, then walk backwards; he walks towards me. I stop again, eyeing him harshly, before stepping sideways. He steps sideways.

Well, this will get annoying fast.

I turn my vision away from the cameraman in the hope he'll disappear. He must, because I can no longer spot him. All I can see is a beach resembling a place I often daydreamed about, which I find strange.

My hands are clammy. Sweat pours from my armpits and leaks from my forehead. My heart hammers in my chest, and with this rapid change in heart rate, my stomach contents hustle up my throat. I'm on the verge of being sick.

The cameraman returns. The big lens is focused

right on me. I swallow with a gulp, then glimpse over my shoulder in search of the yacht, only to find Conrad with my suitcase tucked under one arm making his way up the beach behind me.

"Melinda Grant. Hello. You made it. How wonderful to finally meet you."

I flick my head in the direction of a voice I've never heard before.

"I'm Daniel Knight."

I say nothing. I stare. He's tall, medium-built, with fair skin and jet black hair. His straight white teeth fill his broad smile. *This is the guy?*

I eye him up and down and conclude he's most definitely attractive, but in a rugged understated way, and he's really, really, really tall. If I were to guess his height, I'd think six-foot-three, or even four. To me, he looks like a scruffy basketballer, wearing a cheesecloth shirt and long tan slacks instead of his everyday sports uniform.

Good God, I'm judgmental. Arlie was right in his observation, and I realise this more and more each day.

"Welcome, welcome," he announces.

"Hi." It's barely audible.

A gust of wind sweeps between us like a mini tornado, and the force of it is enough to send the bottom of my dress fanning outwards. I'm in so much shock, my reaction time becomes diminished to the point where I don't move my arms at all—well, not until the bottom of my dress reaches over bust height. When I realise my lacey white knickers are fully exposed, I fight the material of my dress in the only way I know how—erratically. From the corner of my eye, I spy the cameraman again, and I cringe. Well, I've been here for all of two seconds, and my arse is about to be televised. *Fuck my life.*

Daniel wraps his arm around my shoulder and pulls me along the beach in a somewhat jogging fashion.

"Don't mind those little wind channels. They happen all the time." He speaks loudly, so loudly you'd think he was trying to talk over the sound of moving chopper blades. "There you go. We're out of it now," he says, rushing away from me in pursuit of what I can see is a tumbling white hat. A hat I'd forgotten I was even wearing. I watch as he bends over and picks it up. *He has a cute butt, so there's that.* He turns around and jogs back in my direction.

"There you go." He speaks much quieter than he did previously. I take the hat from his hand and place it on my head to cover what I believe will be a head full of horrible hat hair. *Great start, Mindy. Sheesh.*

"I'm Daniel Knight," he announces again.

"Hi Daniel." I hold out my hand, and he accepts it in a handshake.

"Let me show you to where you'll be staying." I

watch his mouth move, and then focus on the clef hollowing out a portion of his chin.

"Thank you," I reply hesitantly.

"If you have any questions on the way up, feel free to ask. if I can answer them, I will."

"I do have one." I pause trying to stop nerves from rattling my voice. "Will we be living in the same house?"

"No."

"Oh, good."

"You and the other contestant will."

"There's more than just you here?"

His eyebrows dip downwards. His mouth pulls together. He seems confused by my question. "I don't stay on the island. I come in when I need to do my job."

"Job? Do we get paid? I thought there was only a chance of winning prize money at the end?"

"There is, but I'm not entitled to any of the money because I get paid."

"So if we do the tasks and finish the experiment, or whatever this show is trying to prove, I'll get all the money and you'll get none because you're already getting paid?" I don't give him a chance to reply. "But if one of the other couples on one of the other islands does a better job than us at falling in love, I don't get any prize money, but they do, and you still walk away with payment?"

His expression of confusion becomes more

apparent when his eyes narrow. "I think you're misunderstanding my role. I'm not on the show as a contestant. I'm the host."

My mouth creates an '0' shape.

"But what you said is right. However, nobody is getting paid to be here. Only the couple voted by the public to be the perfect match wins the prize money."

"Oh okay. Well, this makes more sense. It's fine, though. The money doesn't bother me anyway. I wasn't even aware you could win money until the other day when I was reading through the forms I signed."

Daniel doesn't say a word in response. He turns and walks up the beach, and I follow, wondering why he didn't respond, and who in the hell is my perfect catch if it isn't this Daniel guy?

Chapter Fifteen

There are eight dirty brown stairs. I count each one as I make my way to the top. "What a climb," I puff.

"There's not that many steps." Daniel brushes off my lagging fitness.

"No, not too many at all. Honestly, I would have preferred thirteen of these thick, high suckers." There's sarcasm in my tone.

Daniel doesn't reply.

"This is where I leave you, Dr Grant." Conrad's voice travels from behind me. I twist on my heel to find my suitcase held at arm's length.

"Thank you," I pant when I take my belongings from his grip.

"You're welcome. Have fun."

"I'll try to."

"Excellent." He gifts me a reassuring nod.

"Thank you, Conny," Daniel adds, as if they're great

mates.

Again, Conrad bobs his head, then he turns and races down the incline we just took, missing every second step as he goes. *Shit! I'm unfit.*

"Welcome to paradise. Welcome to Heart Key, Ms Grant." Daniel's voice projects the superb infomercial tone. His hand shifts slowly across the vision laid out in front of me.

Baby Jesus, Joseph, and Mary. I've stepped into a dream.

"This is where you'll be staying." His hand stops roaming the lush green scenery and stills on a crisp white house.

I crane my neck back as my eyes travel into the blue abyss of the sky above. "Talk about a mansion. It's huge. For two people? This home is all for two people?"

"Yes."

"Wowzer. Well, I never." I drop my suitcase at my feet. I slowly lower my chin, taking in the cute navy shutters and the flowerpots residing under every single window ... there are a lot of windows. The house is huge, slightly old-fashioned, yet magnificent. This would be my dream home if I could ever afford it.

"It's one hell of a beauty, isn't it?" Daniel asks.

"It really is. Not your modern-day mansion, but a mansion nevertheless."

"This way." Daniel points towards the front door. I

return my vision to the house stretching four stories high. It looks more like a resort than living quarters for two people.

"Come along." Daniel strides in front of me as we move onto a grey-stoned path. The noise of my suitcase wheels bumping and jumping against the small stones interrupts the sound of crashing waves.

That can't be good for the wheels.

"This is the most beautiful place on Earth." Daniel doesn't slow down or peek back over his shoulder at me. It's like he's talking to someone who's keeping up with him.

I'm not keeping up. In fact, I'm lagging farther behind. I quicken my pace. Not quite a jog, but not a walk either.

Suddenly, Daniel flings out his arm, almost barrelling me over. My knees buckle. I manage to stop without falling, but my hair whips my face, and my breath catches in my throat.

There's a settled silence.

Brushing my hair from my eyes, I catch the opening of the front door. My heart pounds. My teeth clamp together.

He's wearing a black suit. It's all I can tell while his face stays in the shadows.

One step, two steps, three steps. The sun catches something metal because beams of light spread like a rainbow after a storm in front of him. He's angelic as he takes another step, and I squint to see more of him.

Black suit. Tall. Muscular. A white rose is attached to his lapel. I follow his silhouette upwards.

I gasp. I gasp so loud it could scatter chirping birds from their homes.

"Oh, hell no," I screech. "Are you kidding me? Nope. Nope. Nope. Not a chance." I drop my hand from the suitcase handle, leaving it where it stands. I turn abruptly, and I stomp in a fury back the way I came. Well, until I halt due to a video camera shoved in my face.

I dip my chin and put my hands in front of my head to offer myself shelter. Brown hair. Big white teeth inside a broad smile. Those eyes, familiar, kind, unique ...

He never called.

He made me want him, and then he never called.

I can't spend three weeks with him.

Not now, not ever.

Chapter Sixteen

I push my hand outwards and step to my left to pass the lens capturing the moment when I realised Arlie was the man on this island waiting for me.

"Melinda, STOP! Let me explain," Arlie shouts.

Stop? He wants to explain? He couldn't have sent a message saying, 'Oh, by the way, I'm going on some show to meet some dumb-arse bimbo who I'll fall in love with, and I won't be in contact because it'll be pointless'. Or, 'I won't ask for your number after this enjoyable meal with you because I'm going on a television show and won't be available'?

"Hey! Stop."

The sound of racing footsteps causes me to stomp faster, harder.

"Give me a chance," he says breathlessly, right before his hand grasps my shoulder. "I can explain. Give me a chance."

"Why?" I jerk from his grip, staring at the top of the stairs leading back to the beach.

"I'm sorry. I was going to call you, I was." He pauses. "Look, I chose you the moment your profile came up as a match."

I clap my hands. "Bravo," I spit.

"Can you fuck off with the cameras? Please." His tone is filled with anger. "Dude, will you back up and give us some space?"

I twist with my anger to face Arlie. His eyes are slits. His nostrils are flared.

"Why did you ask for my number if you knew you were coming on this thing?"

"I didn't know I was. I wasn't even originally chosen to do so. I swear. One of the guys pulled out, and they called me. I-I-I wanted to give the show a chance and see what happened."

"Okay. So, what if it didn't work out here with the bimbo? I'd be a choice for you once you got home?"

"No. No, I didn't see it like that, not at all."

"Really?"

"Honest. I swear. I was given four envelopes with matches. As soon as I saw you were in there, it seemed like the universe was telling me something I may have already known ..."

"What?"

"That our run-ins haven't been only a coincidence." His eyes become wider. His tense jaw relaxes. "I think I'm supposed to get to know you better, Melinda

Grant."

"What's your last name?"

The corner of his lips lifts slightly. "Blight. I'm Arlie Blight."

"I knew it." I throw my arms into the air.

"You did?"

"Fort Knox social media profile? Harder to crack than a nut? The one with the dachshund picture?"

His smile grows. "Yeah." He places his hand on the back of his neck and rubs. "So will you stay, please?" He turns his eyes to his feet.

I should say no. So what if he chose me? He should have chosen to call me days ago.

But what if he's right? What if this is fate?

And what if Chris kicks my butt when I get home for not taking a chance?

"Fine. I'll stay."

"Good." Our eyes reconnect. He breathes a long sigh of relief. "Can we possibly go inside? This suit is scratchy and becoming an oven under this sun."

I nod.

He holds out his hand, palm up. "Are you ready to do this? Are you ready to find out what it is that's happening between us?"

I bite my lower lip as my heart leaps with joy in my chest, then nod.

"I'll take that as a yes." His eyes smoulder.

I gulp as I lace my fingers with his.

"Paradise." It's what Arlie says as we walk side by

side, hand in hand, up the stone path. We stop momentarily when Arlie takes possession of my suitcase. "I'll help you get this inside," he mumbles.

Daniel stands by the front door with a camera pointed in his direction. "Are you ready to see inside the house, Melinda?"

"Sure," I say.

"Well, in you go. Arlie, you can take it from here. Remember, every inch of the house has cameras except the bathrooms. Due to privacy laws, we're not allowed to fit those with cameras. However, the bathrooms along with the rest of the house are fully miced."

"So you guys don't come in?" I'm curious.

"No. Not inside the house, but any outdoor recreations will be filmed by the crew who are staying on the island with you."

"Where?"

"Now that, Dr Grant, is a secret."

I nod, completely unaware of how any of this works.

"So that cameraman is filming this?" I'm again curious.

"We are, and we'll capture you entering."

I nod.

"Then the inside cameras will take over once—"

"Thank you." Arlie interrupts me. "Let's go in ... this suit ..." He pulls at his collar in a way which says his tie is strangling him.

"I'm ready." I'm not, but it's now or never.

"Have a great time. Your first task will take place this afternoon. You'll find everything you need to know about the rules on the table inside. Settle in, unpack, and relax," Daniel says.

I fake a smile and step through the doorway, still holding Arlie's hand.

Bang!

The door shuts quickly, and with its closing Arlie's grip disappears from both my hand and the suitcase. He takes two steps down a large and plain-walled foyer. He turns to face me, then stills momentarily. He appears agitated, uncomfortable, and overwhelmed.

A flick of his arms has the jacket he was wearing falling on the floor. He takes the knot of the tie between two fingers and, with a quick pull, loosens it. One further tug has the tie dangling from his fingertips until he also discards it on the floor. His eyes find mine. He clears his throat. "I was burning up." Arlie rubs his hand down his jawline and continues down his neck.

I break eye contact and follow the movement of his hand. *One button, two buttons, three buttons.* I gulp. *Four buttons, five buttons, six ...* the two sides of his shirt separate. His chest is hairless. His stomach is ripped beyond anything I've ever seen in the flesh before. His pants rest low on hips. A defined 'V', an actual fucking 'V' is created from muscle and points to his manhood, still covered by his slacks. I gulp even harder.

Arlie undoes the button on his pants and pulls down the zipper without any concern for me standing right in front of him. I should look away—I know I should—but I can't because it has been so long since I've seen a man's body in this way. Well, unless you count Chris, but his doesn't really count, considering he doesn't do chicks. His body holds no value to me.

Don't look, I warn myself. *Keep your eyes above Arlie's waist. Be respectful, Mindy. Be a goddamn lady.* I close my eyes briefly to stop my roaming vision, but it doesn't work. I flash open my eyes and look at the one place I warned myself not to.

Surprise lifts my brows. Not because the bulge in his briefs is more than impressive, but because his briefs are a fuchsia pink. Arlie is wearing hot pink cotton shorts under his slacks.

"That's so much better." He follows his statement with a satisfying moan as he kicks off his shoes and reefs off his socks.

I find myself squeezing my thighs together at the same time as I beg my racing heart to get a grip and slow the heck down.

It's a body.

A man's body.

I've seen men's bodies before.

But nothing like this.

"I'm going to put something more comfortable on. The rooms are upstairs." Arlie bends at his midsection, retrieving the clothing he shed.

"Hmm." I'm rendered speechless. Good lordy, his body is fine, so freaking fine, and I would like nothing more than for him to stay in a state of undress for the entire three weeks we're here. I, on the other hand, need to remain wholly clothed day and night, because what I've got under this pretty material will hold no value to someone like Arlie.

"Are you coming? It's this way." He holds his bundled belongings against his abdomen with one hand and my luggage with the other.

I nod.

His bare feet tap against the tiled flooring. His tight arse moves hypnotically in front of me. I shift my vision to his calf in search of the tribal tattoo I know to be there. It is. Arlie Blight is really here, on this island, with me. Is fate about to play a horrible trick on the both of us, or is it leading me down the right road?

Maybe the bus to Happily-Ever-After Land has finally arrived. And standing behind its closed doors this entire time was the hunkiest guy I've ever laid eyes on … Arlie Blight.

Chapter Seventeen

We take to an over-polished staircase the colour of mahogany. I don't scan our surroundings as we climb. Instead, I keep my eyes planted on Arlie's arse because that'll be the only way I'm going to survive this stint of physical activity.

We make our way along some tiled flooring, then swiftly turn up another set of smooth, varnished wooden stairs.

You've got to be kidding me. I hope this is the tour and welcoming portion of the day because if this is the hike to our bedrooms, then I don't see me coming down often or at all. "Are the bedrooms all the way up here?"

"Our bedrooms are on level three. They've been allocated to us, although there are rooms on all levels from what I've found." We continue taking each step. "The pool, sauna, and a fully equipped gym fill level four. Oh, and I think there's a beauty parlour, but I didn't gawk inside. There's one big bedroom up there too. It appears to be some type of honeymoon suite, and let me tell you, the view of the beach is far better than the one I have." He takes a breath, then continues, "Level one is the lounge, cooking quarters, formal dining area, library, sunroom ..." He pauses, as if thinking. "There's a bathroom on level one. Well, there are bathrooms on every level, I think." We make it to the top of the stairs. I look to my left, then my right.

A long hallway. Only two doors coming off it at either end.

"Level two is a cinema and a stack-load of guest bedrooms. Well, that's what they look like to me."

"This place is gigantic."

"It is, but if you search for this big winding staircase, I've found you won't get lost inside it."

"Find the staircase. That I can do."

"Our rooms are down different ends of this floor. Yours is to the right and mine is to the left."

Keep your eyes on his. Don't look down at his junk. Don't look at his crotch.

I flick my vision to his crotch. His cock is so well defined against that material. Big, too. Could I fit it in my mouth?

"Melinda?"

"Hmm?" I reply, and—

Oh, shit. I'm still looking at his crotch.

I shoot my eyes to his.

There's a quiet snickering. "Melinda."

"Yes?" I clear my throat.

"Our rooms are at different ends of the floor." He pauses, the corners of his lips rise, but swiftly fall. "My room is massive. It's the one they said I was to take, but if yours isn't up to scratch, then feel free to check out mine, and if you like it better, we'll swap. I want you to be comfortable."

"Comfortable. Right."

He smiles.

I bite my lower lip when my eyes greedily scan past his mouth, his clean-shaven chin, and stop on the only part of his broad chest not covered by his belongings. The top of his pecks.

"I'm going to get dressed. I'll be back in a minute. Do you want me to take your luggage to your room before I head off, or are you all right?"

"I'm fine." Again, with the dreamy reply. *Stop it, Mindy. Just stop it.*

"I'll leave it here for you then." Arlie's free hand now skirts my upper arm. "See you in a minute or two."

I nod.

He turns and walks down a carpeted hallway. I don't shift my sight from his bare back, because it's beautiful. Even the small brown birthmark marking his skin like a tramp stamp in the small of his back is perfect.

Snap out of it before he sees you staring at him.

I blink excessively, then grab my suitcase and make my way to the right and the bedroom I was told was mine, dragging my luggage behind me. "Thank you, God," I whisper under my breath, still thinking about the sudden strip show I was gifted.

The door to my quarters is cracked open. I push against the wood until it widens farther. It's dark, which I'm not expecting due to the time of the day. However, after adjusting my sight, I spy two huge curtains pulled along the farthest wall. I leave my belongings inside the door, including the hat I take off. *Is it bad luck to wear a hat indoors? Or is that only if you open an umbrella inside? I can't remember.*

I make the vast distance from the room's entry to the curtains. I take one of the two metal sticks hanging from the point where the curtains meet and pull.

Step by step, I draw back the dense material. Sunshine blasts through the gap it creates like an eclipse. It's bright enough that I could wear sunglasses. Perhaps I'll leave here with Amazonian skin and not the milky white complexion I currently have. *That would be a bonus.*

Once I have one side completely drawn, I make my way to the other curtain but stop before I finish the trek. The view—the view is so captivating. It has me holding my breath. Trees sway, waves ripple onto the shore, and there's so much white sand. The sky glows a brilliant blue above, and it almost appears as if it's been hand-painted there.

"Wow," I mouth, noticing the sea is absent of boats, vessels, and people. I'm really on a deserted island. My breath gets faster. Whoa. Did I even realise that before now? It rains down on me like a tonne of bricks. Every breath I take becomes harder. *Oh God, am I hyperventilating?*

"Melinda, are you happy with your room?" Arlie says over the sound of light tapping.

"I am," I reply, with my eyes glued to the view laid out in front of me as I attempt to control my sudden bout of anxiety.

"It's pretty impressive, yeah?"

"It is."

I don't hear his footsteps, but I know he's standing behind me because I can feel his breath cascading across the back of my neck. "I don't think I'll want to leave here when it's all said and done."

I shake my head, slowly, hesitating. I'm mesmerised.

Arlie's presence disappears. I catch him striding past me from the corner of my eye. He pulls the opposing curtain away.

"Our rooms are pretty much identical. Even the view is similar," he says.

"How is that possible? Didn't you say you're down the opposite end of the hall?"

"I am, but it appears the scenery is similar from both ends of the property."

"Do you see the mountains, too?" I point towards

the high green peaks in the distance.

"I do, although one of mine looks like a crooked nose on a face." He half laughs. "Well, that sounded stupid, but to me it does. What do yours look like?" He comes to stand beside me. I scan peak after peak until I'm left looking at a rock face with a protruding mound.

"A boob." I giggle. "Doesn't that one there look like a boob?" I stretch my finger in its direction.

He mimics my movement and uses his extended finger to trace the shape of a breast against the glass sliding door which separates us from the circular veranda. "With a nipple and all. I think we should swap rooms. I want to admire the boob mountain. You can have the crooked nose mountain?"

"No dice. If you'd said it was shaped like a giant peen ..." I snap my teeth together and curl my lips shut.

"Peen? Were you going to say pen?" Arlie grins in a way that says he knew exactly what I had intended to say.

I'm blushing. I know I am because my face becomes overheated.

"What's so endearing about a pen? Are you a stationery collector or something?" He nudges into me softly. "I know—you've got a thousand pens scattered from arsehole to breakfast around your home, don't you? Sticky notes, oh la la! They're stuck to every wall, too, I bet. Go on. You can share."

I clear my throat, trying not to laugh.

"I should go down to level two. There's a conference room there. If my memory serves me correctly, I think there's a few pens with the Heart Key logo on them. I could get you some, if it'll tickle your fancy."

My determination falters, and I giggle. "Stop it." I fold my arms defensively across my chest and dramatically huff.

"What? You're the one who loves pens, not me."

I turn my eyes in his direction. Big wide teeth. A gorgeous broad smile. A face so handsome it should be carved into the side of a mountain for every person on Earth to admire.

"So is that a yes to me getting you those pens?" His banter is cheeky.

"Noooo!" I place my hand on my forehead. "You make me so embarrassed."

"Me?" He stops. "There's no need to be all blushing and overwhelmed. We all have things that, you know, turn us on. Personally, I love me some balloons. All colours, every shape. They feel …"

"Stop taking the mickey out of me. You don't even have a thing for balloons. I think you teasing me is what turns you on here, Mr Blight."

He shrugs. "I guess time will tell."

"Arrrgh. You're terrible."

"I am. It's true. I'm a monster."

Arlie's quick-witted, handsome, and funny with a

hot-arse body. I can mess around with him with such ease, and, apart from Chris, I typically don't let any man see that relaxed side of me. But with Arlie, it comes easily. He's everything I hoped for and more, which is why I need to tread carefully because I don't want to get hurt.

I don't want Arlie to leave me with scars.

Chapter Eighteen

I've opened every drawer and run my fingertips across each surface; there's not a speck of dust to be located in this room.

I've lain on an extremely comfortable four-poster bed and peered out at Boob Mountain from a pillow that feels like it's been handmade out of the stuffing you'd only be able to pluck from a cloud ... It's the softest pillow my head has ever encountered.

Every switch in the room has been flicked on and off at my hand, including the chandelier, which remains lit. I watch the many dangling crystals sparkle above until I spot two red lights in either corner of the room. *The camera's.*

Exploration of the walk-in robe was the best part of these impromptu tasks because it's gigantic and fan-tab-ulous ... It would have been even more rewarding if I had the clothes, shoes, and accessories to fill every square inch of it. The wardrobe is about the size of my bedroom back home, which makes me instantly feel like a pauper. The fact we were only allowed to bring one piece of luggage to Heart Key means not even one percent of this lavish space can be filled, which is wasteful in my book. I wonder if the show takes requests for custom clothing?

Arlie stands in the centre of the room as I continue to move from task to task. He doesn't say a word, but I sense his eyes travelling with my movements. Usually, I'd find this creepy or even stalkerish, but I don't with him because I like thinking someone like Arlie could enjoy what he sees when he's looking at me.

Chris said I could change my life story to end how I like, so why can't I create a tale where Arlie finds me to be enough? Where following me everywhere will bring him happiness while living out his life?

Opening the patio doors allows a light breeze to wrap around my skin. It's refreshing—not cold, but not hot either. "I'm going to leave these ajar."

"Sounds like a good idea."

Oh, his voice. It's soft yet profound. I could listen to Arlie Blight speak all day and night.

"Did you unpack?" I ask, spinning around to face him.

"Yes, two days ago. I've been all over the island and the house—not your room, though ... I thought I'd wait for you."

"The door was ajar," I comment with a hint of accusation in my tone.

"I know it was. It was like that when I arrived. I did come down this way, but I didn't enter the room. As I said, I wanted to wait for you. I wanted to see it through your eyes. You're pleased?"

"Pleased? Arlie, it's the most amazing bedroom I've ever clapped eyes on. I could live in here forever. Hey, do you have a big television on your wall?" I point in the direction of the screen across from my bed.

"I do. Our rooms are pretty much identical. The only difference is your drapes, bedspread, and décor are reds and golds, and mine are dark blues and silvers."

"Wow! Matching king and queen rooms."

"It seems so." Arlie walks around to the right side of the bed, the side I prefer to sleep on. "Watch the television. I want to show you something."

"Porn?" Oh God. I did not just say that ... did I?

Arlie chuckles. "No. Not porn. Watch." He grabs a silver remote from off a small cabinet below it, and I quickly twist until I stare at the blank screen. The television suddenly lifts and disappears into the wall, only to be replaced by a large portrait of Audrey Hepburn, one of the people I admire.

My chin drops. My mouth hangs open. "Incredible," I say on a ragged breath.

"I have Frank Sinatra in mine." There's silence. "Do you want me to put the TV back the way it was for you?"

"No, no," I rush in saying. "I love Audrey."

"Okay."

"I should probably unpack."

"Sounds good. After, though, we'll need to read through those binders on the table downstairs."

"Have you read them?"

"No. Just the welcome letter and some of the manuals for operating the stove and oven." He shrugs. "I've only been here for two nights, but I needed to cook and eat."

"How do we even get food to cook here?"

"There's a small convenient store."

"Huh?"

"There's also a chemist and clothing stores." His eyebrows lift, and he grins. "There's also a nice jewellery shop as well … So many things."

Is he having me on again?

"It's true, I swear."

"Wait, what? It's a deserted island. There are not supposed to be other people here." I'll go along with his little white lies and see how far he goes with them.

"There are no people running them."

I cock one eyebrow. "Well, who makes sure people pay for what they buy then?"

"Us. It's all ours. There was a master key to open everything whenever we wanted included with the welcome letter. We don't need money."

"Get the fudge out of here. No! You're fooling me

again. I'm not buying what you're throwing down, Mr—"

"It's true. I swear. I'll take you for a spin around."

"We have a car?"

He chuckles. "No, but we do have a golf buggy."

"Do not."

"Do so. Why do you think everything I'm telling you is BS?"

"Because you seem like a bit of a trickster. I can tell that pulling pranks would be right up your alley."

He laughs. "Well, what I've said is the truth. I guess you'll need to see it for yourself to believe it." Arlie rocks on his heels, comfortable and not at all looking guilty. "I might leave you to unpack."

"You can stay and chat if you want to. I don't mind."

"If you're sure?"

"Yes. You've probably been lonely if you've been the only occupant on the island for the past two days."

"It wasn't bad, but the conversation was extremely lagging. There are only so many times I could answer myself back before it became weird and borderline insane."

I snort. "Well, settle in then and tell me some more about yourself while I put my stuff away." I throw the suitcase up onto the mattress, then pull it towards me until it rests against the edge of the bed.

"What do you want to know?"

"What about your niece? The one who makes you smell like ginger when you bake. The only niece you have."

His lips tug upwards. "Okay. Well, I can tell you she wasn't thrilled I was going on holidays."

"I could imagine she wouldn't have been."

Arlie treads around the left side of the bed as I finish unzipping and opening my suitcase. He faces me before plonking himself against the mattress.

I gasp. No! I reach out my arms to attempt to catch the flying missile but miss. I wrap my hand over my mouth and muffle a scream. "Oh, fuck! Why, CHRIS? Why?" I yell behind my palm.

The rainbow-coloured dildo lands flat-end down, tip-end up. It sways like a bowling pin on the cusp of falling over, but it doesn't. It remains erect and at attention on the carpet below.

Please God, strike me down with a bolt of electricity. A heart attack … I'll take a heart attack right about now. My heart pounds hard enough for it to happen.

I stare at the vibrator, then slowly rotate my head towards Arlie who's now crawled across the bed. He's knelt on all fours like a dog beside my suitcase. I follow the direction of his eyes and pray he's either suddenly blind, or for my quick and timely death to arrive.

"What were the chances of your prick stick launching out of your luggage at the same time I threw myself on the bed? I wouldn't have thought high until now. That's insane."

I'm horrified. My stomach launches into my chest

and up my airway. I don't know what to do or say, so I do what any woman in my position would do. I race towards the rogue piece of equipment and swing my foot back, kicking it, launching it like a stiff torpedo towards the pulled curtains in hope they'll swallow it whole in the way a deep-throating professional would.

This doesn't happen. Instead, the torpedoing dildo bashes into the frame of the glass sliding doors where we just parted the curtains and comes hurtling back in my direction. I scream. I leap up onto the bed, then fall, landing on Arlie's back. My arms wrap around his body for dear life, like if I didn't hold on to him, the dildo would go on attack. We both tumble to the bed in a heap. Arlie chortles.

"Oh my God, I'm sorry. I'm so sorry." I'm on the brink of tears when I attempt to roll off the back of the man I was honestly entertaining the possibility of a relationship with. Well, that dream's gone down the shitter, no thanks to Chris and the eight speeds of pleasure he obviously stuffed inside my suitcase before I even left the apartment.

I'm going to kill him. I'm going to kill Chris the moment I lay eyes on his stupid face.

"Are you okay?" Arlie chokes out between his hysterical rumblings.

"I'm stuck." My voice shakes. My throat tightens farther when impending tears roll up, knocking on my tear-duct door. "The suitcase is in my way. I can't roll over it, and your leg has mine pinned so I can't sit up."

"Don't move," he says before untangling his leg from mine. With a loud huff expelling from his lips, he rolls underneath me, and I flop like a sausage against his chest.

My entire body weight rests on top of Arlie as his eyes find mine.

"I'm so sorry." Apologising is all I can think to do.

"Melinda! Are you often that rough with things replicating the male appendage?"

A tear rushes down my cheek.

"Hey! Don't cry. It's okay." His thumb swipes my tear away as he keeps his eyes on mine.

"I-I-I ..." I stutter "I'm ..." I don't say another word, because without warning or notice of his intentions, Arlie presses his full lips against mine.

Arlie kisses me in the most embarrassing moment of my life, and I'm left brainless. At first, my mouth remains unmoving, but soon his lips become so enticing I find myself kissing him back. Every swirl of his tongue in my mouth has our kiss deepening, and I know it needs to end, but I don't want to stop kissing Arlie because it feels so right it can't be wrong.

He wraps his arms tightly around me and moulds his body into mine. There's so much passion at this moment I feel as though my heart will explode. Our limbs entwine, and soon, Arlie rolls over with me in his arms until his lips pull away and he's left looking down on me.

This is where it needs to stop, Mindy. You need to stop this now. Slow and steady wins the race, not fast and furious. My mind is screaming, but my heart soars.

Arlie lowers his mouth towards mine.

"Stop," I whisper.

He pulls himself away. His eyes disappear. His lips go, too.

What do I do now?

Chapter Nineteen

One large room. A vibrator lying on the carpeting in front of me, and one massive and embarrassing moment playing over and over in my mind.

Tears flood my face as I sit alone on the bed beside my belongings, not at all disappointed Arlie hightailed it out of here the moment I said to stop. I would have too if I were him. I bet he's already on a boat back to civilization, and I'll become the heroine of the dildo girl story he'll tell his friends about in years to come.

How could he possibly leave this deserted island without a craft to do so? That would be with the use of a get-out-of-jail-free card, the very cards I was informed of before I came to Heart Key. *"You can leave whenever you want. All you need to do is hold up your out card and say, 'I'm leaving paradise'."* It's what Susan said.

Where do I find one of these cards? Because I need

to leave this place too. As it is, I can already imagine the headlines with my name on them.

Melinda Grant: Screw up. Fuck up. Everything that can go wrong will. Good or bad, she'll find a way to make it worse.

Why did Arlie kiss me? Why did he have to do such a thing? I close the lid of my suitcase, zip it back up, and pull it off the bed.

Tap, tap, tap, tap.

"I come bearing tissues. Can I come in?"

Arlie. What? Why?

"Please stop crying. I'm sorry," he pleads.

He's sorry? Why's he sorry? He didn't do anything wrong.

"I'm coming in. I want to make sure you're okay."

I turn my blurred sight to the partly opened door.

Arlie steps through the gap with a box of tissues held out in front of him. "I shouldn't have done what I did. It was ... well, you were about to cry. I didn't want you to cry." He pauses. "I made it worse."

I shake my head. *Is this guy a saint?*

Arlie plucks a tissue from the box and waves it in retreat.

"You left." My voice quivers.

"I did. I had to ..." He clears his throat. "I had to fix myself."

"Fix yourself?"

He points downwards. "A male thing."

I suck my cheeks inwards. "Oh."

"I'm really sorry."

"You don't need to be. It's me who should be sorry."

Arlie drops the box of tissues to the floor and marches towards me, closing the gap quicker than I can blink. His hands wrap around my body. His heart beats against my ear. He kisses the top of my hair.

And with this one display of pure affection, comfort, and kindness, my embarrassment drifts away, and my body relaxes.

"Do you want to put your suitcase back on the bed and unpack? I'll leave you to do so on your own and wait downstairs at the table for you."

I nod against his chest.

"I'm going to let you go now."

Before he has a chance to step away, I snake my arms around his waist and hug him back. I hold Arlie as tightly as I do Chris when I'm upset. Arlie holds me as tightly as Chris does in return.

There's a glass of water to my right and a plate of assorted cheese and crackers to my left. Arlie sits across from me with a binder open, reading through the rules and regulations of the island out loud.

When he gets to the part about the get-out-of-jail-free cards, I tense. Not long ago, I planned to whip one out so I could go home. Arlie, on the other hand, did not. I need to get a grip and relax more. I'm in paradise. With the first little hiccup, I planned to bolt.

I can't bolt. I can't run from this island.

"The cards are in the back of the binder," he says.

"Okay."

"We need to open an envelope each day that will have a task for us. Today's one is here." He holds a blue envelope in the air.

"Okay."

Arlie tears the paper. He pulls out a matching blue-coloured piece of paper from inside.

"Arlie and Melinda," he reads. "Your first task is to take a canoe out to the middle of the ocean. Once there, you're to share three things about yourself with each other, things which have meaning and significance to who you are as people. There's nowhere to run. No place to hide. Be honest. Be understanding. Once completed, you'll receive a prize."

"A prize? Exciting."

He nods.

"Just one thing: do you know how to canoe?"

"Yes."

"I don't."

"You've never been on a canoe?"

I shake my head.

"Well, today you will be an expert."

I half laugh.

"It also says in the letter that if you don't want to complete this task you can use one of your out cards to abandon it, but we need to use them wisely, because once they're gone you get no more."

"How do these cards work exactly? You get one to leave, and two to remove yourself from tasks?"

"No. My understanding is you get three cards, and you can either use any of them to leave or to sit out a task."

"Oh, okay. Are you going to use yours?"

"No." He sounds surprised. "You?"

"No. I'll give it a go."

"Good. We better head out soon before it gets too late. We don't want to be on the sea at dusk."

"Why?"

"It'll get dark quickly. And sharks."

I gulp. "I see. Well, let's start because I don't want to be some sea creature's dinner."

Arlie smiles. "Bathers it is. There are towels in the bathroom."

"Where's the bathroom?"

"There's a door against the wall in my room off from the bed."

"Hmm. I didn't see one in mine."

"Well, looks like you'll be using my bathroom." His voice rises. A smile touches the corner of his lips.

"You said there are heaps of other bathrooms in the house?"

"There is. But mine is the only one on our level."

"Oh."

"It's up to you which one you use. I don't mind if you use mine."

"Okay."

"Go get changed, and I'll bring you down a towel. You brought bathers, yeah?"

I nod.

"We'll meet back here in five?"

"Sounds good."

I open the suitcase from where I shoved it in the wardrobe, still fully packed. I dig through my clothes in search of my black tankini and boardshorts. Turns out I no longer have either of these items in my luggage.

"Chris," I groan. Not only has he put the vibrator he purchased for me in my bag, but he's also removed all my bathing suits, bar the yellow bikini I swore to myself I wouldn't wear. His death will be the first task I complete when I get back to Melbourne.

I stand inside the closet to change and make sure I'm facing the wall.

I must not let these cameras see me naked.

Once I tie the back of the two-piece into place, I make my way into the bedroom and nervously pace back and forward. There's no mirror in here. What if I look ridiculous?

I wrap my hands around my naked belly, and cross one thigh in front of the other to hide my curves, curves I couldn't remove even if I was to exercise. I have a naturally curvaceous frame. Big boobs, wider hips, chunkier thighs … I've been like this since I started puberty at twelve years old. How do I cover these unattractive qualities? How does a girl like me impress a guy like Arlie who's cover model material? I can't.

The kiss we shared earlier will be as far as our romance goes. I know this; he probably does, too.

"Melinda," Arlie calls with an air of excitement. I freak out. I jump on the spot, then hop from foot to foot in an un-coordinated jig, hightailing it into the wardrobe. I dig through my case and pull out a strappy, casual white dress. I'm quick to rip it over my head before I walk in a circle like a dog chasing its tail in search of the sunglasses I wore on the yacht. I can't find them. Did I leave them behind?

I dig through my stuff again, this time in search of the spare pair I know I placed in there. I find the thick black frames and slip them onto my head.

The white hat Conrad gifted me still lies on the ground near the bedroom door. I dip down and retrieve it on my way out.

"I'm here," I puff. I'm flustered. It's obvious. How do you turn fluster off?

"Towels, water bottles, and sunscreen." Arlie nods toward the backpack slung over his shoulder. "Can you think of anything else we'll need?"

"No," I say, shifting my eyes from his bare chest to the waistband of his boardshorts, which hang from his hips in just the right way.

"Hat. I need a hat." He turns on his heel and jogs down to his room.

"Hat, sure, hat," I mutter to myself feeling self-conscious, nervous, and very intimidated.

"Ready?" he asks, jogging towards me wearing a black baseball cap which match his boardies.

"I am," I lie.

"I can't wait to get out in the surf. How about you?"

"Super excited," I lie again.

"Great. After you." He waves me in front of him.

I place my sunglasses over my eyes and put the hat on my head. I hate the surf. I hate bikinis. I hate Chris right now, but most of all, I hate everything about myself and the way my body continues to betray me.

Chapter Twenty

The moment we reach the soft sand, I see the canoe by the water's edge. It wasn't there when I arrived on the island, but it is now.

Headaches: They're something I rarely experience, but right now, my head pounds excessively, and it makes me feel like throwing up. I'm putting the dull ache which has turned into drumming against my skull down to the champagne I had on the way over here. Champagne and my brain never mix well.

"Are you okay?" Arlie asks.

I rub my fingers against my temple. "Hmm."

"A headache?"

"A little one. I'm probably a bit dehydrated."

"Do you want to get some paracetamol?"

"No, no, it's okay. We've already reached the beach. No point turning back."

"Do you want to wait a bit before heading out? Wait for the headache to die down?"

"Yes. Can I just sit here for a bit and drink some water? Do we have time?"

"Sure. I might go for a swim. Unless you want me to stay with you."

"No, you go swim, and when you get out, we'll get the task over and done with."

"Are you sure?"

"Positive."

"Okay," he says, placing the backpack and his hat beside me. "Be back soon."

I nod.

Every step he takes has the tattoo on his calf drawing my attention. I don't know what it is about, but I like looking at it. In fact, I love it. It suits him. Maybe I should get a tattoo. What would I get? Where would I even put it?

Arlie dives under the water and disappears for a moment.

"It's lovely," he yells when he resurfaces.

I give him a thumbs up before placing two fingertips against my temple and rolling them around in a small circle. I feel sick, and I still can't figure out if I should get a tattoo or not.

Water. More water. I'm so thirsty I drink from one of the bottles Arlie packed until my belly is as full as a camel's would be when taking to the desert. The more I drink, the less pain I experience.

Note to self: Drink more H20 to prevent future headaches.

No sooner do I think this than I see Arlie swimming back into shore. I jet my head in every direction, looking for the cameraman I expect to see down by the shoreline—after all, we've left the house—but he's nowhere I can see him.

It's strange. Everything about this beach feels bizarre to me at this moment. That is, until I scan the water's edge and see a man with a camera standing there. *Where did he come from?*

Arlie stands. His tanned skin glistens. *Good God, he's gorgeous.*

Arlie runs his hand through his hair, and my eyes glue to his bulging bicep. He must work out a lot to have arms like tree trunks. I watch as he looks towards the camera I'd not long ago spotted myself. I pull the sunglasses down the bridge of my nose, tipping my chin slightly before peering through a small gap. Just because I've put limits on where our time together can go doesn't mean I can't perv. I'm human, after all.

Every step Arlie takes has me drooling because he's the best type of eye candy imaginable. The waistband of his boardies appear, then a little more material creeps out from the water as it sinks farther down the tops of his legs. *Yeah, baby, work it*, I think, right before I burst into a fit of laughter at the sight of his very defined buffalo. Arlie's pants have wedged so far up his front, the seam has split his balls into two defined bulges, one on each side.

I snort, then cough, then fall to my side. The camel toe for men. Who knew it was a thing that happened?

By the time Arlie reaches me, I'm crying and laughing at the same time.

"What's so funny, you?"

"Oh, I don't know." I continue my laughter not able to look up at him. After a minute or two, I rein in my amusement. "You know how my flying trapeze vibrator is going to make it into every single lounge room across Australia?"

There's a slight chuckle coming from above me.

"Well, now your buffalo is too."

"What?" He screeches, causing me to laugh again. "I knew I shouldn't have packed these fucking shorts because they have a habit of riding my junk."

My laughter grows until I'm crying again.

"Oh, this is really funny to you, isn't it?"

I nod.

A piercing squeal explodes from my mouth when he wraps his arms around my waist, and he lifts me until my pointed toes can't touch the ground. "Let me go," I squawk.

"Yeah, no. Not until you stop laughing at me."

"Okay, okay, I'll stop," I choke out.

Slowly, my body is lowered until I'm flat-footed and held against his cold chest.

"You see, I don't embarrass easy ..." His lips are

close to mine. His eyes narrow and appear more serious in reflection. "I don't care if I was sporting a man toe for the world to see." Arlie steps away.

"Okay," I whisper, finding myself mesmerised by the colour change in Arlie's eyes, so much brighter, darker in colour than they were before he set off for a swim. There's something about the way his eyes change to different shades of blue and grey under differing circumstances ... I find this fascinating. My eyes don't do such a thing, so why do his?

"Are you ready to get this task completed yet?"

"Yes." I'm all breathy and absent of thought.

"Good. Get your kit off, and let's head out."

Take my dress off? I'm not taking it off. I'm heading out as I am.

"What's wrong?" He must sense my sudden change of heart.

"Nothing. I'm ready to go."

"Okay, rip your dress off, and tuck it in the bag."

"No, no. I'm wearing it out."

"What?"

"I'm wearing it. We're going in a canoe. I'm not going to get wet."

"Yes, you will. Trust me, the less you wear, the better. Plus, you'll need the traction your skin offers to keep you seated securely as we row."

"What? Why?"

"Because the canoe is fibreglass, and the material of your dress will have you slip-sliding out of your seat."

What the hell? "Okay," I say, turning my back to Arlie. One deep breath has my hands reaching for the bottom of the material. Another deep breath has me sliding it up my stomach. A hesitant and shaky breath has the dress ripped over my head.

Then it hits me—if he's wearing boardshorts, won't he slip and slide too?

"Hang on. You're wearing ..." I rip my body around to face Arlie, who has the cheekiest smile lifting his lips.

"Yellow's a good colour on you. You shouldn't believe everything you're told. Now, let's go before we're shark bait."

What an arse hat. I totally fell for Arlie's cock-a-bull story.

My arms are burning when we come to a stop out in the middle of the sea. The shoreline is only just visible, the island much too far away for my liking. My stomach becomes awash with nerves as I rotate my head and look at the mountains, which appear so close I feel as though I could swim the distance remaining between them and us. We're not alone out here, though, because there's a speedboat hovering not far away.

Arlie points at a microphone attached to the canoe with his outstretched finger.

"I guess this is how they hear us," he says, matter-of-factly.

"Do you keep forgetting there are cameras around and then suddenly remember, like I do?"

"Yep. I took a step back when I saw old mate on the beach."

There's a moment of silence between us. The only noise I hear is the shutting down of a boat engine.

"At least the water is calm out here," Arlie says.

"Eerily." I shiver.

"Okay, I'm going to say this before you think it."

Think what?

"I'm trying hard not to stare at your boobs right now, but I'm a man, and your boobs are, you know, boobs."

A smile touches my lips as my face warms, and I know I'm blushing.

"Boobs," he says again, childishly.

"I get it, and it's okay."

"Good." And without even blinking, his eyes roam from my face to my tits. "Thank you, God," he whispers so softly I almost don't catch it.

I giggle. It seems we pray in the same way. I'll mark that in the 'pro' column of my time with Arlie Blight. He's open and honest, and doesn't hide how he feels. I'll add that to my list, too. "Do you want to go first with these three truths, or should I?"

"What would you like?"

"I'd like you to go first."

"Okay. I'll do it."

Arlie crosses his hands over his lap. His vision remains on my bust until he lifts his chin and stares into my eyes.

"I was once engaged to a woman named Elissa Samuels. It didn't work out because she cheated on me with my best friend. I haven't had a serious relationship since. Betrayal is my least favourite word, and I have trust issues because of the situation. It's one of the reasons I came on the show. The other reason is that by admitting this in front of the whole world, I can't hide from it anymore. I hope it'll mean I'm more comfortable with dating again."

Holy fuck. That's a huge fucking truth. "I'm sorry that happened to you. Can I ask some questions about it, or would you prefer not to discuss it any further?"

His eyes narrow, his lips pinched together, and then he crosses his arms over his chest. I can see he doesn't want to talk about it. He's likely hurting, so maybe it's still raw. "Sure, ask whatever you'd like, but if I don't want to answer something, can I say pass and you'll move on?"

I nod.

Closing my eyes, I ask myself if it's best to drop the twenty questions and move on, sparing him any further discomfort, but I want to know. I want to know Arlie Blight, and the good, the bad, and the ugly that comes with him. "How long were you together?" I say, opening my eyes and looking down at my legs tucked to the side.

"Ten years."

"Holy ffff ..." I mush my lips together to prevent myself from completing the word. *Not in front of my parents.*

"A long time. I thought we were going to get married. It turns out she'd been screwing my best friend for the past four years we were together. I should have seen it, but I was blind, naïve, and stupid."

"No, no, I'm sure you weren't." I lift my head and reach out my arm until I place my hand against his leg.

"I was, but that's love. Sometimes, it's blinding."

"I'm so sorry."

"It's okay."

"Can I ask how long you've been apart?"

"Five years."

I try to do the math to figure out how old Arlie is. I conclude he must be in his late twenties.

"I'm thirty-one, Melinda." It's like he reads my mind. "We were high school sweethearts. We started officially dating when we were sixteen but had been friends from the age of twelve."

Double holy fuck. "I don't know what to say."

"I know. Nobody does." He pauses. "Any more questions?"

I have a million, but I can hear the annoyance and sadness in his tone, so I decide to drop it before I ask too much of him. "No, none. Thank you for sharing with me."

He nods.

"My turn?"

He nods again.

"Okay, here goes." I'm nervous to share, but after what Arlie's admitted, I feel comfortable to offer something of myself that I haven't told anyone apart from Chris. "I've never been engaged or married, but I've also never dated. Well, that's technically a lie. I've been on two dates with two different guys, but I never went on to date them afterwards."

Arlie's posture completely changes from down in the dumps and slumped at the midsection to curious, intrigued, and seated upright. "Who did you date?"

"Alec. I was sixteen."

"And?"

"And the blind date from the night I bumped into you at the Chinese shop, but he turned out to be a cat-killing psycho, so—"

"Cat-killing psycho?"

"You don't even want to know."

"But I do."

There are a lot of laughs between the both of us as I explain the ordeal of the evening before I made it to the Chinese restaurant and subsequently ended up eating a meal with the man seated across from me now.

"He was crazy," Arlie says.

"Told you."

"And the Alec fellow?"

"Well, that one stung a lot. Alec and his friends humiliated me. He was the popular boy. I wasn't popular at all, and the date was a prank."

"That's sad."

"Yeah, but the weird part is it wasn't because of the date, I don't think, that I never went on to date again in my life. I think it's because I find myself nervous around men, and my brain-to-mouth functionality falters a lot."

"You talk to me just fine."

"I know, which is weird for me, if I'm honest."

"I'll take that as a compliment."

I smile, then nod.

"So, does this mean you've never had a boyfriend or a partner?"

"You are correct," I say, drawing a big invisible tick in the air.

Arlie's eyes grow wide. His eyebrows lift high on his forehead. "Melinda, are you a virgin?"

I didn't see the question coming because I hadn't put all the pieces of what we discussed together. Of course, Arlie would get such an impression. "No, no, no! Nooooo! I'm not a virgin. I've been involved like that."

Arlie's eyebrows dip. His lips narrow. "With?"

And then it dawns on me. Strange men when I'm drunk. I can't say that out loud. "Pass."

"Okay, okay. Sorry. Too far."

I place each hand on the opposing arm, creating a

cross of protection across my chest. I'm a floozy. A skanky floozy.

"My turn again," Arlie says.

"Please."

Arlie lets out a long sigh. "The worst thing that's ever happened to me is my mother dying. She was mugged in a train station late at night. It was my fault because I had a project due for school I hadn't told her about until right before it needed to be handed in. My mother, being the type of person she was, went into town to get supplies so she could make it while I slept. If only I'd done the damn project, she wouldn't have been killed. Maybe then she'd have been around to stop my sister from getting knocked up so young, and I wouldn't have gone off the rails and rebelled against everything for the next year of my life."

My heart hammers in my chest. Arlie has had some horrible things happen to him, yet he seems so reasonable, not whiny and all 'woe is me' like I tend to do when things aren't going right in my life.

"Arlie, I'm so sorry." I slowly try to stand.

"I wouldn't do that, Melinda," he warns.

I don't listen. I need to hug him. I need to do something. His mother was murdered in a subway station.

"Melinda," he says my name louder and with more dominance.

I crouch down due to his tone.

"Camel toe." A twinge of humour lines his voice,

causing me to shoot right back to my feet before turning my eyes down to Miss Priscilla. *I don't have a camel toe. What's he talking about?*

The canoe wobbles. I throw out my arms to regain balance, but before I get a chance to sit back down the canoe rocks and then overturns, throwing both Arlie and me into the cold water below.

"Oh, shit," I say when my head bobs above the surface.

Arlie's laughing.

I tread water to stay afloat as I glare in Arlie's direction. It's like a thousand knives suddenly stab into my skin from my shoulder to my navel. *Somethings biting me. A jellyfish?* "Ouch, oh God, ouch. Fuck!" I scream. I can no longer hear the deep chuckles coming from Arlie. All I can listen to is my pulse beating in my head.

His arm curls under my legs, his other arm around my back.

"It stings. It frickin' stings." Tears roll down my cheeks as I clench my teeth and hiss out my pain.

"Help! Help!" Arlie yells.

The sound of a boat engine starting brings with it the sensation that my body is being pushed through the water.

"It's okay. I'll get us on the boat."

I don't feel anything bar the searing heat through my midsection when I find myself lying on the boat with Arlie hunched over the top of me.

"Jellyfish," he yells. "Take the fucking camera off her now." Instant anger.

"Get the stingers off. Get them off," I hiss.

"They are. The tentacles are gone. Lie still." Arlie's incredibly calm. His touch is gentle. His presence is helpful.

I close my eyes and groan, one long sound. "My heart hurts. My arm hurts too. My stomach is burning like acid."

"I've got you." Arlie's tone is confident.

It feels like forever until I hear the engine beginning to slow. A different warmth, unlike the fires of hell previously spreading across my skin, takes over. I open one eye. "What the fuck? Arlie, no!" I choke out.

"It'll stop it. I promise." His pants are no longer around his waist. Part of his penis fills my vision. A forceful stream of pee is flowing from its tip.

Arlie is fucking peeing on me.

"Stop!" I cry. "Stop peeing on me."

Of course. The old story that peeing on a jellyfish sting will make the pain go away. Arlie doesn't reply, and he doesn't stop either.

Oh my God, just let me die.

Chapter Twenty-one

I'm lying on the couch with a towel soaked in vinegar rested across my midsection, and an ice pack pressed to my forehead.

Arlie sits in a chair opposite me, staring at me with a look of worry scrunching up his face.

He should be worried, because the moment I can get up, I'm going to slap him stupid.

First, my dress lifted above my head back on the beach, showing the world my knickers. Then I mistook the host of this stupid show for the mystery guy I was supposed to be meeting. I attacked a flying dildo. I kicked that same flying dildo. I kissed a man I barely knew in a moment of tears that turned into passion. Now that same man has peed all over me after I sustained a jellyfish sting.

What the hell are my mother, father, and sister going to think when they see this? Hell, what are my work colleagues and my friends at The Quarter going to say?

Chris? I know he'll find this funny as hell, and he'll never let me live a minute of it down.

Arrrrgh! What a mess.

How much does it cost to blackmail a director? What figure will it take to prevent this embarrassing footage from making it to the air? If I don't stop this, I'll never be able to show my face in public for as long as I live.

Day one: Everything's gone to shit. Everything that can go wrong is, has, and I believe will continue to do so.

"Are you okay?" Arlie says hesitantly.

"Um … vinegar, bright spark. You use vinegar on a jellyfish sting, not urine." I flare my nostrils as I contain my anger. "Arlie, you peed on me."

He chuckles.

"It's not funny."

"Some of my piss pooled in your belly button, and I had to kind of roll you onto your side so that it would empty."

I cover my face with my hands and suck back a harsh mouthful of air. His booming laughter follows. "Arlie, it's not funny. None of this is funny."

"Oh, but it is." He continues to laugh.

"I didn't even have a camel toe. I rocked the damn canoe for no reason at all."

"I'm sorry. I swear I am." There's still humour in his

tone.

"So why are you laughing?"

"Because it's funny." And there he goes again. Deep laughter fills the room.

I close my eyes and hope when I open them none of this has even occurred. I hope that this has been a horrible nightmare, and when I wake, I'll be home, curled into a ball on my bed, wearing a fluffy bunny outfit. There'll be a needy cat tucked under my arse, hogging the bed like he usually does.

One long, steady breath has my limbs relaxing.

I bet we failed the task, and due to this sting, we won't receive the prize. Another slow inhale sees the last of my pain disappear.

I don't want the stupid prize anyway. I want to go home.

My eyelids grow heavy, my heart slows, and the need for sleep overcomes me. I attempt to fight it, but I fail.

Birds chirping have my eyelids fluttering open. The sunlight is bright, so bright I squeeze my eyes shut before rolling onto my side to escape the glare. A piece of fabric as soft as silk rests against my cheek; my head is supported by what I can only describe as a mink blanket balled underneath it.

Where am I?

I open my eyes as I run my hand in a semi-circle

beside me. Sheets—I can feel the thread count of expensive sheets below my fingertips. The last thing I remember is lying on a suede lounge chair with a towel against my belly in a two-piece swimsuit.

The pressure to my neck from the string of my bikini top is absent, which has my hand shifting across my chest. I gasp. I drag my hand farther down over my chest, my stomach, and only stop when I reach my mid-thigh. What's happening? I'm wearing a long cotton T-shirt.

I launch my body upright. My eyes shoot open. I hold my breath.

What the hell?

I flick the blankets off. I'm wearing a blue T-shirt with nipples erect and bosoms unholstered. *Holy shit! I'm completely naked under here.* My beaver is roaming free and loose, and that's not the way this beaver likes to roll. It's a modest creature who enjoys the security that covering it brings. So, if I'm dressed like this, it can mean only one thing: someone who was not me has changed me.

Arlie?

I leap from the mattress, tucking the material of the T-shirt between my legs. My head pounds like it does after I've downed a bottle of scotch.

Where is my underwear? Where's my bra? Where's my memory? What the hell happened last night? Can a jellyfish sting give you a hangover? Can it erase memories like dancing the mumbo with a bottle of liquor can? Why don't I know the answer to these questions? Why is my head not only pounding, but so freaking fuzzy too? Why do I feel like I do after I've drunk myself stupid and woken up to the realisation I've had sex?

I swallow in a gulp.

Did I have sex?

Chapter Twenty-Two

I hear a doorknob turn. I walk backwards. I wrap my arms around my chest as I hunch my body and flick one leg in front of the other, being mindful to keep the material of the T-shirt tucked across Miss Priscilla.

"You're awake. How did you sleep?" Arlie stands in front of me, bare-chested, wearing only a pair of green boxer briefs. There's a silver tray held between his hands, and a cool, calm, and collected look planted to his handsome face.

I take a step back and eye him cautiously.

"What are you doing?" he asks.

"I think the better question here is what have you done?"

"Me?" His voice rises. "I brought you breakfast. I figured you'd be starving."

"And ...?" I wait for the 'and' ... the and that comes

with the explanation as to how I've found myself dressed as I am. Surely, there are a lot of innocent reasons for my current attire. I passed out after a long day and the jellyfish sting I sustained. I came upstairs and undressed myself in my tired state, somehow finding a T-shirt that doesn't belong to me, and forgot I did these things. However, my mind is focused on just one terrible thing. Did we perform the horizontal tango and that's why I feel like I do, as I have on occasions before today?

"And ... what?"

"And ...?" I point at the T-shirt.

"My shirt?"

"So, you admit it?" I stab my pointer finger into the air.

"Admit it? That you're wearing my surf tee?"

"Yes." In my need for justice, I forget about protecting my crown jewels and widen my stance.

"You fell asleep on the lounge. I tried to wake you, but you were out like a light, so I thought it best to tuck you into bed."

"It doesn't explain why I'm ..." I pause and adopt a low, whispered tone, "It doesn't explain why I'm naked under here."

"You fell asleep in wet bathers, and I didn't want you to get sick. I was already freaking out over the jellyfish sting and the fact you were so out of it. I had to call the emergency number in the binder to let the show know we needed a doctor to come out to check on you."

"What?" My eyes grow large. My blood pressure soars. "You invited a strange person to come check on me while panty-less and asleep?"

"What was I supposed to do?" Arlie steps to his right and places the tray on the cabinet under the television.

"Leave me in my wet bathers to sleep it off."

"No! What if you got sick or something? It would've been my fault." He places his hands on his hips. "After all, it was my camel toe joke that caused you to plummet into the sea and got you stung in the first place."

"I was fine. I'm a doctor. I knew I was fine."

"About that ..."

"What?"

"Being a doctor. You said you were a receptionist. Your submission form doesn't reflect what you told me at the restaurant that night."

I drop my shoulders. I stare into his sexy-as-fuck eyes, and I realise this horn dog is changing the subject and turning this all back on me. "Hold up there, buddy, that's not up for discussion right now. How I'm currently practically naked is."

Arlie places his hand to his forehead before dropping his head. "Look, the doctor checked the sting and your vitals, then said you were fine, and to let you sleep."

"Dude, you ..." I huff. "You let them check my

stomach while I had no knickers on, and you did this full knowing it could be filmed."

Arlie lengthens his neck. His eyes find mine. There's a slight grin tugging his lips upwards. "Actually, I forgot about the cameras, but you still needed to be checked."

"Oh my God, you're killing me. Haven't I already had enough embarrassment?"

"It was a doctor. I'm sure he's seen enough vaginas in his day. I bet you've seen your fair share of vaginas, right? Being a doctor and all." He bobs his head.

I gasp. "The number of vaginas I've seen has nothing to do with the fact you should have just left me sleep ... left me be."

"Melinda, I was worried about you. I was so worried that even after the doctor said you were okay, I still sat beside you the entire night making sure you kept breathing."

Warmth floods me. He ... he did that?

"You did?" I mumble, all dreamy.

"I did."

That's so lovely of him. So kind. So sweet. So—

He still saw you naked.

He let the world see you naked.

"Did you look?" I completely disregard the kindness he's expressed and decide to ramp my mood back to its previous pissed off status. I'm going for his perfectly formed manly jugular this time. His sweet nothings are not going to derail my upset. No, siree

Bob.

"I'm the one who changed you, so kind of."

"Kind of?" *What the hell, man?*

"Well, it's not like I laid you out stark naked, spread your legs, then grabbed a torch and a microscope so I could inspect your bits. I did glance. I'm a man—it's hard not to when the chick looks as hot as you."

"I can't believe you did ..." I stop mid-sentence. I replay what he said over in my mind. Did I hear him correctly? "You think I'm hot?"

He turns his eyes to his feet. "Yes," he says, barely audible.

My entire demeanour changes. I've never been called hot before, not by anyone. Not even by Chris. *That's so sweet.* "It was kind of you to care so much," I say sweetly.

"I was doing what anyone would do, Melinda."

"Thank you."

"It's okay. I'm sorry if carrying you upstairs, putting you in your bed, and getting you changed has upset you."

"It's okay. I shouldn't have bit your head off ..."

He raises his hand in the air, rendering me speechless. "I get it. Men can be creeps. I didn't do anything, I swear. I got you dried, covered in something I thought would be comfortable, and put you into bed." He shifts on his feet. "I didn't think rummaging through your belongings would be right. I didn't want to invade your privacy."

"You carried me all the way up two flights of stairs? Me?" I don't give him a chance to answer. "How? I'm not a petite or slender woman. Put it this way: if I was to try out to be a cheerleader, it's obvious my role would be the anchor at the bottom of the pyramid. There's no way I'd be the one at the top playing the role of the bright, glittering star."

Arlie's eyes narrow to slits. *"Okay."* He pauses. "It wasn't hard to carry you up here."

"Pffft. How's your back after such a hike? Is it broken?"

"Melinda, I'm serious. It wasn't a hard task at all. I lift weights much heavier than you." His eyes grow wide. He steps towards me.

"What are you doing?"

"Showing you I can lift you." He marches and closes the gap between us, and before I can even scream out the word 'no', I'm cradled in his arms, and he's walking around the room.

"Put me down," I yell as I twist my legs, and my body follows. Arlie stumbles, and I feel myself falling until I no longer do. I'm again held securely against his chest. I worm like a toddler in a tantrum and resume kicking my feet.

"I'll put you down. Stop flinging yourself around, would—" Arlie goes silent.

I gasp and shudder before holding my breath. Shock travels through my limbs as fast as a shooting star flashes through the night sky.

"Holy shit, I'm so sorry." He's apologetic and mortified as he removes what I believe to be his wayward finger that found itself entering my no-fly zone in the scuffle.

Arlie puts me down, then jumps in the opposite direction to me. His pointer finger is held in the air like evidence he needs to dispose of.

I leap backwards with disbelief rattling around my brain.

"I can't believe I did that. Why did ...?" Arlie stops talking mid-sentence. His jaw drops low.

"Oh my God!" I screech. "The first time you KFC my box is like this? What? How? Why?"

Arlie snaps his teeth together before tilting his head slightly to the side. "KFC your box? What does that even mean?" His tone is soft, confused, and unthreatening.

I stand there with a blank look on my face, unsure how in the heck I even answer his question because I'm not sure I truly understand the expression I've just used myself. KFC my box? It's something Chris has said to me before. *"Girl, every time a guy KFCs my goodies box, you know he's not going anywhere fast, because I'm that fucking finger-licking good."*

Slowly, I raise my arms until I face-plant my palms.

"Melinda, I'm sorry. I don't know how it happened."

"It's not your fault, it was an accident, but I'm humiliated and need a moment to think," I mumble into my hands. I cross one leg in front of the other.

Miss Priscilla got an accidental jabbing, and right now, her response is one of throbbing.

"I understood about two words of what you've just said," Arlie says in a hush.

I drop my arms. I keep my vision to the carpet. "Can I have a moment alone please?"

"Of course! Again, I'm truly, truly sorry that my finger slipped—"

"Don't say it," I rush.

"Okay," he replies just as fast.

I haven't been able to look Arlie in the eyes since his finger stabbed my lady taco this morning in what'll be forever known in my mind as the accidental oops-my-finger-slipped-in-your-va-jay-jay-and-I'm-not-sure-who's-more-shocked-you-or-me incident.

Day two, and our first complete day here on the island has been a significant bust. It's pouring rain and has been since ten a.m. This island seems strange; one minute, the sky is the same brilliant and bright blue as it was the day prior, then in a shake of a lamb's tail, it's a ferocious grey, eerie, and mad as hell.

Tropical island: Equals tropical weather it seems.

I lie on the couch with a novel between my hands. My comfortable and straightforward fire red day-dress keeps me mostly covered until the blanket I've thrown over my legs takes over. I need to be careful because E.T. fingers could strike at any time, be it with an innocent slip or a deliberate attack.

Did Arlie mean to do what he did? I don't think so. Okay, I know he didn't, because he seemed more shocked than a nun having an encounter with a flasher's penis. So why am I still so freaked out?

I've not seen Arlie since I brought the empty tray containing the breakfast he made me back down to the kitchen. It's probably a good thing for us.

The kitchen: It's the entire width and length of the inside dining area of The Quarter. Boasting three huge ovens, a massive centre island, and a breakfast bar … I couldn't help but stand in awe.

The three microwaves, the upright deep fryer, the two side-by-side deep freezers, and the four double-door fridges have left me wondering who in hell even needs this many appliances in one place.

Two fully stocked wine fridges, an industrial-sized dishwasher, fourteen stove burners, and the five sinks … Well, that seals the deal in my mind that this is not a kitchen for the rich and famous, but in fact, a facility only a chef would be accustomed to.

Arlie looked comfortable in such a space, which had me questioning if he can even cook? Is Arlie a food artist who makes your tongue orgasm and your stomach want to light up an orgasmic cigarette after digestion? Is Arlie Blight even who he says he is?

I turn the page even though I haven't read a word, and I tell myself one thing: I won't be fiddling with any of the buttons, switches, or do-be-maracas residing in the kitchen. The last thing I need is to start a fire that has Arlie carrying me out and finger banging me due to my awkward leg positioning.

Why did I fight him as I did? Why did Arlie being able to lift me cause me such distress? These two questions I know I'm going to need to save for the shrink I hire when I arrive back home.

Chris was right. I need some serious professional help. I'm a total Nutter Butter.

Chapter Twenty-Three

Arlie clears his throat. I turn my eyes away from the pages of Delilah and Hugh's story, the one I'm hoping will find the two of them married and living happily ever after. I'm not holding my breath, though, because I've been reading all day and there are not many pages left, and Hugh is still nowhere to be found. God, that hunky, messed up, loveable man turned into a total chicken shit on the run. Hugh makes me mad.

"Would you like some dinner, Melinda?"

I don't look at Arlie.

"Would you like something to eat?" he repeats.

"I would." There's an awkward and unsettling tension filling the air around Arlie and me, and there has been all day. Every time he's come and gone, I've pretended I'm too engrossed in this story to notice.

"Would you like anything to eat in particular?"

"I'll make a sandwich."

There's a small huff like sound which has me sitting upright. "Why did you just huff?"

"Because you're frustrating, woman."

"Woman? Woman? You called me woman. I don't like it."

He huffs again.

"You huffed again."

"Because you're impossible. I'm trying to be nice. Make you something to eat. Make up for what happened."

"There's no need. It was what it was."

"Yeah ..." He places his hand on the back of his neck. "But I feel like I've violated you most horrifically." His hand moves from his neck to the waistband of his jeans.

I break eye contact. *I don't feel violated, do I?* I take a moment to think about what Arlie said. To consider how he's feeling. To ask myself why I'm acting like an absolute bitch to him.

I can see why he'd feel like he did violate me. I'm treating him like garbage.

I place the bookmark between the pages and snap the cover closed. "I'll help you make dinner if you want? On one condition, though. I don't have to touch any of those gadgets and appliances. There are a lot— too many for me." I offer an innocent smile in the hope it'll break this strain.

It must work because Arlie smiles back. "Okay, I'll

work the gadgets, and you can do the slicing and dicing."

"Deal."

Arlie holds out his hand. I hesitate, then cup my palm to his.

"We'll need supplies. Do you want to take the golf buggy for a spin?" He helps me up from the lounge.

I nod.

"Do you want to go now while it's not raining?"

"I'll grab my shoes—"

"I'll meet you out front—"

"Okay."

It's a four-seater golf buggy, white in colour with red leather seats. A few minutes later, I climb in beside Arlie, who's sitting on the passenger's side.

"I'm driving?" I'm shocked because I thought men liked to play the role of driving Miss Daisy when accompanied by a lady. Well, it's what I see in the movies anyways. Plus, my dad never lets my mum drive when they're together.

"I thought you'd want a bit of fun, and riding around in this is fun."

I return his infectious smile as I turn the key. "Okay, Daisy, which way do I go?"

"Daisy?"

"Just go with it."

"Okay. Daisy, I am." Arlie laughs. "We need to go down the path between those coconut trees." Arlie points in front of us. "It's a straight drive."

"Hold your bootstraps because I'm about to handle this bad boy like a pro."

Arlie laughs again.

I inhale deeply and sort through the different fragrances in my mind. Clean, crisp-like mountain air, but nowhere near as strong. It's not bland, nor rich like spice, and it's less subtle than rosemary or thyme, or any herb for that matter. The smell of the earth after rain doesn't have a description—it just brings with it a feeling of peace.

I drive at a moderate pace, glancing at my surroundings and listening to the ocean's waves and the wildlife chirping and squawking above. The sky is once again a brilliant blue, no longer the colour of steel metal, no longer angry. The only evidence of the torrential downpours we experienced for a majority of the day lies in the curled white tops of the waves now folding over each other in a battle before smacking against the shoreline.

Arlie takes a series of loud, deep breaths. I instantly smile. There's no better air to breathe than that which follows a storm.

"Can you smell vanilla?" He sniffs loudly.

My smile grows.

"We must be coming nearer to the flower gardens because what I'm smelling is sweet."

"Flower gardens? The tropical island has a park?"

He nods.

I inhale deeply. He's right; the air is now sweet.

Purples, reds, blues, pinks, yellows, and oranges tie together in a large open area. Flower gardens with roaming paths between become my view. "Wow! That's crazy pretty, right?"

Arlie grins, then causally jumps from the moving buggy.

I stomp my foot on the brake. "What are you doing? You can't jump ..."

"It's fine."

Of course, it is.

I don't know what it is about Arlie that at this moment shows me I need to take more risks. I need to climb out of the bubble I've spent years and years shielding myself with. *I want to feel as free as it appears he does.*

Arlie jogs towards the garden on my left. He bends, and I can't help but glance at his shapely rounded arse covered by tight blue jeans.

When he pops his head up, then twists, I spot the handful of flowers he's plucked from the ground.

"For you." He smiles, handing me a brightly coloured arrangement.

"Aww." I gush like a love-struck teenager hopped up on hormones and soppy emotion.

"To the convenient store. Daisy is getting hungry." Arlie plucks a single yellow daisy from my grip and puts it between his teeth. "Let's hunt and gather so I can eat," he mumbles with the flower laid across his mouth and cheeks.

I giggle, while slowly pressing my foot to the accelerator.

Arlie wasn't lying when he said there were stores. He also wasn't lying when he said it was a straight drive to arrive at them.

A long row of navy blue doors and big glass windowfronts takes over my sight. I turn the steering wheel a hard right with one hand. Arlie throws his arms and legs to the side in the most dramatic way when I do. "Crazy women drivers, am I right?"

I clear my throat.

He winks.

Cheeky shit!

There are three aisles, and from those three aisles, we select items from the shelves and place them into a shopping trolley Arlie has taken dominance over.

This moment: Nostalgic! I'm instantly reminded of the very moment I met Arlie Blight in a supermarket back home.

"So, what do we still need?" Arlie dips his head into the trolley. "Men's deodorant? Yes. Condoms? I'm thinking about eight or nine packs. Toilet paper? Lots of toilet paper." He bolts upright, shifting until he's facing me. "Melinda, are you going to steal a cake today? Because if you are, we'll need to grab a cake."

I launch out my arm and tap his chest. "Stop it. There's probably not even toilet paper or condoms here. They're already in the house. I saw them."

He laughs, a low toned sound.

"Stop it!" I warn again.

"Okay, I'll stop after we select a cake."

A shelf is filled with a few decadent desserts, and I'm standing in front of a chocolate mud cake. I've not gorged on anything sweet since I've been here. That's a record for me.

"Chocolate or vanilla? What are you thinking?" Arlie interrupts my thoughts.

"Chocolate?"

"Agreed." Arlie snatches the container from the shelf and rests it in the seat of the cart, just how I had the red velvet cake on the day we met. "Cream. We need whipped cream and ice cream." Arlie pushes the trolley down the aisle towards a fridge stood against the back wall. I follow. "This can be dessert," he mumbles, as if speaking to himself.

There's no checkout to line up at or conveyor belt to load our groceries on, but that doesn't stop Arlie from pretending there is when we're finished selecting our supplies.

"What's that you've got there? Fifty packs of condoms. Oh, and enough toilet paper to stock a public restroom. Do you live in a share house like me?" Arlie smirks.

I roll my eyes as I grab the cake from the seat of the

trolley. I hold it against my chest. I race to the doors like a criminal in escape mode.

Arlie's laughter drifts from behind me.

"I'm stealing this damn cake."

Arlie and I get each other. We're comfortable in one another's presence. It seems right even though it's likely wrong.

Maybe Arlie Blight is my happily-ever-after guy.

I mean, stranger things have happened, right?

Chapter Twenty-Four

"Blue satin totally makes your eyes pop, babe." It's what Chris said when I stepped out of the dressing room in the knee-length gown with the peep-shoulder neckline now covering my skin.

I hope I look as pretty as Chris told me I did when I purchased this dress because I'm not wearing any make-up, and I'm in a hurry to get downstairs for dinner.

Today's task: Arlie Blight has officially asked me out on a date, as per the instructions from inside the purple envelope I ripped open when we returned home from our shopping adventure.

Dear Arlie and Melinda,

Inviting another to spend time with you can lift spirits and increase confidence. Tonight is date night. One contestant must ask the other to be their date and provide a night to be remembered.

Who will it be?

That's up to you.

There'll be a prize if you complete this task successfully. If unsuccessful, like the canoe challenge, you'll receive nothing.

Good luck, and may love be with you.

Perfect Catch

Every step I take has my heart throbbing and my feet unsteady even though I'm barefoot and not challenged by stilettos. I tiptoe across the tiles and head towards the dining room.

It's bare. What the hell?

The table is undressed and missing a feast.

A piquant scent wafts by my nose. "Barbecue," I breathe. He's cooking on a barbecue.

I follow the smell until I reach a patio lit by candlelight. "Hello," I say softly.

There's nobody here, yet two pieces of steak sizzle away on a large grill. A table for two is set in the middle of the space, and on the table rests a crystal vase with the flowers Arlie picked this afternoon.

Do I wait? Do I sit? Do I look for Arlie? I'm not sure what the appropriate action to take is. I pull out the seat closest to the door and sit.

"You're here. I was just in the kitchen, and those potatoes you cut up burnt. Never fear, though; we can do without the added starch." Arlie's holding a basket filled with bread rolls in one hand and a gravy boat in the other. He places them both beside the vase.

Holy mother of God.

Tailored black suit pants. A white collared shirt unbuttoned to the middle of his chest. How in the world am I going to be able to keep it together with him dressed so devilishly?

When Arlie disappears, I find myself swallowing hard, then flapping my hand in front of my face. Just the vision of this man dressed in such a way has me hot, bothered, and fanning myself, and I don't get long to lower my searing temperature before he returns with two plates full of vegetables in hand.

"How would you like your steak cooked?" He's dressed to impress, but incredibly casual in his demeanour, which makes him sexier than hell when he points at the open grill.

"Medium," I croak.

"Perfect," he replies before turning off the hot plate, then returning to the table with our dinner served.

"It looks amazing," I compliment.

"Thank you." Arlie picks up the basket containing the bread rolls and holds it in my direction. "Bread?"

"Please." I take one and place it on the small plate to my right as Arlie nicks one for himself.

"I'm starving." He licks his lips as he did in the Chinese restaurant, and immediately I'm overcome by ravaging heat once more.

I turn my eyes down and stare at polished cutlery,

watching the candlelight dance across the knife blades, hoping I can find composure in a moment when my mind is busy creating images of hot, sweaty, and satisfying sex.

Arlie is going to be my undoing. He has me exploring possibilities I'd never normally find myself contemplating, and I want nothing more than to tear his clothes off as desperately as he tears into a bread roll with his teeth. *Why is he so goddamn good looking? Is this a test of self-control? Am I being tested?*

"No. Stop it. You will not sleep with him. He's all sorts of fine wrapped in a bow. Oh, is he good looking, but you placed a 'no access' pass on Miss Priscilla before you even stepped foot onto this patio. Sex is off the table, Mindy. There'll be no side dish of lady taco for Mr Gorgeous tonight." I swallow hard, as hard as I press my thighs together, then slowly compose myself so as I can get through our dinner conversation without any more impure thoughts.

Arlie clears his throat before slipping his finger under his collar. Our eyes connect until I see him press his lips together as one would when stifling laughter.

"Is something funny?" I want nothing more than to race my hand to my nose to ensure there's no boogers hanging out of it. My insecurities hammer me in one fell swoop.

"No, not at all." I can hear humour laced in his tone. "But ..."

There's always a but.

"At least I know where you stand, and I promise I'll make no advances when dropping you to your bedroom door. I won't even request a side dish of lady taco." His smile touches his eyes. "I believe that's what you called it."

"Oh, dear God. I said all of that out loud?" I leap from my seat. I bump the table. A napkin falls to the floor. "I need to go."

I take two steps before his hand wraps around my arm. Warmth travels through my fingers in the same way it spreads across my cheeks.

"It's okay. I'm glad you were honest. I appreciate honesty."

I can't look at him.

I need to leave.

I'm such an idiot.

"I'm sorry." There's humiliation in my apology.

"It's okay." His tender gaze confirms his sentiment. "How about we sit back down and enjoy the rest of our dinner?" There's a long pause. "I'm sure you're hungry, and I'm curious whether Miss Priscilla means what I think a KFC box does."

I can't breathe. I can't breathe.

Laughter explodes through his lips. It takes me a moment to comprehend what's happening before I find myself laughing too.

It's a warm night; so warm I choose a pair of cotton summer pyjamas to wear after I shed my dress, shower, then head back downstairs. I plonk on the couch with my book in hand as a puff of air is expelled forcefully through my pinched lips.

Arlie steps from out of nowhere into my line of sight. He too has changed. No longer is Arlie wearing a business shirt and perfectly fitted slacks. Instead, he's shirtless and sporting a pair of blue jeans which hangs low off his hips, low enough that I can see his black boxer briefs peeking out from underneath.

"Did you have a lovely night?" He seems genuine as he places the vase of flowers from our dinner for two onto a coffee table he drags into the centre of the room.

"I did. Thank you."

Dinner conversation with Arlie was never lagging, and even in the silent moments, there was still an air of comfortability surrounding us. I like being around this guy in the same way I enjoy being around Chris. So why am I fighting so goddamn hard to ward off my feelings for him?

I am fighting it. I know me well enough to know I am. I'm trying to control and rein in my needs and desires so I can keep the protective bubble around myself intact. Arlie Blight is threatening to pop my bubble, and I'm not sure if this will result in something rewarding for me or something terribly disastrous.

"What you said at dinner ..." Arlie curiously eyes me. One hand pistol grips his chin while the other hangs by his side.

I take my book from my chest and hold it in the air, then open it.

"What you said about ..." He clears his throat as if he's uncomfortable. "The sex stuff ..."

I gulp, then open to the page in my book where the bookmark resides.

"I have no expectations from you. We don't need ... you know, there's no ..." He pauses and seems to take a moment to think. "There's no pressure, is what I'm trying to say." Arlie takes a shaky breath. "I'm not one of those guys, you know." He steps towards me. "I'm not a player. I don't see you as a sex object. In fact, it's the opposite, because I think sex is something that happens naturally and is an evolutionary thing that comes naturally when two people like each other, not something just to get your rocks off." He scrunches his face, and even with a scrunched-up face, he looks as handsome as hell. "Am I making any sense?"

I nod before shifting my eyes to the page.

"I want you to know I'm not expecting anything like that from you. That's all."

My heart grows heavy. My top lip tucks under my bottom one, and I'm suddenly pouting. Is Arlie saying that although he has previously stated he finds me hot, he's not interested in me sexually? Or is he saying he's not in a hurry to have sex with me, but it might happen as things evolve? Or is he stating he's not some horn dog who slips his Peter Pecker into every girl who has a landing strip? *What the hell is he saying?*

"Okay." I'm not sure what else I'm supposed to say.

Arlie exhales a loud breath. "Okay, that clears that up then." His lips make a horse type sound before he resumes speaking. "The fact you were thinking sex must be what I want ... it rattled me. I'm glad you spoke your truth instead of keeping it in even though it's obvious you hadn't intended to."

"Me too." That's a lie. Now I wish my stupid brain-to-mouth function hadn't faltered so epically because Arlie is skirting around the situation like a frigid teenager who can't sort his thoughts out, and he has said the word sex far too many times in a matter of minutes for me to handle.

When Arlie leaves the room, I breathe in and out, slow and steady.

Hang on. I think I just got rejected in the politest way possible.

Turning my eyes to page three hundred and twenty-four, I drown out my sudden feelings of sadness and instead focus on Hugh and Delilah. I hope these two get their shit together.

I read the first line.

The rain pours so heavily, and its force blinds me.

I'm losing hope Delilah and Hugh will work this out. My gut says Hugh will crash and die in the storm. My brain agrees. My heart? My heart holds on to the hope that Delilah will find a way to save him.

I continue reading until I make it through the next chapter, then bolt upright into a seated position, holding the book to my chest. A single tear leaks from behind my eyelashes when I come to close my eyes. Hugh did precisely what he told himself he wouldn't do. He scarred Delilah. "No fucking way," I breathe.

"Are you okay?" Arlie's voice is distant. "Melinda, are you okay?" he says again, worry lifting the pitch of his voice.

"Fine," I mutter as I lie back down and try to compose myself. *This book is killing me. I must know how it ends.*

I flip the page, engrossed in the words rushing across them. I hiss. I scowl. Adrenaline has my pulse beating. I'm enthralled and reacting to what I'm reading.

Arlie clears his throat, and for a split second, I glimpse in his direction. He's sitting in the chair across from me with a book of his own in front of his face.

Arlie reads? A gym-owning, hot-as-fuck guy such as Arlie reads?

I turn to the next page.

God, Arlie is even more sexy than he was only moments before. A guy who reads is beyond hot.

"You look like you're enjoying your book?" Arlie suddenly says, interrupting my thoughts.

"Yes."

He lowers his novel until it stops below his chin. He

gifts me a toothy smile. "What are you reading anyway?"

"Um. Just a story."

"Okay." His smile grows. "It must be action-packed, because you're tensing and flinching nonstop."

"I am?"

"Let me have a gander." Arlie stands.

"You probably wouldn't like this type of story."

"Why?"

"Romance." I smile awkwardly.

"Are you always so single-minded, Melinda?"

My lips curl upwards. "Sometimes." I don't lie this time.

"Here." Arlie rushes towards me with his hand extended. "Let me read." He plucks the book from my fingertips, causing me to sit upright and cradle my knees. Arlie drops down beside me. He turns his eyes to the page and reads aloud.

"Delilah said not two words to me as I drove her to my penthouse ..." Arlie reads with a tender tone. He dips the cover down. His eyes find mine as I tilt my head to the side, resting my cheek against my kneecaps. "Can I keep reading?"

"Sure," I gulp, hugging my knees tighter.

He swiftly returns his sight to the page. "I can't believe I've hurt her so harshly, so unthinkably. Tonight, the woman I loved threw herself at the mercy of God in a bustling street, in front of cars who would have struggled to see her if some man had not screamed out her presence ..."

Arlie pauses. He takes a deep breath, then continues. "I did the one thing I said I wouldn't: I scarred Delilah, and now she's soaked through, shivering and staring out the windshield of my car. What have I done to her?"

I bite my lower lip in hopes I stop it from quivering.

Arlie continues reading. "I carry Delilah from the car to the elevator. She's wet, cold, but looking at me like I'm her saviour."

Arlie suddenly clears his throat, and my breath hitches in mine. He reads beautifully and with emotion, and I'm heating up in places I shouldn't be. "Once inside the penthouse, Delilah presses her cheek against my chest over my heart. 'Put me down please,' she says quietly.

"I lower her to the floor. Water drips from her dress to the marble flooring below, and when she shakes her head, her mangled hair disperses more water. 'Why did you bring me here, Hugh? Why did it have to be you who saved me?'"

Suddenly, I'm overcome with a sense of hope that these two frustrating idiots will finally work this out. "Keep reading," I whisper.

"I'm not sure what to say to Delilah. I gaze at her in the same way I would a wounded puppy seeking safety, guidance, care, shelter, and love.

"'Because I love you, Delilah,' I declare with full conviction. 'I love you. I've only ever truly loved you, and I did so from the very first moment I laid eyes on your perfect face.'

"Delilah's eyes find mine, and the look she delivers is tender and forgiving. 'You love me,' she says softly.

"'I do. I always have. I-I-I just wanted to protect you.'

"'From what?' she asks forcefully.

"'From me ...'" Arlie seems to search me in the same way I picture Hugh looking at Delilah—like I'm a wounded puppy. "This is some heavy shit," he mumbles.

"It's frustrating and powerful and heartbreaking," I confess.

"Should I keep going?"

I nod as the corners of my lips raise. Arlie continues to read tenderly, and I'm so taken by him I know I could listen to him read every day of my life.

"Okay," he says as he turns the page. "Delilah rushes towards me. Her arms fling around my neck, and she squeezes tightly, like if she didn't hold me in such a way, I might disappear and abandon her again. Her lips hover an inch from mine. I want nothing more than to kiss her, but I won't because I don't think it's what she truly needs from me at this moment ..." Arlie seems as engrossed as I am. "He needs to kiss her, right?"

"Uh-huh. Like, right now."

"Well, let's see if he does." Arlie turns his eyes back to the page. "'You love me?' she asks in a way that tells me she doesn't believe my initial confession of love for her.

"'I do,' I whisper.

"Delilah's lips move even closer, to the point where they're almost touching mine. I can't hold back. I must taste her. I must devour her mouth with my love. I must have Delilah again. I'm going to fuck her like it's the last time I'll ever get to ..."

I flick my head upwards; my knees fall until my feet thump against the floor. "Okay, and that's the end of the story. Thank you for reading it to me."

I reach out my hand to claim the book back. I know I'm blushing because I understand, given the previous scenes in this story, that a very descriptive sex scene is about to play out, and I can't have Arlie speaking it out loud. I'm already twitching in my seat from the smooth way in which his voice speaks these words.

"Oh, no, no, no. This story is just getting good."

"Arlie." I grit my teeth at the same time I press my thighs together and swipe for the novel once more.

He draws his arm back. "I want to know what happens."

"I'll tell you the end when I get there."

"How about I read you the end?" His tone is filled with desire.

I graze my teeth against my bottom lip as I pray for the sudden throbbing between my legs to halt from its current whorey state.

Arlie moves the pages in front of his face before

continuing. "She tastes like lemonade on a hot summer's afternoon, yet her skin is as cold as a chill brought on by a winter snowstorm. I need to have Delilah right here on this floor. It's been five long months since I've been inside her ... since I've felt her tight grip and warmth around my cock..."

I gulp. I reach out my hands. "Give it to me."

Arlie chuckles.

I scowl.

Arlie continues. "'I want you, Delilah,' I groan as my cock rises in my trousers.

"Delilah steps away from me. Her arms fold across her chest as if she's protecting her heart.

"'I'm sorry,' I say. 'What am I thinking, asking this of you after all I've done?'

"One of Delilah's arms falls from her chest. The other hand moves to her shoulder blade. Slowly, sensually, Delilah peels one of the straps from her dress away, allowing it to slide freely down her arm. She repeats the same movement on the other side. I hold my breath as the material once covering her drops to the ground below. Her waistline is so small. Her breasts heave. She's more beautiful than I remembered her to be ..."

I shuffle in the seat. Heat rips through my veins. I need Arlie to stop reading. I can't take it.

He doesn't stop. Instead, he softens his tone further as he reads. "'You're beautiful, Delilah,' I whisper as she undoes her bra and then slips her panties away.

She's naked in front of me. Exposed, and wanting me to own her like I once did.

"This time, I can't run away. This time, I must claim her as my love, my forever love. Delilah is mine from this day forth, and nobody will ever hurt her again, especially not me ..." Arlie turns the page.

"Okay, so now they'll have sex and live happily ever after. The end."

"Hang on."

I lift my hand in a final attempt to take the chance of him continuing away.

Arlie bats my hand. "Not so fast."

"Please don't." I can hear the pleading in my tone.

Arlie shuffles until he faces me. "Please don't read? Or please don't do this?"

The novel flies through the air. Arlie tucks his arm behind my back. One pull against my waistline has my body close to his. He dips his chin. His lips move quickly towards mine, and at the precise moment our mouths connect, I wrap my hands around his neck and kiss him with every ounce of passion thumping through my veins.

Arlie perches between my legs, hovering above me. His erection pushes against Miss Priscilla, causing my knees to fall farther apart. I want him, all of him, but the more I think about what's happening, the more I remember we're on a television show and cameras are filming us.

I can't have sex on television. Hell, I've never had sex

sober.

When Arlie's lips leave a trail of kisses from my neck to my cleavage, I scream, "Stop! I can't do this. Get off."

Arlie does. He throws himself away from me.

I leap to my feet. One step, two steps, three steps back create a more considerable distance between us.

"I'm sorry," he rushes in saying.

"I've never had sex sober." It flies out of my mouth so fast I can't reel it back in. *I can't believe I just said that to him, and on television.*

"You haven't had sex sober?"

"No!" I shout.

"Okay. It's okay." His tone is compassionate and reassuring.

"I'm an idiot," I spit out before turning on my heel and running towards the staircase. "Just leave me."

Tomorrow is my thirtieth birthday. I'm not sure if Arlie even realises I'm facing the next decade of my life and hitting the start of digits beginning with three, but if he knew about my doctor status from my submission form, then I'm sure he saw my date of birth.

The thing is, I can't stay here with him and turn another year older, even though throughout the night, the night that dragged on forever, I heard Arlie's footsteps going up and down the hallway between our two bedrooms.

Today, I'll go home. Tomorrow, I'll turn the dirty thirty, clean and without his bodily fluids forever staining my heart, and with Chris and Fletcher by my side, just how it was supposed to happen.

I'm nervous as I retrieve my suitcase from the wardrobe. My stomach twists and turns as acid creeps up my oesophagus every time I find myself bending over.

How could I spend my birthday here after what's happened? I can't.

I take the oversized white hat in one hand, and the handle of my suitcase in the other before I walk out the bedroom door. There's no point in delaying the inevitable. It's like pulling off a fucking Band-Aid— best done quick and fast. Whatever's festering underneath this sore, I'll deal with later. Right now, my only focus is leaving this island as quickly as possible.

I reach the top of the staircase and halt when I spot Arlie standing at its bottom. He's all red-faced and blotchy. I guess he's been out for a run, considering the workout gear and sneakers he's wearing.

His eyes narrow. His stance becomes rigid. "What the fuck, Melinda?" His eyes narrow farther. His nostrils flare. He glares at me. "You're leaving? You're not even going to give me a chance to—"

"I have to go."

"Run? You need to run away?"

"No. That's not ..."

"It's what you're doing, though. You're running away." Arlie jogs halfway up the stairs, but stops, maintaining a distance between us.

"I'm not. This isn't going to work, and I'm wasting your time."

"Says who?"

"Me!"

"I don't get a say?"

"I don't even know you," I snap.

"So you won't even give yourself the chance to get to know me?"

"No."

"I really like you," he confesses. "Like, a lot." Arlie places his hands on either hip. "I don't kiss any girl. I hope you know."

"I didn't say you did." I squeeze my lips together and grunt. "Look, it's not you, it's me."

"Really? You're going to pull out the 'it's not you, it's me' line?"

"Arlie, if there were lots of girls here, trust me, you wouldn't even be kissing me. You'd have your mouth all over some skinny minnie who has a tramp stamp and legs that stretch up under her armpits." I huff. "You're only fond of me because of the island and the fact there's only two of us here."

Arlie cocks his eyebrows high on his forehead. "Nice! Okay, well you've made up your mind it seems."

"Arlie, like, have you seen yourself in the mirror?

Have you?"

"Yes!" he shouts unexpectedly, causing me to jolt. "Why are you so hung up on looks? Do you want to know why I stay in shape?"

I don't answer.

"I work out because I've been doing so since the year after my mother passed. It's what kept me out of the trouble I found myself spiralling into. It's what kept me focused and took away my anger. It's what continues to keep me on the straight and narrow."

I place my hand on my chest. *Arlie's mum dying.*

"I don't do it for appearances or to score pussy; I do it for me. It's good for me."

Anger burns like a flaming red sword stabbing through my stomach. I'm mad, but I'm not mad at Arlie. I'm mad at myself.

"You haven't even given yourself a chance to get to know me. You haven't even—"

"Do you want to know why I run?" I interrupt. "Do you want to know why it's what I need to do?"

Arlie nods.

"Fine, I'll tell you." I drop my hand away from the suitcase and take one step down. "I run because it's what I do to survive. I'm not a doctor anymore because I killed someone. There, now you know. I killed someone in my job, and I live with the guilt of that every single day. Running works for me. If I take off before anyone gets hurt, then I'm doing myself and that person a service. Let me spare you from me."

"So you are running away?"

"No. I'm not."

"Yes, you are." Arlie takes one step towards me.

"I'm not," I say, stepping down.

"You are." Arlie stomps his foot to the next step.

"I'm not."

"You are."

"I'm not."

"Yes, you fucking are." He grabs my waist and pulls my body against his. "Don't run," he whispers against my lips. "Stay and see where this is going."

I brush my lips across Arlie's as his hand moves up my spine until his fingers tangle in my hair.

"I'm going to kiss you now," he says.

"Uh-huh."

And when his mouth takes mine, all my fears melt away as my body moulds against his.

Chapter Twenty-Five

Today is my birthday. I'm thirty. *Thirty.* And the task we've been given is to hike to the top of Mount Serendipity or, as I like to refer to it, Boob Mountain. I'm assuming it's the boob we're about to scale, the one I laid in bed gazing at this morning after Arlie left my side and took his cradling arms with him. I could be wrong, though; there are so many mountains surrounding this little paradise hideaway.

Last night was the first time I've ever slept in a bed with a man while sober ... well, a man who wasn't Chris. It felt incredibly good just to be held.

When Arlie suddenly left hours ago, I felt lost and needed to be resting against his body once more. I stare at the mountain, waiting for him to return. He doesn't. Where is he? Does he even know today is a day of celebration? That it's the day of my birth?

I climb out of bed. I huff, then groan; I don't like

hiking or any outdoorsy-type activities, so I think a sudden-onset illness is about to overcome me, one that renders me incapable of mountain climbing, and one that keeps sex well and truly off the table until I leave this island. The last thing I need is to find myself in a place where Miss Priscilla battles with my logic, and if Arlie and I continue to sleep in the same bed each night, I'm not sure I'll be able to keep my pasty-looking dinner roll quiet.

Arlie's more delicious than any sweet treat. Arlie's cake for my snatch.

I grab the towel hung over the end of the bed and drag my feet down the hallway. I need to pee so bad that my bladder feels like it might burst. The only place I can go is in the en suite inside Arlie's bedroom.

The bathroom: A hike of its own when you have a tiny bladder and a mile to trot.

Fancy gold taps, marble tiling and flooring ... it's a bathroom straight out of a billionaire's magazine. We're still yet to find the door allowing access to it from within my room, the door we both went in search of last night. Maybe my room just didn't come with one full stop. The only way for me to bathe on this level is to gain access through the room Arlie's occupying.

I reach the open entry of the bedroom that's decorated in blues and silver. My stomach roils like a tidal wave. What if he's back and in the bathroom? What if he's naked? Or worse, what if he's rubbing one out with Mrs Palmer and her five daughters?

There's been a lot of sexual tension between us. It would take a highly statured virgin priest not to recognise its velocity, and I hear men like to destress by masturbating. Well, it's what my reliable source Chris tells me anyway. Chris should know, he owns a spout, and he's also man meat for other man meat.

"Hello," I call out like a nosy neighbour as I peek my head around the doorframe and scan the room. *No Arlie.* "Arlie, are you in here?" I say, treading quietly. Again, no answer.

Every step I take is hesitant. I'm waiting for this hunky man to appear out of thin air and scare the crap out of me due to his sudden presence. He doesn't.

At least I don't have to do my morning business knowing he's close by. I'm such a nervous pooper. The thought of anyone residing within hearing distance makes my butthole pucker, and my arse cheeks snap together like a vise. This morning, when I sit on that loo, I will poo freely and without worry. I reach for the toilet spray kept on a shelf above the loo.

Placing the towel on the triple-bowel basin, I tiptoe to the toilet and put the spray down on the floor beside me. I'm not sure if my body's waste will stink, but last night I ate garlic, and garlic is like a vampire's kryptonite to my bowels. The last thing I need right now is to pong up this entire area and find myself further traumatised by my time here at Heart Key.

I shuffle down my pyjama bottoms and let them fall

to my ankles. I sit on a seat that's regulated to a perfect temperature. Who knew toilet seats came with temperature controls? Not me. But Arlie explained what all the buttons on the tiles behind me meant when I got my first glimpse of this glorious space.

Sitting on the loo, I let my mind roam. Hiking adventure! More like unnecessary heart strain, stinky sweat, and muscle pain. How do I get out of this without using one of my get-out-of-jail-free cards? I come up with no plausible solution as I scan the considerable space surrounding me. When my vision stops on the jacuzzi, my thoughts shift from hiking to bathing. I'm quick to decide that tonight I'll soak in the tub.

Today's my birthday, and I may as well start my thirties off on a high. *Tonight, I'll relax in a jacuzzi built for ten.*

Reaching for the toilet paper has me shifting my attention to the screen of a television taking up a significant portion of the wall space in front of me. Who needs a television in the bathroom? It puzzles me. I won't be waste vacating and watching, that's for sure, but maybe I could enjoy a little viewing pleasure from the jacuzzi. Now there's a thought.

With toilet paper in hand, I reach between my legs, but before I have a chance to wipe, I freeze. There's no warning, no sound of someone approaching, but when Arlie suddenly bursts through the door at a fast pace, my heart launches into my throat.

"Morning. How'd you sleep?" He looks right at me.

Holy fuck! What is he doing? Can't he see I'm on the toilet doing my business? Why is he talking to me?

"Good." My voice rattles. "You?"

"Yeah, great. I needed a good night's sleep after the one before it."

"Oh."

He places his hands out in front of him, waving them. "No, no, that's not what I meant. It's not your fault I didn't ..." He stops speaking. "I'm putting my foot in my mouth. I'll stop."

"Um, so, I'm kind of, you know, using the loo."

"I saw. Don't mind me. I'm going to wash up." Arlie rips his shirt over his head, discarding it on the floor. He places his thumbs into the top of his shorts.

"Whoa, whoa, whoa. No! Stop. Leave your pants on."

"Huh?" His face scrunches tight. He seems puzzled by my outburst.

"Me, girl. You, boy. Me, on the loo. You, getting naked. Big problem." I speak to him like I'm Tarzan because Arlie's behaviour replicates that of an uncivilised caveman.

"Oh shit! Of course. Sorry." He removes his thumbs from his waistband. "What was I thinking? I'm so used to living with the lads." He places his palm into the middle of his forehead. "I can't believe I just did that. Let me know when you're done."

"O-k-a-y!" I draw out the word as he races out the way he entered.

What the hell?

Clutching the can of spray in hand, I mist the air with the scent of lavender. I cough when I inhale a deep breath that tastes like poisoned toilet spray. *Too much! I've sprayed too much!* I wipe, pull up my pants and flush.

"I'm going to take a shower." I cough through the haze of chemicals that are still present. It's all I can do to communicate my intentions with Mr Loo Peeper.

"Did you call for me?" He opens the door.

"Um. Yeah, no. I was letting you know I'm going to bathe real quick."

"Okay!" He grins, but it's not his usual cheeky grin. It's more like a hungry, needy expression.

"So, that means you leave."

"I know." He doesn't move. He stares.

I wave my hand in the air in front of me. "Hello?"

"You're really pretty in the morning."

I dart my head back. I bite my lip, trying to prevent the broad smile taking ownership of my face.

"Yeah, pretty," he says, as if talking to himself, as he takes a step forward.

"You're pretty in the morning, too," I say in this very awkward situation. But I'm not lying. Even with sweat dripping from his brow, he's a vision.

Arlie suddenly curtseys, which causes me to laugh. "Have a good shower. I'll jump in after you."

Ask him to join you? My head jerks back again. "I'm not asking him to join me. That's wrong on so many levels."

Arlie turns. "What did you say?"

"Join me," I blurt out before swallowing hard. My heart races. My legs shake. My stomach fills with a million butterflies. What the hell is wrong with me?

Arlie cocks one eyebrow, then licks his lips most seductively.

I'm petrified, excited, overwhelmed—I'm a ball of emotion, and I'm not sure which one of the many feelings bouncing around my insides will win and project in my expression.

Arlie swaggers towards me. His eyes do not leave mine. He stops short of my trembling legs. Long fingers move in my direction ... long fingers that are clearly shaking.

Arlie's shaking. Why?

His hand splays across my back as he pulls my body gently to his. Arlie's lips brush against my temple. "Are you sure?"

My throat instantly becomes bone dry as my heart thrums out of control. I can't find words, so I nod against him.

"I have a confession," he says breathlessly. "I've not had sex in more than two years."

I'm instantly smiling.

"So, Melinda, this won't become sexual. We're only taking a shower together, okay?"

That works for me. I nod again.

"If we do, you know, get physical, I'd like for it to be special ... memorable."

I melt into Arlie Blight. He's a dream: funny, kind, polite, gentle, caring, and so fucking gorgeous. "Just a shower." My voice rattles.

"Just a shower,' he repeats, letting me go and taking a step back.

I'm scared to break eye contact or even move when his head bobbles slightly. His subtle movements are enough to tell me he's no longer wearing any clothing.

He gazes deep into my eyes. "Do you bathe with your clothes on?"

I mechanically shake my head.

"Do you need help?"

I bite my lower lip.

His pupils grow. The blue of his eyes darkens.

I nod.

One step, two steps ... his fingertips skirt my arms, causing me to shiver. His eyes leave mine when he runs his hand over my stomach. The material of my shirt lifts, causing me to shake even more.

Arlie's hands tremble against my skin when he slowly, carefully pulls my shirt upwards until everything disappears from my sight. As quickly as his image vanishes, it reappears, and I'm suddenly standing topless. "Are you okay?" he says in a hush.

"Uh-huh," I breathe.

I squirm to my right, then my left when his

fingertips skim my sides before they still at the top of my shorts waistband.

"Keep your eyes on mine," he whispers.

I hold my breath. My mind is vacant of thought, yet I still can't seem to draw a breath.

It's a flash of time which no longer exists that has me completely naked. Arlie, too, is in a complete state of undress, and I can't undo this decision now. For the first time in a long time, I've decided I don't want to change my mind anyway.

I want Arlie Blight. No matter how long it takes for us to arrive at a place of togetherness, I know I need this guy in my life.

Arlie takes my hand and helps me under the warm running water that sprays down from the faucet above me. I turn my body away from his and face a window that's inside the shower. Gentle waves rolling in to shore becomes my view as my heart hammers in my chest.

"Are you okay?" he says softly.

"Yes," I say quietly.

"Would you like me to wash your back?"

I nod as I catch water in my palms and wipe it over my face.

"Good."

The soap is smooth as Arlie rubs small circles against my back. His touch is gentle. The smell of coconut wafts around me.

"Hmm."

"It feels good?"

"So good." I drop my head and look at the tiles below.

"I'm glad."

I'm not sure how long Arlie runs his hands over my skin, but when he stops, I feel a sense of loss.

I like Arlie touching me as much as I like touching him.

"Would you like me to wash your back?" My voice becomes hoarse on asking.

"Please."

I turn, expecting Arlie to have his back to me, but he doesn't. Instead, his eyes await mine.

"Hi," he says.

"Hi." I smile, trying so hard not to turn my vision down to what's between his legs. I fail, then suck a breath of air in, trapping it in my throat. I immediately take sex completely off the table. Arlie's endowed.

I bite my lower lip as I lift my chin.

"The body wash." Arlie's grin is unmistakeable.

"Thank you." My hands shake when I take the bottle from him.

Squeezing a small amount into my palm, I snake my other hand still holding the bottle around Arlie's waist. "Can you put this on the ledge please."

"Sure."

I rub my hands together then slowly place them onto his back. My movements almost become rhythmic as I work a lather against his skin. The smell of coconut is now stronger. I move down lower, and lower until my fingers brush over his birthmark.

Arlie drops his head. I lower my hand further.

I jolt when Arlie grabs my wrist and turns into me.

"I like you washing me."

"I like washing you," I say breathless.

"I'm glad."

And without warning, his lips connect with mine.

Chapter Twenty-Six

Why did Chris have to remove my fucking boardshorts? What am I going to wear on this hike?

I stand in the wardrobe, pulling items of clothing from my suitcase before folding them and putting them away.

The large shelving and deep coves remain relatively empty, but at least a few items are now filling some of the space.

I can't run away from Arlie. I no longer want to, so I may as well unpack.

Our shower together seems to have been a turning point for me. Perhaps it is due to Arlie's subtle glances at my naked body, and the respectful way in which he did so. Maybe it's because he treats me with a level of worship I'd always hoped I'd find in a guy. Or it's very likely that I'm incredibly horny, and in love with the idea of possibly having a boyfriend at my sexual disposal for once. Quite frankly, it could be all three.

"Hallelujah," I huff when I locate the only pair of hiking-appropriate bottoms in my belongings. They're not boardshorts, but they are knee-length capris.

I clip my sports bra in place, throw on a surf T-shirt, and slip on my underwear and pants before I secure my feet into a pair of white sneakers. Blowing out a forceful breath, I fold at my mid-section, letting my hair dangle towards the floor until I gather it and tie the untamed locks into a ponytail.

Tap, tap, tap, tap.

"Melinda."

"I'm ready," I say as I straighten to an upright position.

The door opens. Arlie appears wearing a pair of loose-fitting basketball shorts and a muscle tee. He stands with both hands behind his back. "Stand in the middle of the room."

"Why?"

"Just do it ..." He pauses. "Please?"

"Okay." *What is he up to?*

Unhurriedly, his hands appear. A pink iced cupcake with a love-heart candle rests in one of his palms. "Hang on." He's smiling when he exposes the lighter in his other hand.

There's a small flame burning at the top of the cupcake when Arlie closes the gap between us. "Happy thirtieth Birthday."

An ache fills my chest. It's not painful or upsetting. It's an ache brought on by an explosion of happiness. *He did know!*

"I made a bunch of these cupcakes this morning. There are plenty more where this one came from."

"You shouldn't have."

"I wanted to. I was going to wake you up with one when I got done and went for my run, but, you know, I walked in on you, and then the shower stuff ..." His big white teeth shine between his stretched lips.

"Thank you. You're very thoughtful." I'm smiling so big my cheeks burn.

Arlie hands me the cupcake. Pink icing is smoothed over the top of a vanilla base. It's perfect.

"Blow out the candle and make a wish."

I suck back a breath and circle my lips, but before I get a chance to blow out the dancing flame Arlie sings "Happy Birthday" to me.

Arlie can hold a tune. It's apparent he can bake. Is there anything this man can't do?

The flame is extinguished by my breath, and Arlie's quick to pluck the candle from the cupcake. After days of not consuming any sugar, I pull back the paper like a ravenous wolf and take a significant bite. "So good. Do you want some?"

He nods.

I hold out the remnants of the cake, and Arlie's quick to chew a chunk away. "You better finish that. You're going to need energy for this climb," he mumbles, licking icing from his finger.

The mountain. Do I have to do it?

We didn't even get a prize for yesterday's task, so why even bother?

I was wrong. We're not hiking Boob Mountain. We're climbing a winding track on a much smaller slope.

"We're halfway." Arlie seems in his element as we tread along a dirt track.

I feel the life draining out of me as I hunch at my midsection and suck back a needy breath before straightening my shoulders in time to come face-to-face with a massive spiderweb. I hate spiderwebs, spiders, bugs, twigs … I hate everything to do with bushwalking, but I manage to manoeuvre around the web's sticky strands and rein in my need to scream at its presence.

"Do you need another drink?" Arlie's barely puffing.

I, on the other hand, am huffing like I've knocked back a few bongs, and smoke is squeezing my lungs, holding them for ransom from oxygen.

"You'll get dehydrated on a walk like this if you don't keep replenishing your fluids."

I don't disagree and take the water bottle from Arlie's outstretched hand. I suck from the spout in the same way I apparently did from my mother's breast at the age of two: like a crack whore.

"Let's keep going," Arlie chimes, upbeat and relaxed. I hand him back the water bottle.

This mountain will be the death of me. I declare it to be named The Life Snatcher because lord knows I'm going to drop dead before we make it to the top.

My heart is pounding as my mind screams for me to pull up stumps and never, ever move again. The sensation ripping down my thighs can only be compared to a million hands twisting violent Chinese burns against my skin. *Yep! I'm going to die here.*

"Are you ready to keep going?"

Noooooooooo! my brain cries. "Sure!" My lying tongue is a traitor. I continue to walk for what feels like hours even though it's more likely minutes.

"Watch out. After this bend, there's a fallen branch; I can see it farther in front." Arlie takes large strides. I'm barely shuffling.

"Watch out for the branch, got ya," I pant. I no longer have any saliva in my mouth.

"We might take a break when we get back onto a straight path."

"Sounds good." I gasp for air.

Arlie slightly chuckles. I want to kick his backside for exposing his humour at my near-death experience, but that would mean I'd need to pick up the pace, and my leg to boot his butt, and that isn't going to fucking happen.

We round the bend. I barely scramble over the fallen branch he alerted me to. My feet are dragging, and Arlie's getting farther and farther in front of me. I have no air. I can't keep up. I need to stop.

"Break time," I bellow, falling to the ground and lying on my back, closing my eyes to shield them from the sun.

There's laughter, booming laughter, coming from above me.

"Shut up," I groan, thinking about cocktails and deck chairs laid out across white sand.

"Just take some deep breaths. It'll pass."

The feeling of death lurking? Or the pain in every part of my body, Arlie? What's going to pass?

"We'll sit for a bit. Catch our breath. It's not too far to go."

"We have to come back down, you realise."

Arlie laughs.

"Stop laughing at me."

"You're very cute when you groan and moan like you're doing."

"You're very fit and annoying," I tease.

"Noted."

I catch my breath. Arlie takes my hands, helping me into a seated position.

"Have another drink," he says, passing me the water bottle from the backpack he's got slung to his front and is lugging up the mountain with us. "Watch the ground for ants. Those suckers can cause a nasty sting."

I spring to my feet. "Thank you." My lips, mouth,

and chalky tongue taste the sweet, sweet water when I drink as if I don't my limbs will wither and fall off.

Arlie sits across the path from me in front of some long strands of grass. He takes a deep breath and closes his eyes. "Mountain air. It's so good for the lungs."

Fucking gloater. He can breathe. I can't.

I continue to sip from the water bottle and watch as Arlie's eyes roam our surroundings. I drop my head to the ground below and find myself stuck in a long-drawn-out gasp. I choke on the water, then cough and splutter.

"Are there bones in your water?" Arlie questions with humour in his tone.

"Don't move," I choke out.

"Huh?"

"Don't move." My eyes bug from my head as I see the slippery sucker sliding in Arlie's direction, poking out its tongue with a long hiss. "Snake," I spit.

"Snake? Where?"

"Seriously, don't move. It's about to ..." I squeal and use all my strength to fight away the urge to run.

"Where is it?"

"To your left. About to slither onto your lap."

"Fuck," he breathes, slowly rotating his head.

"Oh God, it's on your lap."

"I know. I can see it," Arlie hisses through his visibly clinched teeth. "Fuck," he curses again.

"I'll get a stick."

"No! Don't move. Stay still."

"Okay," I whisper.

The snake slithers farther onto Arlie's lap. It's not a baby, not even a little brother- or sister-sized snake. It's a big sucker, and its flat bowhead is now directly on top of Arlie's man junk.

"Are you hanging in there?" I'm not sure what else to say to a man who has a snake head perched on top of his cock.

"I've had better days," he groans.

"Whatever you do, don't move."

"No shit!" There's fear in Arlie's tone.

I'm not sure how much time passes, but it feels like forever before this uninvited slippery critter completes its body drag across Arlie's groin. As the last of the snake's tail slides to the ground, Arlie remains still.

"It's gone," I say.

"Hang on."

The snake disappears into the brush, and with its vanishing act, Arlie suddenly leaps from the ground and runs towards me, smacking at his legs and flinging his arms around.

I laugh. I can't help it. This manly built man's limbs are being flung every which way.

"Stop laughing. Fucking snakes," he scolds.

I laugh harder.

"It could have bitten my cock. Seriously, this isn't funny."

I bend at my midsection with tears rushing down my cheeks.

"Let's get the hell out of here."

A loud, piercing scream explodes from my lips when Arlie lifts me from the ground unexpectedly. "What are you doing?"

"You're going too slow," he says, moving me until I'm clinging to his back.

"You can't piggyback me to the top."

"You want to fucking bet? I'd rather that than get my dick bitten off by a hungry serpent."

Throwing my head back has my laughter returning.

"Payback, Melinda. There'll be some epic payback coming your way. You mark my words."

"Bring it on."

"Oh, it's brought."

Chapter Twenty-Seven

Arlie hikes to the top with me perched on his back just as he said he would. When we reach the peak of the mountain, my jaw drops, and my eyes bulge from their sockets. The view is unlike anything I've ever seen before.

Trees that line the shore as small as ants. The ocean is smaller than the mass number of hills surrounding it.

"It's definitely a boob." Arlie laughs as I slide down his back, my feet again back on land. "Nipple and all. How about that?" He points to our right where the boob that once appeared the size of a B-cup is now as large as a D-cup.

"Too funny."

"I wonder where the nose is?"

I scan the rock faces and spot it to our left. I point in its direction. "There."

There is a lot of shrubbery in the fissures that make up the rock formation's nostrils.

"Nose hair," we blurt out simultaneously in laughter.

Crack, crack, crack.

I flick my head to my right. Did a branch just break? A man wearing a bright red baseball cap appears from the bushes like a peeping Tom, holding a big video camera.

The television show. I forgot again. How do I keep forgetting I'm here being filmed?

"Do you want to race me to the bottom?" Arlie wiggles his eyebrows.

"No! No, I don't." *Is Arlie insane?*

"Come on." Arlie points at the cameraman, who has obviously been following us. "It'll be fun."

"Only if you carry me."

Arlie's eyebrows lift high on his forehead. "Nope."

I half-heartedly laugh. "Spoilsport."

"Ready?"

"Nope."

We return to the path in front of the house. I'm hot, sweaty, and still laughing from the tumble I took as I attempted to run down the side of the mountain. My knee has a graze, but other than that, I'm unscathed. Running down the hill of death was satisfying, even if it was exhausting.

"A swim?" Arlie puffs as he folds at his midsection with his hands braced against his knees.

"Yes! Oh, God, yes. I'm melting."

"It'll have to be in your underwear because I'm not running back to the house to get you bathers unless you are?"

"No. I'm too stuffed."

Arlie throws the backpack on the ground. He kicks off his shoes, I follow suit, and suddenly, he grabs my hand; without warning, we're running again.

When we reach the fine sand, I hop from foot to foot. The sand is hot beneath my feet. I continue to hop, skip, and jump on the spot as the sun shines in my eyes, causing me to twist away from its blinding rays.

Arlie, too, is shifting from foot to foot in front of me as he rips his sweat-drenched shirt over his head. It takes not a second for him to drop his pants also.

Arlie's naked—stark naked. His arms are the size of tree trunks. His legs … well, he doesn't skip leg day, that's for sure. They're huge.

"Shit, I'm hot," he groans.

He is hot, but it's not his body temperature I'm referring to. The sun is blistering, burning, and my own body is overheated to the point where I feel as though I'm in a sauna.

"Are you coming?" Arlie's arse doesn't jiggle when he walks towards the calm ocean that barely contains ripples. "Are you coming?" he calls out a little farther down the beach.

I am. In my knickers, because Arlie Blight has me on the verge of an orgasm just from the way he moves in his birthday suit down a long, white sandy beach.

Happy birthday to me. "Coming," I moan, frustrated.

Arlie's laughing by the time he reaches the edge of the water, and with his laughter, I hesitate for a moment before I impulsively decide to shed my panties too. Crossing my arms across my bust, I take off. I can't believe I'm doing this. Running naked down a beach where cameras are filming. It's so wrong yet liberating at the same time. The faster I reach the water, the less my feet burn and the less time I'm naked in public. I run into the ocean, and make sure to keep a distance between Arlie and me.

The water is crystal clear, though, so the ocean offers no protection to my nakedness. Arlie must have the same realisation because when I flash my sight upwards, I see him staring at the water below. I know he's looking at my body, and he's not discreet at all.

I watch Arlie watching me. An overwhelming rush of hormones shoot down my throat and to my nether region. I bring my thighs together swiftly. Arlie's lips curl upwards.

I pant. I can't help it. I want him so badly the throbbing between my legs intensifies.

Arlie takes three steps towards me. My breath catches in my throat.

"Melinda," he says my name with a possessive growl.

"Hmm?"

"I want to kiss you." His arm sweeps around my waist. He pulls my body against his chest. "I fucking want to kiss you so bad." His lips are less than an inch from mine.

I curl my arms around his neck. I press my breasts firmer against his chest.

"Kiss me," I beg.

His lips are soft, full, and comforting when they press to mine. Every inch of my skin ignites with a desire I've never felt before. Arlie lifts me, and I instantly wrap my legs around his waist. His erection pulses against me. His mouth devours mine like he's saying goodbye and he'll never get to kiss me again.

I can't sleep with him. I want to sleep with him. I need to get out of the water.

Our lips part. "Don't run," Arlie rushes in saying as he presses his forehead against mine.

"I can't ..."

"I'm not going to fuck you here. I just want you to let your muscles relax and be with me. I want you to trust me."

"Okay." It's almost inaudible.

"Be with me. Promise that you won't run." He lifts his head. His gaze finds mine. "Be with me," he repeats, tipping his head to the side and kissing my neck. He lifts me higher and kisses the fullness of my breast.

"I'm with you," I moan, clutching either side of his head and bringing his lips to mine.

We make love in that ocean. Not love in its physical state, but in a way that speaks of an intense connection between two people unable to be fully controlled. I've fallen hard for Arlie Blight, so hard I fear I'll never be able to run away from him even if I want to.

Chapter Twenty-Eight

We're curled up on the lounge chair. Arlie reads from the very book he threw the day prior in our moment of passion here on this lounge.

Was it the book that invoked our passion? Or is there a real love affair beginning to unfold between us?

Am I going to finally find myself in a position where I'll actually date a guy? Is Arlie my future boyfriend? My first boyfriend?

As Arlie continues reading, every word he says tells me I never want to read another book for myself again. Who needs an audiobook when you have an Arlie Blight?

Arlie's voice. The words. Him. It's perfect. *He's* perfect. And right now, I think Arlie is, in fact, my perfect catch.

He turns to the second to last page. Hugh and

Delilah have sorted through the messy relationship that unfolded throughout the hundreds of pages prior, and I find myself hoping for a fairy-tale ending. I have a feeling, though, that this rollercoaster ride will complete with anything but. Chris never gave away the ending, but something in the way he spoke about this story has led me to think I won't be happy with its conclusion.

"Are you ready for the ending?" Arlie runs his fingers back and forward across my stomach.

"I'm ready," I breathe, not feeling ready at all.

"Okay." He continues. "Watching Delilah stand by the dresser, brushing her long locks each night, has me pinching myself. She's a vision, angelic, pure ... and she's mine. How I'm going to last without her when I travel to New York next week, I can't fathom. But we do need to part even though it's only for seven days.

"A week is too long for me to be without *Delilah*. She's the light which invades the darkness of my broken soul. She's the hope I never thought I deserved but wished to hold ..."

Arlie shifts his hand from my stomach to my hair, running his fingers through my untamed locks as I relax farther back against his chest.

He continues reading. "Delilah places her hairbrush on the dresser. She turns to face me. Her smile is sexy, inviting ... I know I'm going to have her over and over. I've a week of lost time approaching, and I've only eight hours to hold her before I'm gone

..."

I tilt my head slightly, so I can hear Arlie's heart beating more clearly as he keeps reading.

"'I wish you weren't leaving in the morning,' *Delilah* says. 'I wish, mon, free, fly, turning start.'

"*Delilah* 's words make no sense as her eyes grow. Her arms fall limply to her sides. There's this imminent fear taking over her expression ..."

I gasp.

"What just happened?" Arlie says.

I swallow hard. My heart thumps one intense beat. "Keep going."

He does. "'Baby, baby, are you okay?' I leap from the bed.

"*Delilah* steps forward. Her eyes roll back into her head. 'Love,' she moans before her legs give way, and I catch her slumped body before it hits the floor ..."

I bolt upright. I flick my head towards Arlie overcome with shock. It feels as though I'm Hugh, left holding the love of my life in my arms. This must be a joke. Arlie must be messing with me. "It doesn't say that, does it?"

He nods.

"Give it here." I snatch the paperback from his hands. The sense of happiness I felt for this fictional couple has disappeared, now replaced with a painful ache that's tearing my heart in two. *Instant sadness.*

I trace my finger down the page, trying to find the last line Arlie read. I know I'm trembling. I can feel the tears welling in my eyes. I read on silently.

"Baby, no. Come back to me. No!" I scream so forcefully I can taste the blood at the back of my throat. "Help me! Somebody help me! She's dying. She's dying."

No matter how hard I pump Delilah's chest with my desperate hands, or how many times I place my lips to hers and give her my breath, my life, she doesn't open her eyes.

Delilah doesn't speak a word.

Her heart doesn't beat again.

She's gone.

I spent a lifetime running away. I ran because losing someone to the angel of death again wasn't an option.

Why did I think things would be different this time? Why did I think my curse would be lifted?

I should've kept running when I had the chance. I won't survive this heartache. I won't survive losing Delilah.

I can't live without her.

"Baby, please open your eyes. Don't leave me," I howl. Don't leave me.

To be continued ...

"Fuck off! Who the hell does this crazy bitch author think she is? You can't do something like that. You can't," I shout, ripping my arm backwards and hurtling the paperback across the room. "I seriously hope this author chokes on a dick and dies." I pull myself upright. I stomp towards the front doors.

"Where are you going?" Arlie says.

"Away from that damn book. It's horrible. The story is horrible." I pause. "To be continued! What tripe is that?" I open the door. "To be continued," I mutter, stepping out onto the verandah.

You can't end a story by ripping a person's heart out. Why did this author kill the lead character? It's cruel. So freaking cruel.

I'm never reading another book for as long as I live.

Well, except for the next one in this damn series, because what happens to Hugh now?

I trek down the stairs. I don't know where I'm going, but I stomp my feet and continue to mutter curse words under my breath as I go.

A catamaran sails across the ocean. I catch sight of it in my peripheral vision. What in the hell? Naturally, I change my direction and march towards the beach.

Jet skis, sailboats, canoes, a windsurfer, surfboards … the sand is littered with them.

I'm confused.

There's not a person in sight, apart from two camera operators who seem to be filming the arrival of the catamaran heading towards them, and the shore.

I shift my attention to my right and spot a pop-up bar, just like the one I sat in front of for an entire afternoon when I took a vacation to the USA and had a layover in Hawaii.

There's a grass hut with a roof and brightly coloured flags flapping in the breeze around it. Small tables beside long deck chairs with beach umbrellas placed between them. There's even a big sign which reads, *Happy Birthday, Melinda.*

This is all for me. Get out of here.

As I manoeuvre the stairs, I change my stomp-like march to a relaxed stride. When I reach the sand, I note it's much cooler than it was when I was down here earlier and more pleasant on the soles of my feet. Scanning the ocean, I'm surprised by the thick whitewash being forced in my direction. The sea is nowhere near as tame as it was earlier either.

This ever-changing island suddenly excites me. These watercrafts and activities laid out in front of me cause butterflies to flutter in my stomach.

Maybe the outdoors isn't as bad as I thought. I can drink, Arlie can play with the boy's toys; the afternoon promises a change of pace to our current quiet retreat.

A clearing of a throat has me swivelling on my heels until I can see over my shoulder. Arlie stands with an excited smile lifting his lips.

"How cool is this?" I can hear the happiness in my tone.

"Very. I think we'll need to get changed into our bathers."

"Agreed." I flick my vision back to the tiki-type hut,

and the chairs set out around it; I can't think of any way I'd want to spend the rest of this afternoon than drinking cocktails and relaxing.

"Arlie, Melinda." The familiar voice of Daniel has my eyes travelling in the opposite direction from the cocktail bar.

"How are you enjoying paradise?" he says when he stops in front of us.

I laugh. How am I enjoying it? Am I enjoying it? I've no frickin' idea. So many crazy things have happened in such a short amount of time. My head is spinning.

"It's been interesting," Arlie states.

"I agree." I do agree. It has been interesting and a little crazy.

"How are you feeling, Melinda? That was a nasty sting you received." Daniel adjusts the collar on his button-down shirt.

"Much better."

"Good. And a Happy Birthday to you."

"Thank you."

"This is the gift you've won for completing the mountain hike. Unfortunately, you failed the canoe task, and the date night task as you only prepared a meal in the home, so you lucked out on the prize for both of those."

There are no surprises on the canoe task, but I happened to enjoy our date night.

"You get to keep this equipment for ten days. Then they're gone."

"Okay," Arlie and I say simultaneously.

"The cameras have caught your reactions to the big reveal ..."

"How? They weren't facing me," I say.

Daniel points over my shoulder. I twist my head and see a long-lensed camera peeking through some trees.

"Sneaky little sucker."

"The point of the show is that you don't see them or the crewmen as much as possible. It's the deserted island experience. I only came over to make sure you two were well and doing fine, and to film my segments for your island for the show. We weren't expecting you down on the beach quite so soon, but it's worked out. We've captured what was needed."

"Sex," I blurt out, like the word is used commonly and openly amongst strangers in such a manner.

Daniel's eyes widen as he stifles a smile I can see trying to lift his lips.

"Sex can't go on television, right?"

Arlie clears his throat.

Daniel's attempt to keep his humour cloaked fails. His smile flickers brightly.

"It can't, right?"

"No. We don't air nudity or sex," Daniel says matter-of-factly.

Arlie clears his throat again.

"Okay." *I had to know. I just had to know definitively.*

"We'll go get changed then and leave you to your

job," Arlie says with a hint of humour.

"Have a good time, you two."

I intend to, now. I plan to drink to my heart's content, then bang this man who has me so sexually frustrated. I've no choice but to put an end to this situation with a much-needed fuck fest. First, I must get drunk. Second, I must complete my mission. I've never had sex sober, and I'm not about to start with Arlie Blight.

Chapter Twenty-Nine

The best afternoon of my life began the moment I wrapped my lips around a straw and sucked back the sweet nectar combination of many spirits mixed with juice.

Cocktails: Angel's brew. The best creation to ever be concocted by some man—I'm guessing it was a man, whose hand I must find and shake with gratitude, even if by now it's skeletal.

I've skulled five tall glasses, and who knows how many will follow? With this liquid courage, I've found myself doing things I'd have been too frightened to do otherwise. Like ride a jet ski, and attempt—and by attempt, I mean fail miserably—to ride a wave on a surfboard. I'm having a blast, and from the laughter now coming from the guy with the stunning blue eyes, I'd say Arlie is too.

He's probably pissing himself from laughing at my

expense, but it doesn't bother me because right now, nothing bothers me. I feel good. I'm free, having fun, and enjoying the big three zero like a woman no longer worried she's turned the big three zero at all.

"Do you want to try again?" Arlie chuckles.

"Fuck yes, I do," I cheer, grabbing the strap dangling from my beached surfboard and dragging it back towards the water.

"This time, you need to put your back foot farther to the back end of the board."

"Got ya." I make a gun with my thumb and pointer finger and shoot it in Arlie's direction before blowing pretend smoke from my imaginary gun's end. Arlie laughs. So do I.

We paddle out, side by side. Arlie winks at me when a wave grows in the distance.

"This one," I shout.

"I think so. Remember, get your back foot as far back as you can."

"Back foot back. On it." I turn and face the board and myself toward the shore. I lie flat on my stomach, plucking one side of my yellow bikini bottom out of my hungry arse.

"Let's do this," I chime as I stroke my arms through the water to gain momentum. Jumping upright, I lose my balance instantly, then topple into the water like a massive bag of potatoes.

I'm laughing when I resurface. I can't surf but trying is so much fun.

Arlie rides the wave like a pro surfer who's about to go on tour, and as I watch him swing the board, his arms held out wide, beads of water glistening across his back under the sun's rays, I find Miss Priscilla cheering him on as much as I am.

I'm so turned on right now that if I don't find a way to alleviate the pressure pulsating through my clit, my vagina might explode, and not in a good happy-ending way, more so in a devastating rest-in-peace, your-pink-lady-taco-has-died way. *I need to get my sex on and soon.*

When I swim back to shore, I'm greeted by Arlie's extended arm, and E.T. fingers awaiting me. I take his hand in mine before he pulls me to my feet. There's a moment, a long pause in time when I find myself gazing deep into his eyes—his beautiful dark blue, forever-changing, sparkling eyes.

I want him ... today, tomorrow ... always. I'm in love with Arlie Blight, and I need to have sex with him on a television show that won't show our sexual escapades because it's a modest and kind entity.

I tilt my head slightly to the left as I wrap my hand around the back of his head. "You're one hell of a surfer," I say, perching onto my tiptoes.

"I do alright," he says, wrapping his cold arms around my waist and pulling my body against his.

"I'm having the best time here with you."

"Me too," he whispers.

"I'm ready to take this further, Arlie."

"I know."

I press my mouth towards his, closing my eyelids. Our lips connect, and we kiss in a hungry, possessive manner. My limbs become weak. My heart thumps wildly. Every nerve ending my body possesses is overcome with electrical pulses, because kissing Arlie Blight is more magical than a rainbow-coloured dildo with eight speeds of delight. It's so much better. I lift my leg and curl it around his arse, taking all my weight through only one foot.

Arlie suddenly pulls his mouth away.

What just happened?

"Is everything okay?" I ask, winded.

"Of course."

My leg falls back to the ground.

"What do you want to do now?" He lets go of my waist, steps back, and turns side on, and discreetly fixes himself below the waistline.

I want to have sex, dumb arse, is what I want to say, but I don't. Instead, I reply with, "I might have another drink."

"Okay, well I'm going to take the jet ski out again. Do you want to join me this time?"

"No! I'm fine. I might relax on one of those chairs." I raise my hand and point in the direction of the chairs in front of the cocktail bar.

"I'll see you when I get back." Arlie takes one step forward, dips his head, and kisses me softly on the cheek before turning his back to me.

What the fuck? He seriously just rejected me.

My brain is not one to be messed with. When not distracted, it works at a full pace, questions everything I do and say, and takes me down winding paths of doubt I can't seem to trek back out of. Right now, my mind is working in overdrive, and no matter how many cocktails I find myself downing, it won't stop racing.

I need Chris. I need Chris so badly right now I could cry.

Chapter Thirty

Pouring yellow liquid into a tall glass has my body swaying. I skull the drink in one go and top the glass again. My level of drunkenness escalates. I'm no longer happily tipsy. I'm more unsure and unbalanced, and my body is numb. *I wish my stupid brain would go numb. That would help.*

I bend to retrieve a straw, and when I do, "Never Be the Same" by Camila Cabello plays from within the hut. My hips instantly begin to move to the beat, but I'm confused as to how it began playing in the first place. *Where are the player and the sound system?*

While slowly dancing, I search the bench and surroundings of the hut for a system. I don't find one and give up looking straight away. I'm much too shitfaced to go on a hunt.

When the previous song ends, and Sam Smith's "Too Good At Goodbyes" takes over, I move out onto the soft sand. I'm relaxed. I'm shaking my booty, and I dance along the shore, free from all the worry caused by Arlie's rejection. A canary yellow cocktail fills the tall glass I have wrapped securely in my hand. I throw my head back and smell the sea air. The breeze is so refreshing. The beach is alight with warm sunrays. I admire the water for its crystal patterns, which sparkle like diamonds. The sound of Arlie speeding over the waves on the jet ski drifts far, far away ... The music's all I hear. *Who cares if Arlie doesn't love me back? Not me. I'm fine on my own and always have been.*

The track changes to "Break Free" by Ariana Grande, causing my movements to grow more extensive and upbeat, and for a split moment, I get the sense the songs playing are replicating my current mental state, but I'm quick to squash these thoughts because they're insane, and I'm enjoying the fact I'm currently having a dance party for one beachside.

Puffed, and with an empty glass, I stumble towards the deck chairs. I'm halted on the spot. *Arlie.*

He's lying on a chair with the stupidest grin planted on his face.

"You really are a groover and a shaker." His grin grows. "How'd you get music playing?" he yells above the beat.

I shrug. "I bumped something and ... voila." I throw one hand into the air. "Do you want a drink?" I shout with one eye all scrunched like a pirate.

Arlie shakes his head. "I'll pass."

"Your loss."

Finding the jug full of the concoction I made, I pour another glass and walk towards the deck chair beside the one Arlie's stretched out on.

I plonk down. Half the contents of my glass spill down my leg and onto the sand. "Bugger," I groan before tucking the straw between my teeth and sucking away on the sweet, sweet juice, not caring I'm covered in alcohol.

"You're enjoying those, aren't you?"

"You bet your sweet arse I am."

"Hang on." Arlie climbs off the chair. "Let me turn this music down; it's blaring."

"Whatevs." I giggle. *Holy hell, I'm drunk.* My head's spinning. The beach is spinning, but Arlie's not. He's the only object not out of control in my vision.

Arlie disappears from my view. I close my eyes, relax back into the chair, and keep sipping away.

The volume of the music becomes minimal.

I instantly miss it and want the volume turned louder. I need to turn it back up.

I can't get up. I don't move.

"That's better," Arlie says, causing me to open my eyes.

We lie side by side in silence. The sun lowers toward the horizon. My drink's empty, and my body's so relaxed I feel like I'm floating on the gentle waves filling my vision. This is paradise.

"Can I ask you something?" Arlie suddenly says.

"Uh-huh." Nothing's going to ruin my state of relaxation.

"You don't have to tell me about it, but I'm hoping you will."

I don't reply.

"When you were planning to leave, you said, well, you blurted out you weren't a doctor anymore."

"Yep!"

"You said you were a receptionist when we were back home in Melbourne."

"Spot on."

"So you're a receptionist?"

"Not just any receptionist." I roll onto my side. "I'm a receptionist for an escort agency," I whisper, wiggling my eyebrows.

Arlie doesn't react.

"Right? Pretty epic, huh?"

Arlie half-heartedly laughs. "Well, it's definitely interesting. So, what, you answer phones, and you book jobs?"

"Nope!" I lie. "I have phone sex daily."

"What?" Arlie reacts this time by straightening his torso and staring.

"1800-I'm-A-Whore, Melinda speaking." I portray my sexiest voice. "How may I service you?"

Arlie swings his legs over the side of the chair. He's now wholly sitting and staring.

"It makes for some super long days, but it's

rewarding for someone who doesn't get laid like me."

"Hold up. Hold up. What?"

"You asked. I told. It's my job."

There's a long silence, and I struggle to contain the laughter trying to force itself from behind my pressed lips.

"I don't believe you. I think you're messing with me."

"You'll never know." I laugh, relieved to have parted with the pressure of my humour.

"No seriously, is that what you do?"

"Yep." I laugh harder.

"Well, fuck!"

"Fuck with my mouth is right."

Arlie doesn't seem amused when I hopelessly struggle to sit the same way he is. "Are you lying again?"

"Yep."

Arlie blows out a sigh of relief. "Seriously, you had me going then."

"Good."

"You answer phones and take bookings, right?"

I nod.

"For an escort company?"

"Yep. That part was true. But I'm not even sure if I have a job anymore."

"Why?"

"Because my boss did not seem impressed I was taking this time off to come here. Plus, things there have been so weird. Like, my boss is acting strange. I think she's had botched plastic surgery or something. I don't know."

"I'm sure you have a job to go back to."

"I'm not even sure I want to go back when I go home. I hate that job."

"You hate it?"

"Yep."

"Okay then. Will you go back into medicine do you think? You're also a doctor, or were a doctor?"

"Was. Am. I can still practice medicine. Like, I'm still registered, but I don't."

"How drunk are you?"

"Very."

"Do you want to talk about this?"

"Whatever floats your boat. I'm cool, dude."

Arlie laughs.

I fall back into the chair.

"So you stopped practicing because of a death."

"Not because of a death, but because I caused the death."

"That's what I wanted to ask you about. I wanted to ask at the time you said it, but you were trying to flee and were worked up. However, I'd like to know."

"I don't talk about it."

"Maybe you should."

"Maybe."

"I'll listen if you want to tell me."

Tell Arlie about the life I took. Explain everything.

I think not. It'll kill my current impressive buzz.

"Another time," I say, kicking my feet into the air and shuffling until I'm comfortable. I again watch the gentle waves skirting into shore.

Arlie doesn't say another word. The sun drops even farther towards the horizon. It'll be night soon, but that doesn't mean the party needs to end. I must find the energy to clamber over to the bar, find out how to turn the music back up, and do it.

I don't move. Instead, I think about the life I took in detail, like I didn't want to.

"Have you ever killed someone?" I say, almost inaudibly.

"Apart from my mother, no."

"You didn't kill her. Someone at a train station did," I reply without emotion or sensitively.

There's a long pause. "He took her life, yes, but I sent her. Now he does twenty years in a jail cell, and I get to be on this island with you. It doesn't seem right, does it?"

I laugh. I shouldn't laugh, but I do. "You never killed her—he did. You also never sent her there—it's what happened. You couldn't control the situation." I find Arlie's response ridiculous in my booze-soaked state.

Arlie doesn't reply.

"You know what, Arlie? A wise, highly flamboyant gay dude once told me that when our number ticks over, that's it, and no matter what we do, the result will always be the same. So you can lock yourself into eternal damnation until your number arrives and blame yourself, or you can grow some lady balls and live your life."

"Chris?" he asks.

"Yeah, Chris. He says Leon Drucelli would have died that day regardless if I had made the call or not. Do you believe we can't change the course of someone's untimely death? Do you think it'll happen anyway?"

"My sister does. Me? I'm still undecided."

"Your sister should meet Chris."

Arlie chuckles lowly.

"It's the guilt. It's too much to handle." I roll onto my side to face Arlie.

"Why do you feel guilty?"

There's a long silence.

"He was very sick when he arrived at the hospital. Diagnostics was kind of my talent as a doctor. Between you and me, I failed at surgery and emergency medicine. Too clumsy." I let out a sharp, short laugh. "But on the medical ward, when tough cases came in, I always seemed to find the answer."

"That's a good thing." Arlie stares into my eyes.

"It is until you get it really wrong." I stop, take a deep breath, then continue. "That day, the day Leon came in, I'd concluded we were looking at two different bacterial-type illnesses. Leon was deteriorating fast, and I had to make a call. If I didn't, he wouldn't see the morning." I take another long, steady breath. "I decided to administer a highly controversial drug, which nowadays works wonders in saving lives. Back then, though, it was still going through the trial stages. If I was right, he'd live. If I was wrong, he'd die."

"And on this occasion, you were wrong?" Arlie says softly.

"No, I wasn't—that's the thing. In his autopsy, it turned out I was right."

"So how is it your fault?"

"Because I intubated him. I'd done it a million times before, and every single time, I'd nailed it. That day, I shoved the tube down his oesophagus and took the wrong track. I placed it in his food pipe, not his windpipe. He died from suffocation. So it was my fault."

"And you're human," Arlie says matter-of-factly.

"I had a duty of care to not only him but also to his family. By the time I realised what I'd done, it was too late. He passed away, and no matter how many times I pumped his chest and wished I could bring him back, it never happened. I couldn't call time of death. I couldn't even move from his bedside. In the end, I was led out by my colleagues."

"I'm sorry this happened to you. I can imagine how making those calls and performing those procedures do come with huge amounts of stress."

"I'd never felt stressed by my job. The thought of going back, helping people—now that's a whole bundle of killer heart attack stress for me now."

"Did you love being a doctor?"

"With every beat of my heart. It's all I ever wanted to do."

"So go back and do it. Life's too short."

"And kill someone all over again? I don't think so."

"And save someone all over again." Arlie's eyes don't leave mine when he stands and then sits beside me.

"I can't, Arlie, even though I wish I could." A single tear drips from my eye down my cheek.

Arlie's quick to swipe it away. "How about another drink? I'll turn the music back up." He grabs my hand. I need someone to hold my hand right now.

"Okay," I whisper.

And as Arlie lets go of me, then walks away, I find myself shocked at the fact I spilled the details of the most horrible thing I've ever done in my life to him. Apart from Chris, I've never told anyone the complete story before.

Holy shit! I just told the entire world.

What is it about Arlie that makes me want to confess to him everything about my life, everything I feel, and everything I am?

Chapter Thirty-One

The once warm sun treks so low now, it's all but the size of a thin golden disc. Its lack of glow amongst the pinks and purples rising from behind it dims the water I once tried to surf in. Heart Key is a breathtaking place, one I'll never forget when my time here has come to an end, and as the once fleecy clouds that appear more like puffs of smoke in the sky roll by, I take a deep breath and turn my sight back to a face I know I'll never forget either: Arlie's.

"What have you put in this drink?" Arlie presses his hand against the bar and pokes out his tongue as he scrunches up his nose.

"A little bit of this, a little bit of that, and some pineapple juice."

"It's sickly sweet."

I laugh. "Tell me more about your sister, Hazel. She seems like a lot of fun." I lean against the bar as Arlie again scrunches up his face.

"Hazel's fun. A little too much fun sometimes. Hence my niece's existence."

"You seem disappointed she has a child."

"I'm not. I just wish she'd been ready for a child. Don't get me wrong, she's a fantastic mum to Agatha, but Hazel missed a lot of the stuff you get to do when you're young, and she's terrible at choosing men. Some say she's a bit of a mess."

"I'm a bit of a mess. Actually, I'm a full-fledged emotional train wreck, and I have no kids. However, I wish I did. I think it's what life's supposed to be about, you know? Creating the next generation, seeing the world through eyes we've long left behind."

Arlie smiles. "You want to be a mother?"

"Yep! I'd love a bunch of rug rats nipping at my ankles. It would work for me."

"They don't nip ankles. I think what you're describing is like a chihuahua."

I laugh.

"So you want a bunch of chihuahua dogs. What else do you want?"

"To be happy. That's it."

"To practice medicine again?"

"Maybe, if I can get my shit together."

"I think you should give it a go."

"Maybe. I can't say no because I'm not sure of anything happening in my life right now. This escape—it's just what I needed, I think."

"Me too."

"Really?" My eyebrows hitch high on my forehead.

"Yeah. I've been walking through life aimlessly of late. The gym's going well. My clients are great. My friends are a fantastic bunch of people, but something's missing."

"Chihuahua dogs?" I giggle.

"No! Not chihuahua dogs." Arlie's smile reaches his eyes. "Life is missing."

"Life?"

"Yeah, like the next stage of it. The love, living-with-a-woman thing. I was with a woman for a long time, and I never once asked her to move in with me. You know, it never dawned on me to do so."

"Maybe because you were young, and she wasn't the one you were supposed to end up with."

"Maybe. I thought I'd marry her, you know."

"What was her name again?"

"Elissa."

"Pretty name. Stupid girl to turn someone like you down."

"She was a beautiful girl. Always was."

"Do you still love her?"

There's a long silence. "Do I still love her? Yes, but I'm no longer in love with her, if that makes sense."

"Do you still see her?" I know I should stop probing, but I can't help myself.

"No! I don't. She married my best mate, Flint, and they moved to the UK."

"So no contact at all, then?"

Arlie's upper lip curls. "My best friend slept with my high school sweetheart and girlfriend of ten years. Would you speak to either of them?"

"Oh, hell no." I snap my fingers in front of my chest.

"There's your answer."

"I couldn't imagine what being broken-hearted from love would even feel like because I've never known love."

"It feels like a thousand flaming swords slicing through every inch of your heart."

"Fuck!"

"Yeah." Arlie pushes the drink across the bar. "I still can't believe you've never dated."

"It's the God's honest truth."

"Love isn't anything to be scared of, even if you feel like you're dying when it goes horribly astray."

"Reading about it is hard enough."

"You are an emotional reader. I'll give you that."

"Like, Delilah dies in the book. How frickin' horrible."

Arlie chuckles in a low tone.

"Do you want another drink?" I offer.

"I'll pass." Arlie sticks out his tongue and shivers like someone has walked over his grave. "I'm more of a beer guy, and even having a beer is a stretch for me. I'm not really a drinker."

"Fair enough. More for me."

Arlie and I talk about his niece, his sister, my sister,

and life up and until this very moment. My alcoholic buzz slowly returns, and before long, a full moon perches high in the sky, and night has arrived.

"We should think about having something to eat? I'm starving," Arlie says as we walk out into the middle of the beach.

"We should, but it's so beautiful out here."

"It is." Arlie's not looking at the night sky when he says this. He's looking at me.

"I'd like to stay down here for a while longer."

"Okay."

We walk, drink, laugh, and talk, and everything is perfect. Slowly, I grow even more intoxicated. I dance freely without concern for the fact Arlie's watching my every move. In fact, I like the fact he views me as he does.

"Come join me," I yell over the top of the now booming music.

One step, two steps, three steps has the gap between us closing. Four steps, five steps, six steps has my heart racing. Seven steps, eight steps has Arlie pulling me against his body and our fingers lacing together. Leisurely, we dance in a circle, our eyes connected, our bodies close, and our lips even closer.

"You're so good looking," I blurt out. "Like, hot beyond any hotness I've ever seen."

Arlie laughs, but he also blushes, which I find endearing.

"Thank you," he finally replies.

"I want you so bad it hurts." I run my fingers down his abs, resting them against his waistband.

"Melinda," he whispers my name.

"Arlie," I breathe, sliding my fingertips behind the material of his boardshorts.

A low groan vibrates in his throat.

I slip my hand a little lower. "I want you." I'm breathless when I reach farther into his pants.

Arlie's hand clasps my wrist, and just as tenderly as I slid my hand inside his pants, he removes it. "We can't." His teeth grind together. There's a growl of frustration held between his pinched lips. "You're drinking. I don't want to be another man you add to the list of men you've fucked while intoxicated. I want to be more than that."

"You will be. You are ..."

"Not tonight."

"But ..."

Arlie places his lips softly against mine, smothering the following words I try to speak.

My head pounds, my mouth tastes like arse, and my body feels like I've been wrestling a crocodile while being punched in the face by a boxing kangaroo.

"Ooooow," I moan, rolling onto my side, placing my balled fist against my forehead at the exact moment my stomach does a push-up into my throat. I'm going to hurl.

I leap to my feet, press my hand over my lips, and try to figure out where I am. I'm in my bedroom.

Running the length of the long hallway sees me busting through the door of Arlie's room, then rushing into the en suite. I don't make it to the toilet. I do, however, make it to the tiled flooring.

Falling to my knees has my body convulsing. I throw down my hands and proceed to hurl bright yellow liquid, which pools around my hands. "Oh, God," I groan before again puking like I'm a powerhouse for the vomiting elite.

Small circles rub against my back. "Here's some water," Arlie says as I straighten my torso and rest my bottom against my heels.

Where did he come from? Where did he get the water from? Was he just waiting for me to come racing in here and hurl up my guts?

"I told you this would happen when you refused to eat more pizza. Getting drunk on an empty stomach— it's not a good thing."

"I know," I whine, turning my eyes down, and immediately noticing I'm clothed once again in a surf tee that doesn't belong to me. Bolting to my feet, I smack both hands against my chest. I'm braless. Removing one hand, I place it below the shirt between my legs. I'm not wearing any panties, and I don't even remember eating pizza.

Did I have sex again while drunk, and I've no memory of it?

Two hands press against my shoulders. "We didn't. You didn't. It's okay." Arlie pauses. "You really shouldn't get drunk like that."

"I know I shouldn't, but drinking is the only way I can bed a man."

"I'm sure it's not."

"It is."

"Do you at least feel better?"

"Arrrrghh." I wince as the sound of untimed bongo drums beat inside my skull.

"Let's get you cleaned up and get some food in your stomach."

"Okay."

"Lift your arms."

I do, allowing Arlie to take off my shirt.

"Step over your vomit."

I do, feeling like I could spew again.

"I've got you, babe. Relax."

Arlie calls me babe, and with this one single word, I feel slightly better in my otherwise very sad and sorry-for-myself state.

Chapter Thirty-Two

One entire week has passed since I got drunk on the beach at my thirtieth birthday party for two, and I've not drank a drop of liquor since, even though the tiki hut remains.

Heart Key. More than one week in: Wonderful— well, apart from an unexpected demon red visitor showing up unplanned and unannounced the moment I stepped out of the shower on the morning of my vomit fest. And thanks to bitchy Aunt Flow's incredibly poor timing, Arlie got to witness the exact moment she burst through the flood gates. *Fuck my life.* Why is it that a woman's period knows how to screw everything up?

Seven days is a long time in paradise, yet it feels like minutes because the time has flown. Making out with Arlie has been a massive feature of the past week. Sleeping in the same bed each night has offered me comfort. The long strolls hand in hand, ocean swims, completing our tasks, preparing meals together, reading books, and watching movies since we don't have access to live television viewing due to the show we're on has felt normal as though we've always done these things together.

Yesterday, I went for a jog, an actual run with Arlie, and I didn't die. I also hit the gym, which I don't dislike as much as I did before I arrived at Heart Key. Fresh air, exercise, eating well, and cuddling up to Arlie Blight have made me feel like a new woman.

As of two days ago, sex is back on the table. I'm holding out because we were told one of our prizes is a family member arriving, and today is the day. Since I only listed Chris as family on the forms, it means he's surely now on his way. Chris is coming. I'm beyond excited.

"Are you ready? I see a boat," Arlie calls out from the lounge room.

"Yes, I'm ready! Okay, so I've chopped the salad, and the fruit platter is in the fridge. You handled the meat stuff, yeah?" I'm nervous, excited, thrilled—I'm a ball of emotion.

Arlie places his hands on my shoulders and leaves a kiss behind my ear. "Babe, relax. We've got it sorted."

"I want to make an impression on your sister."

"She'll love you, just like I—"

I fling my body around and stare into his eyes.

"What were you going to say?" My tone is low, soft.

Arlie moves his hands to my waist. His eyes shift, and I can tell he's thinking. I don't hurry or pressure him, or even move. I keep gazing into his eyes.

"I love you." There's pure honesty in his declaration.

"You do?" My heart thumps hard in my chest, and I worry it'll stop beating because I can't believe this is happening. *Pure shock.*

"I do. This past week. The entire time we've spent together has been the best I've experienced in a very long time."

"Me too."

"I love waking up beside you, and every day feels like an adventure you can't even pre-plan. And, Melinda, you're beautiful. Like, really beautiful."

I press off my heels until I'm on my tiptoes and curl my arms behind Arlie's head. "I love you, too. Like, a lot. Like, it hurts to think about, but in the best way possible."

Arlie's lips find mine, and as his tongue presses into my mouth, I realise I've just been told I'm loved. Another first for me. Another memory to keep stored no matter what the future holds.

Running my fingers through his thick, dark hair, I press my breasts firmly into his chest. Arlie walks backwards with his mouth still owning mine. I move with him.

We tumble onto the couch, and when his hands run

the length of my upper thighs, they don't stop like they've previously done. Instead, Arlie continues to raise them under the material of my blue and white polka-dotted dress. His fingers curl around a portion of my arse, and he squeezes. I moan in response.

I rake my hands frantically through Arlie's hair, and his chest presses forward. He twists and yanks me with him into a seated position. I tuck my legs on either side of his lap. Instantly, I roll my hips in a circular motion before shooting my hands to the bottom of his T-shirt, fiercely lifting it over his head.

Chris and Arlie's sister are about to arrive, but this man just said he loved me, and I want nothing more than to seal the physical deal right here and now.

"Yes," Arlie groans when I push all my weight against the beast risen inside his shorts. His hands cup my breasts, and his fingers tweak my nipples through the material of my dress.

"Upstairs," I moan.

"We can't," Arlie utters breathlessly. "The boat is probably docking."

I stop moving. I let my forehead press against his. "Tonight."

"Definitely tonight."

"I need to change my panties." I giggle.

"I need to have a cold shower." Arlie's smile is the most beautiful smile I've ever seen.

We walk through the front door hand in hand. It feels like we've always been together like this—like not a single day prior have we been apart.

I've no idea if Hazel and Chris will arrive on the same yacht, or if they'll come on separate ones. All I know is a yacht has pulled into shore, and we're now walking towards it.

Conrad enters my vision first. He smiles in my direction. I smile back.

Come on, Chris. Hurry up, you're killing me right now.

Long blond hair, tanned skin peeking out from the areas a soft white dress doesn't cover. She's tall, long-limbed, slender … Arlie's sister is stunning. Like model stunning. I shouldn't be surprised, considering her brother looks the way he does, but I am.

Arlie's grip loosens until his hand falls away. He takes long strides towards his now smiling sister, who has big white teeth and even bigger lips.

"Hey, boo." Arlie strides towards Hazel, who rushes into the space between his extended arms. "I missed you. How's Aggy?"

"She's missing you like crazy," Hazel says.

"She'll be alright. Not too much longer to go now."

"You could always come home today." Hazel's tone is pleading when she steps out of her brother's embrace.

Arlie half-heartedly laughs. "I think I'll stay a little while longer."

"We'll see." There's malice to her words, yet she's smiling innocently.

"Hazel, I'd like you to meet Melinda."

"Sure." Her soft green eyes focus on me.

I put my hand in the air and wave like I'm Queen of fucking England. *Why the hell do I wave in such a way? I'm so nervous.*

"It's nice to meet you." Hazel holds out her hand. I take it in an awkward shake that lasts merely a second before she jerks back and dusts her palms together. *What? I don't have germs.*

"Chris must be coming on another boat," I mutter, more to myself then Arlie or his sister.

"No, he's on there, but he has to wait until they say he can come off." The disgruntled way Hazel tells me this has me wondering what happened on the yacht.

"Oh, you've met Chris?"

"I have." Hazel's eyebrows lift high on her forehead, and her eyes roll beneath them. What the hell is with her expressions? Does Hazel not like Chris? Who wouldn't like Chris? He's a ball of laughs.

Clap, clap, clap!

"Hello." Chris's high-pitched tone is music to my ears. I flash my eyes to the boat. "I have arrived. Paradise, I'm here." Chris holds out his arms like he's Jesus on the cross, and his all-white outfit only causes me to laugh. Two small black duffle bags hang from each of his wrists as he makes his way to the beach.

"Chris," I squeal, running towards him.

"Baby doll, you are a vision," he screeches, folding his arms around my back and squeezing me so tightly my breathing is limited. "I missed you so much."

I'm so happy I could burst. "I know. Me too."

"Let me look at you." Chris shifts me until I'm an arm's length away. "You're not so pasty white. You look sun-kissed and, happily, healthy. You've survived."

"Aww."

"You're as gorgeous as always."

"You look amazing, too. Been working out?" I wink.

He wiggles his eyebrows up and down. "You could say that. With a new friend."

"Oh, who's this new friend?"

"M&M."

I twist my lips. "M&M?"

He leans in close. "Matthew Muller," he whispers for my ears only.

"Get out of here." I smack my hand against his chest. "When? How?"

Chris leans forward, placing his cheek against mine. "I'll fill you in later, babes, okay?"

I'm in shock. I can't believe it. Chris actually found him, just as he said he would. "How's Fletcher?" I ask when Chris folds his fingers around my hand, and we stroll up the beach.

"Your cat has to go." Chris's lips pucker, unimpressed, when I glance at him.

"Why?"

"You wait until I tell you what the little spoilt punk did."

"Oh God. What did he do?" I groan.

Chris purses his lips farther and bobs his head. "He's a little rat, who caught a disgusting rat and brought it into bed with us."

"Ewww."

"Right? Needless to say, your apartment has been fumigated. Fletcher is in my bad books, and I'm still highly disgusted with him."

"Noted. But, like, he's okay?"

"If you think his mental state is right after such a thing, then I suppose he's okay."

"Chris." I release his hand when we get closer to Arlie and Hazel. "It's so good to see you."

"This is the longest we've been apart since we've met, doll face. It's killing me."

"Me too."

"No, seriously. You should come back home with me today."

"I can't. Not yet. I'm still ..."

"Hi, Chris," Arlie says in welcoming.

"Mr Arlie Delight. I was surprised to learn you were the guy here with my bestie, let me tell you."

Arlie smiles like the cat who got the cream.

"You know each other?" Hazel's tone lifts in surprise. Her eyes widen.

"We do indeed." Chris keeps his eyes on Arlie, not shifting his attention to Hazel at all. "So tell me, Mr Handsome, has she been hiding under tables? Oh, and how many times has she tried to run so far?" Chris grins.

"She's been good."

"Well, that's a lie," Chris calls him out.

My jaw drops.

Hazel rolls her eyes.

Arlie? Well, Arlie laughs.

"Do you want a tour of the place?" Arlie says when he's composed himself.

"Do I want a tour? Of course." Chris takes a step forward, then throws one of the bags from his wrist at Hazel's feet. He wraps his arm in mine. "Let's go."

"Chris!" I scoff.

"What? It's hers. I ain't no bellhop, dear."

I mush my lips together and shake my head.

"Onwards and upwards." Chris pulls me along with him. I puff as we take the many stairs from the beach and continue to the house.

Leaving the bags by the front door, the four of us walk down the winding paths, past the gardens, and towards the shops.

Chris gasps, coos, and even smacks Arlie on the arse while on our travels. This is going ... well, it's going.

"It's beautiful." Hazel sighs. "You're so lucky."

"I am." Arlie smiles, looking right at me.

My heart flutters.

When we turn back in the direction we came, Arlie's fingers brush against mine. He takes my hand in his before I tug it away. I have a very strong feeling

Hazel doesn't quite know what to think of me yet, so I want to take things slow around her. I search Arlie's eyes, and I hope to God he can read my mind, but it doesn't appear he can because his sudden scowl makes me feel horrible.

I offer Arlie a smitten smile. His scowl remains.

"So what have you two people of the opposite sex been doing for the past ten days? Spill the beans," Chris says.

"We've done a lot," I state. "I've surfed, rode a jet ski, and I went canoeing."

"Get out of here." Chris's mouth is so wide I can see his tonsils.

"It's the truth. We went on a hike and completed a lot of tasks the show has set for us as well. There have been dinners, and even a board game night where we played for real money. We kind of didn't do so good. I've read some books—"

"Boring." Chris inspects his nails. "Cough up the juicy details, Moo."

"Chris!" I snap in a girly tone.

"What?"

"Shhh." I press my fingers against my lips.

"We've kissed. Skinny-dipped, made out, a lot, and talked for hours on end." Arlie smiles wickedly at me. "Oh, and we've fallen in love, so I'd say that's pretty juicy stuff, wouldn't you?"

I'm instantly blushing, and I realise why Arlie looked at me as wickedly as he did. He's staking his claim and taking control. I'm okay with it because what he said wasn't a lie—none of it.

Arlie reaches for my hand, and this time, I don't let go.

"Now, there's the juicy … hang on, did you say fall in love?" Chris's eyebrows dip to the point where they appear as though they're two caterpillars crawling towards each other. "It's been ten days. You can't fall in love in ten days."

"I guess you can, Chris." Arlie puffs out his chest.

"I agree. Ten days isn't enough time," Hazel chimes in.

Neither of us defends ourselves. We continue walking the entire track back in silence with two clearly confused people by our sides.

Perhaps we dropped this bombshell a little too soon. After all, this declaration only came about a few minutes before Chris and Hazel arrived.

Can you really fall in love in ten days?

Chapter Thirty-Three

When we make it through the front doors of the house, Chris grabs my hand. "Bedroom, now. Just you and me." Chris seems dishevelled and concerned—the deep voice he uses is manly and not at all like Chris's normal tone.

I look at Arlie, who smiles and nods.

"Okay, I'll be back soon." I shrug in Arlie's direction.

"Have fun, you two."

Hazel purses her lips and flutters her eyelashes when I shift my attention her way. I swiftly turn and lead Chris up the stairwell. *This is not going well at all.*

When Chris enters my bedroom, he immediately begins to pace between the glass doors and the bed. He doesn't even gush over the room or the view. He's seriously freaking out.

"You're going to wear a track in the carpet if you keep pacing," I mumble.

"Girl, I think this island has gone and scrambled your brains." He waves his finger in front of him like he's a sassy princess.

"Why?"

"Love? Love? Now that's some serious shit right there."

"I know."

"Well ..." He curls his fingers around his hips. "Do you? Do you love him?"

I bob my head. "I think so. I've never been in love, but what I'm feeling is not like anything I've ever known."

Chris walks towards the bed. He stops running his fingertips over the sheets. "Have you changed these? Or washed them? I'm guessing there has been a ten-day hump-a-thon happening in this space." He circles his arms over top of the bedspread.

I snicker. "The bedding is fine. It's clean."

Chris's jaw drops. His finger points in my direction as his arse meets the blankets. "You didn't even deny it, you dirty humping dog. You have been busy here."

I laugh.

"Sit." He pats the comforter. "Come tell me everything. Do not leave a single detail out."

"Chris ..."

"Is he big? Like does he have a donkey's dick?"

"Chris!" I scold.

"Do me a favour and walk across the room. I need to see if you're bow-legged and all saggy-arsed."

I'm laughing so hard I can't catch my breath.

"Your laughter says it all. His schlong is like a well-hung elephant. Good for you, girlfriend." Chris snaps his fingers three times in front of his chest.

"Stop. Stop it," I snort.

"Come sit. Talk to me. I miss our talks."

I shuffle over to the bed and flop onto my back. Before long, Chris's head is beside mine as I look at the chandelier above.

"So you have fucked a lot, yeah?"

"Not even once."

Chris's gasp is so loud and ridiculously drawn-out that I throw my arm out and backhand him across the chest.

"If you ain't been fucked, you ain't in love." Chris's Southern drawl has me slapping his chest again.

"Sex doesn't define love, Chris."

"Where my cock comes from, it totally does. Like with M&M. My cock is liking what he's got, but is it love? No, no."

I hop onto my knees and stare down at Chris. "M&M? You slept with him? So by working out with him you meant doing that with him? He's not even gay."

Chris snickers. "Oh, but he is. He's at least bi."

I place both my hands to my cheeks. "I can't believe it."

"He's so ..." Chris curls his hands into fists and shakes them with excitement by his face. "Your source was not wrong … I'm dying daily. DAILY."

I flop back onto my back. "I can't believe you're sleeping with him."

"He's my Sugar daddy."

I blow out a long breath of air. This blows my mind.

"So, I'm standing by my initial statement. If you ain't been fucked, you ain't in love."

"You've put your pecker everywhere and anywhere, so I don't think you're a love expert."

"Amen, sister. Love is for fools, but if it's what you want, I'll support your foolishness always."

"You know it's what I want."

"I do."

There's silence.

"You really do love him, don't you?"

"Uh-huh." I chew on my nail.

"This isn't like a 'I'm thirty and desperate' thing?"

"Oh my God, what if it is?"

"I'm toying with you. Get back out of that headspace. Abort, abort."

No, it can't be.

"Is he treating you right?"

"He treats me so good, and I can talk to him, Chris, about everything, and I can lie in the quiet with him and completely relax and switch off. It feels so right."

"Well, you better get your throwdown on before you go making any big decisions, you two-bit hooker, because if he can't get your rocks off, then it's going to be one sad-as-fuck life for you—even sadder than it was before you got here." Chris pauses. "Have you at least seen what he's packing in his pants?"

"Yes." I roll onto myside.

"Well?" Chris flops onto his stomach and perches his head on the backs of his hands. "Spill, spill."

"I'm not telling you."

"Oh, but you will."

There's a moment of quietness.

"So, his sister seems like a royal pain in the arsehole." Chris never holds back what he thinks.

"I don't think she's fond of me so far."

"Mindy, I don't think that snobby cow is fond of anything. Such a sourpuss. She looks like she's been sucking on lemons."

"She's really pretty."

"Oh, she is stunning, but her mouth? A lemon sucker."

"Stop it." I giggle. "Did you two have to travel far together?"

"Yeah, from Brisbane to here."

"Shit."

"It's okay. I talked at her for entertainment—my entertainment."

"Chris!" I spit out, trying not to laugh.

"What? She needs to lighten up and relax. It wouldn't kill her to frickin' smile."

"She's young, and Arlie said she's a really fun-loving girl."

"Fun? Like in a stomped-out-fire-no-longer-burning way? Because if so, Arlie's right."

"Chris!" I tap his head.

"Stop hitting me."

"Stop being a turd."

"Speaking of turds, I hereby declare I'm no longer cleaning them out of Fletcher's kitty litter tray, so you'll need to train him to use the toilet if I ever have to cat-sit again."

"Why?"

"They stink, and they're as long as his tail. He could probably go on a diet."

"Is there anything you can't find to bitch about?"

"I'm gay and picky, so no. Everything is drama, drama, drama in my world."

"God, I've missed you."

"Girl, life is nothing when you're not around. Eleven more days and I get you back, even if it's likely we'll have a tall, handsome, donkey-dicked tagalong."

I laugh, and so does Chris.

The sun is shining. The birds are singing. The air is fresh and clean, and the spread in front of us is mouthwatering. I think Arlie and I created an amazing lunch for our company, which was the task for today. Chris and Hazel only get to stay with us until late afternoon, so I'm not wasting a minute.

Arlie sits beside me at the picnic table on the beach. Chris and Hazel are across from us, and things seem calmer now that we've had a little time with our loved ones alone. Plus, Chris is so overjoyed by the house he has declared that when he finally publishes his brilliant novel he'll be buying this island and residing here.

"Tell me a little bit about yourself, Hazel. Arlie says you have a daughter."

"I do." She places her fork onto her plate. "She's four, and absolutely loves her Unky Larlie."

"Larlie?" I smile.

"Yeah, she hasn't quite gotten his name down pat yet."

"Very cute."

"She is, but she's sad at the moment." Hazel drops her bottom lip. "She needs her Unky Larlie to come home. She's used to not seeing him, but this time it's really bothering her."

"She'll survive." Arlie tears into a bread roll and narrows his eyes at Hazel.

"She likes gingerbread men, too, I hear."

Hazel leans back slightly. You can see the love she has for her daughter in the way her eyes light up as she speaks of her. I think she appreciates the fact Arlie has spoken of them while he's been away, even if it seems she's trying to make him feel bad for his absence.

"So much. She makes us bake them all the time," Hazel says.

"I don't blame her. They're delicious."

"You look like someone who indulges in sweets often, Mindy," Hazel says.

Ouch.

Chris coughs as if he's choking. He takes the glass of wine in front of him and gulps it down.

"Are you okay, Chris?" I go to stand.

He waves in my direction. "Fine." He clears his throat.

I sit back down. "Yes, I do enjoy a little dessert. But I've not had so much over here."

"I'd say you enjoy a little more than you let on. You're not normally the type of girl my brother goes for. Not so fit, athletic, and tiny-waisted."

"Oh, bitch, please." Chris stands from his chair with a look of disgust filling his expression. "You better watch your damn mouth. Just because you look like you've not eaten in a year doesn't mean the rest of the world needs to. Are you hangry? It seems like you're hangry and in need of some sweets. Here. Let me shove some food down your throat so your brain can function more rationally." Chris leans across the table and takes her plate loading it with potato salad before dropping it back in front of her.

"Chris, stop."

"No. What gives her the right? She's acting all like you're fat and unhealthy, and it's bullshit. She needs to eat up."

"Chris, I'm sure she didn't mean anything by it. Down, boy, down."

"Oh, she meant it. Fucking magazines and women thinking skin and bones are attractive. I might be a homo, but I'll have you know it's fucking gross. Hazel, it wouldn't hurt you to eat some cake. You're rake skinny, and God knows you need some. Like, where are ya tits? And your hips? Do you even have an arsehole to shit out of? Because girlfriend, you ain't got no arse. Your butt is flat as a tack."

"Chris!" I snap.

Arlie stands. "Hazel come with me, now." His tone is harsh yet controlled.

Before I even blink, Arlie and Hazel are walking towards the house.

I huff, then puff. "Really? Did you have to tear into her like you did? She's young, and if she thinks I'm a little on the bigger side, then so be it. I don't care what she thinks, Chris. I don't care what anyone thinks anymore. What's the point? Life's way too short."

"Sorry." Chris's head hangs low.

There's a long, strained silence between us. Chris lifts his chin and smiles in my direction. "I'm really proud of you."

"Huh? Why?"

"Because the Mindy I knew ten days ago would have been so butt-hurt after a comment such as Hazel's. She would have burst into tears and ran. You? You've changed, and I'm proud."

I wouldn't have run away all butt-hurt. Would I?

When Arlie and Hazel return, Arlie says in a low

but confident tone, "Well?" The stern look keeping his lips pulled in a straight line is one I've not seen before.

"I'm sorry. I didn't mean to say what I did, Melinda. It was not nice and of poor taste. I hope you accept my apology."

"It's fine, honestly. I know I'm not a size four. I'm a size ten, and I'm okay with being who I am. Curves can be a curse, right?"

Hazel smiles uncomfortably.

Arlie sits beside me. He leans in and leaves a soft kiss against my cheek before picking up his fork. "Eat up. There's plenty more where this comes from." Arlie shifts his eyes to Chris. "You ever speak to my sister like you did again, and you and I'll have words, you hear?"

"Yes." Chris looks at Arlie in a way that tells me he's so turned on, he's about to crawl across the table and mount Arlie where he sits.

I laugh, because I'm as equally frickin' turned on right now.

Arlie Blight is full of surprises, and I'm even more excited to learn about all the sides of Arlie I'm yet to meet.

Chapter Thirty-Four

"It was really good to meet you." Hazel wraps her arms around my shoulders and hugs me gently. I return the sentiment.

She turns to Arlie. "We'll see you when you get home."

"Give Aggy a kiss for me." Arlie pulls Hazel against his chest and kisses her in the middle of her forehead.

"Take care of yourself, big brother."

"Always." His lips curl up in a smile.

"Well, we better go. They're waiting for us to hop on the boat." There's a strain to Hazel's tone. It matches the quivering lip she now sports. Hazel really cares very deeply for Arlie, as I can see he does for her. It's sweet.

I try so hard not to cry when Chris bundles me up in his arms and holds me tightly. "You enjoy your last days here, and I'll be waiting for you at the airport when you get back, okay?"

"Okay." Tears leak from my eyes.

"You're in good hands. I really like Mr Hon with the Buns."

I hear Arlie's subtle laugh.

"I know," I whisper.

"Relax and keep enjoying your time here. This place is a great fit for you."

"I know." I wipe my nose against Chris's shirt.

He sighs. "Really, Snot-a-lot-agus? You wiped your nose on my shirt."

"I'm sad." My voice quivers.

"Oh, sugar tits, you'll forget about me soon enough. Go get your freak on and fall even more in love. You deserve it."

"Sugar tits," Arlie mumbles.

"I love you, bestie." I hug Chris tighter.

"I love you more." He kisses my cheek.

As the boat sails away, I'm left waving as if I'm flagging down a truck on a highway. Instantly, I feel Arlie's hands clamp my shoulders. "Not long now and we'll be home."

I'm not sure if I'm sad because I miss home, life, normalcy, or if it's because I'll miss Chris.

"What do you want to do now? It's almost sunset, so we can go for a quick dip or a walk. Your choice." Arlie slides his hands from my shoulders to my waist.

I turn into him. "I have something in mind."

"You do?"

"Uh-huh." I trail my hand down his T-shirt, then tug the material up from the bottom before dragging it over his muscles and slipping it from his head.

"What do you have in mind?" He eyes me curiously when I skirt my fingers over his abdominal muscles, only stopping when I reach the top of the waistband of his pants. Arlie's breath hitches in his throat. "I'm not sure if I know what you want."

Wiggling my fingers below the material has Arlie's eyes growing wider, and a cheeky-as-fuck smirk tugging at his lips.

"You're beautiful," he mouths, right before I fold my fingers around his very strained erection, causing his lips to slightly part. "Does this mean I'm going to meet Miss Priscilla and possibly eat some KFC for dinner?"

I try not to snicker, but I fail. "Uh-huh."

Arlie runs his hand into the back of my hair as I move mine in an up-and-down motion, gripping him firmly. His pupils grow. His eyes become animalistic when he tugs my hair gently and lays his lips softly upon mine.

I'm sober, I'm scared, but I'm also excited.

We don't get the entire distance from the beach to the bedroom. We only make it through the front door when Arlie pins my body against the wall. His hips move back and forward to the rhythm of his tongue swirling in my mouth. Arlie's hungry, and he's showing me how much with each movement he makes.

He groans when he rips my dress over my head. He curses when he slips his hand inside my panties, pressing his finger against my throbbing bud.

"Bedroom," I moan into his neck.

Arlie doesn't reply. His eyes seek mine as his finger slides over my clit and stills at my opening.

"Oh, fuck," I call out when he lunges deep inside me.

"Are you okay?" His lips hover over mine.

"Uh-huh, uh-huh, uh-huh." I press my mouth to his.

"I want to watch you," he says, tipping his head back and moving another of his fingers deep inside me.

"Arlie." I hold my breath and ride waves of an impending climax rolling through my stomach.

Arlie's lips curl, and his eyes widen farther the more my release builds. I fight it. I'm mentally trapped in a moment of pure heaven and pure hell.

"It's okay. You're okay." He kisses my lips, and it's like Arlie senses my body's resistance. He quickens the pace, and I close my eyes and throw my head back, moaning so loudly I can't seem to stop.

Arlie's free hand tangles in my hair. He gently moves my head forward.

"Oh, God. Oh God, uh, uh." And with an explosion building uncontrollably, I throw my hand down between my legs and cup it on top of his. I instantly shudder. "Holy shit, holy shit," I pant, trying to calm my breathing and my shaking legs.

"I've got you, babe," he whispers right before his lips press to mine.

I'm breathless. I'm trembling, and my brain has left this atmosphere. Holy bananarama. So this is what sex feels like when not intoxicated.

Arlie places two fingers against his lips. His eyes darken in a devilish manner as he slides his fingers into his mouth, curling his lips around them. When he drops his arm by his side, he whispers, "KFC box. I get it now. Finger-licking fucking good."

I bite down on my lip, terribly flushed, slightly uncomfortable, but completely turned on.

I squeal when Arlie scoops one arm around my legs and throws me over his shoulder. He practically runs up the staircase. The mattress catches my body when he rests me down.

Arlie strips away his pants faster than I can blink. He's erect and pre-cum drips from the tip of his cock. "Babe," he says, climbing between my legs and placing his fingers into the lacy panties I'm so glad Chris threw into my luggage. Arlie pulls them down. "This is going to be quick. It's been two years … I'm pretty sure I'm going to be a two-pump chump, but I promise, in another ten minutes, I'll start again and keep going until you're completely satisfied."

Arlie and his honesty—it never ceases to amaze me.

"Protection," I say, as he slides his hand up my back and unclasps my bra, tugging it away.

"I've got some, don't worry." He's moving so fast I can barely catch my breath.

The sound of a drawer opening, then closing has my heart rate increasing and my breathing rapid. Arlie stalks down the bed until his hands splay across the mattress on either side of my head. "Are you ready?"

I nod.

"Are you sure?"

I nod again.

Arlie's weight shifts when he removes one of his hands and traces a line between my breasts and down my stomach. He reaches between my legs, readying himself at my entrance.

I jolt when he presses his hips forward slightly. His hand returns, and his eyes find mine.

"Take a deep breath." His voice deepens to a semi-growl.

I do. Arlie kisses across my jawline, down my neck, and continues to do so until he's kissed every part of my breast around my nipple.

When he flicks his tongue, I moan before he sucks my nipple between his lips and presses his hips forward a little more. I hiss air between my teeth, widening my legs farther.

Arlie jerks his head back. His eyes connect with mine.

I bite down on my lip as he slips his hand behind my neck. The expression in his eyes is one of torture. He's not in pain physically, but I can tell he's trying to refrain from thrusting hard into me even though it appears he wants to.

"I ... I'm okay."

Arlie slowly lifts my head from the bed. He stills, then throws back his head at the same time as he pushes his entire length so deeply inside me I curl my head into his neck and pant excessively.

"Fuck," he roars as he rolls his hips and keeps my head supported. His speed builds much quicker than I thought it would. His movements are faster and harder with every second that passes, and the more he moves the more my insides quiver. Arlie's groan vibrates in his throat, and I'm struggling to breathe.

"You're okay, babe." Arlie's voice is distant but with me. "God, you're beautiful," he growls as I ride the differing sensations ploughing through me, and he suddenly jolts and roars at the same time.

He stills, then rests his forehead against mine. "Worth the wait." His eyes soften, matching his smile and tone.

"Worth the wait." I half laugh, completely and utterly exhausted.

I lie in his arms. He runs his fingers up and down my stomach below the sheets.

"Give me five more minutes, and I'm ready to show you what I can do."

Five more minutes? I'm going to need at least another twenty so I can find my equilibrium and bring it back to Earth.

Chapter Thirty-Five

Sexcapades: Incredible, mind-blowing, earth-shattering. I can't get enough, and I seriously want to jump Arlie's bones every single time my eyes fall to his. Who knew orgasms were so addictive?

For the past four days, Arlie and I have screwed every single moment we could. It's been a sex-a-thon, and last night was no exception. That's probably why I'm beyond exhausted this morning. Day fourteen, and I'm not ready to leave Heart Key in a week. I've learnt so much about myself here, and I'm not sure why it's taken me this long to be comfortable in the presence of a man, but maybe I've needed one guy who is more special than all the rest. Arlie Blight is that guy for me.

"Good morning. I have something for you." Arlie swaggers in my direction in only his hot pink boxer briefs while holding a silver tray.

"What's this? Breakfast in bed again? You spoil me." I scrunch up my nose when I come to sit on my bottom.

"A bit sore?"

"I'm okay."

"You're not. I've told you, you need a little downtime, but you're refusing to hear me."

"I'm fine." *I am fine even though my pink lady taco feels as though she's been stomped on multiple times.*

"Pancakes?"

"You read my mind."

Arlie pecks my lips when he lays the tray onto my lap.

"Are you eating with me or going for a run?"

"I'm staying," he says, climbing onto the bed.

"What's today's task?" I ram a forkful of pancake into my mouth.

"Zip lining."

"What?"

"Zip lining. It's where you throw yourself off somewhere high, like in our instance a mountain, and you zip from the top to the bottom."

"I know what it is, but I've never done it."

"You'll be fine. I promise." Arlie presses his sticky maple syrup-sauced lips to mine. "You said you couldn't ride a horse bareback, and you've done it. You also said you couldn't windsurf, but how much fun was windsurfing?"

"So much fun."

"You've climbed a coconut tree."

"Like Fletcher."

"Yes, like Fletcher ... you told me. You've gone scuba diving."

"I have. Seriously, how beautiful was the coral?"

"Spectacular."

"We'll have to find a way to come back here."

"We will."

"Promise?"

Arlie nods. "I think if you can do all those things, then zip lining will be a piece of cake. If you're too sore, though, use an out card."

"No. I'm not backing down. I'm giving everything a go."

"Good girl."

The harness is pulled tight across my chest before Arlie re-checks the straps at my hips.

"Are you sure you know how to fasten this properly?"

"I've done it a million times, babe. You're going to be fine. I promise." Arlie places his lips to mine and claims my mouth for only a moment.

"I can't do this." I'm rattled.

"You can. I believe in you."

I'm shaking with each step that draws me closer to the edge. I fix the glove on my right hand. I take a deep breath and lean back like Arlie said to do once he connects me to the line.

"Okay. Ready?"

"No."

"Three, two, one, go," he shouts.

I squeeze my eyes together and scream so loud my throat burns. I shoot open my eyelids and laugh.

"It's beautiful," I shout. "So beautiful." A gully of trees below and endless sky surrounds me. "So amazing." I cheer as I soar as freely as a bird, more free than I've been in so long.

The zip line becomes shorter and shorter. I drop my legs and pull my body back, ready for the impact at the bottom, as Arlie instructed I do. It's nowhere near as rough as my mind had tricked me to believe it would be.

I did it.

There are no screams when Arlie comes into view just a lot of woo hoos, laughing and fuck yeahs, but no screaming coming from his lungs.

When he reaches the ground, I rush towards him. He doesn't hesitate to hoist me up until I'm clinging to the front of him.

"Such a rush." His smile says it all.

"I loved it."

"Do you want to do it again?"

I bob my head. "Yep!"

"You're turning into a real adrenaline junky. You know this, yeah?"

I bob my head again.

"Okay, but first I want to give you something, and I want to talk to you about something."

"Me?" I point at my chest.

"Yes, you."

"Okay. What's up?"

Arlie gets down on bended knee.

My heart pounds in my chest. My stomach rolls like the waves we've surfed on. "Arlie, I'm not ready to get engaged." Fear leaches onto my heart and squeezes it tight. I can't marry him yet. I love him, but it's only been two weeks. I don't want to rush into marriage.

"It's okay."

"It's not okay."

He pulls out a square box from his pocket. It's much bigger than a ring box. My fear, although still present, lessens. He opens the lid.

"A key?"

He nods.

It looks identical to the key he's been using to unlock the stores on the island.

"I want you to live with me."

"A key. To your share house?" My hands shake.

"No, not exactly. It's the key to unlock all the treasures of Heart Key."

"Oh, okay." Confusion lifts my brows.

"I have a confession to make."

"Okay." I drop to the ground in front of him. He takes my hand and places the key into my gloved palm.

"Heart Key belongs to me."

"Pardon?"

"Heart Key. It's mine. I own it."

"What now?"

Arlie's lips curl as he takes a deep breath. "Don't be mad."

I can't find any words to say so I say nothing. My brain is working in overdrive. My heart is pumping blood so quickly around my body I feel dizzy.

"There was no television show—only a documentary on my search for love." He keeps his eyes connected to mine. "Twenty-one days to see if I could find the love of my life under the charade of a 'perfect catch' show. It turns out I didn't need twenty-one days. I love you already."

I place my hand to the side of my head. I'm not quite understanding what he's saying. He owns the island. The television show was a sham. Is he even who he said he was?

"Say something."

There's a long period of quiet.

"Do you own a gym?" I don't let him answer. "Do you have a sister, and a niece, and is your mother alive, not deceased?"

Arlie's strong hands clamp my upper arms. "Babe, everything is true. Just not the type of show you're on, or my social standing."

"Social standing?"

"Melinda, I do own a gym, but I own more than one

gym. It's a chain, a worldwide chain." Arlie's eyes narrow. His lips become a thin line. Concern is inked on his face. "I don't live here permanently. I have a place in Melbourne. And I do live with my friends. However, it's a much bigger house than I let on, and when we go home, I'd like to get a place with you."

"Arlie."

My mind races. My heart beats hard. He wants me to live with him? Me? He really does love me like he says. I'm happy, so, so happy.

"Will you move in with me?"

Move in with him. Not marry him. Move in with him. I want to, so why am I not speaking?

I nod, completely gobsmacked at the fact Arlie Blight is not exactly who he said he was. But it all makes sense. His social media account was locked down like Fort Knox. He was already here when I arrived, and he knew his way around the place. He was more than comfortable in these surroundings. The kitchen he's used like a whizz kid, and he surfed the waves as if he had done so many times before. He just launched himself from the cliff above us like a professional.

"Your sister—she's been to this ..."

"Of course. She's been here, many, many times, and Aggy, too. Hazel's protective of me after Elissa. I've been hurt before, as you know, and she doesn't want me to get hurt again."

"So, are we going home to Melbourne tomorrow?"

Arlie swings his head to me and smiles. "No, not if you don't want to. But we can. It's up to you."

"Okay."

"However, you might want to make your decision after this."

"What?"

Arlie leans forward and presses his lips to mine. My eyelids instantly close as our tongues tangle.

I'm staying for at least this week.

When I open my eyes, Arlie whispers, "I love you."

"I love you."

"So you'll move in with me?"

"Yes. I will. I want to very much."

Arlie holds me tightly in his arms. I'm still shaking, but now I'm shaking because the man I've fallen head over heels in love with owns an island. Not any island, but one as amazing as Heart Key. And he wants to live with me.

Rustle, rustle, rustle.

"You can tell the cameraman to bugger off now, Arlie. You've spilled the beans."

"Yeah, not exactly."

I gasp. I leap to my feet. I squeal. "Chris," I yell, running towards him.

"I'm as shocked as you," he says when I throw myself into his arms.

"You know! What the fudge?"

Smiling face after smiling face appear. Hazel's little girl of about four with blond hair and light blue eyes identical to Arlie's. A man I don't know, but soon learn is Arlie's dad. My sister, Bridey, and my mother, who never travels. I'm left completely gobsmacked when Matthew Muller joins them.

"Melinda, I'd like you to meet Matthew." Chris appears smitten.

Holy Jesus, Joseph, and the Mother Mary. Matthew Muller in the flesh.

"It's lovely to finally meet you." He steps towards me. He's wearing a pair of cargo pants and a button-down shirt with a thick gold chain around his neck. He's even more stunning in the flesh. "You too."

I'm trembling. I'm confused. "What does this all mean?" I draw in a ragged breath.

"We have one week to relax and get to know each other. Are you okay with us doing such a thing?" Arlie's eyes find mine.

"Oh my God." I rush towards Arlie, who catches me mid-leap. "I can't believe this."

"I can't believe I finally found you. I thought you were lost and never going to come."

And—I thought he was stuck on a bus bound to Nowhere, somewhere between Single Town and Happily-Ever-After Couple Land with no prospect of ever making the destination. It turns out I was wrong. He finally found his way to me.

Chapter Thirty-Six

Six months later

Reality has been harder than our time on the island, and the place we now call home, a sweet cottage-style house in the suburbs of Melbourne, has nothing on the mansion we often occupy for weekend getaways. Our new place is humble, sweet, and relatively lush, but not overly extravagant.

My life isn't a perfect vacation filled with every luxurious item accessible, but it's the life I want, and the life Arlie knows is important to me. I wouldn't change it for any amount of money in the world even though we have plenty of that.

It's true—even crazy girls can find love, and I found love with Arlie Blight. The man who I met in a grocery store, dined with in a local Chinese restaurant, and unknowingly followed to a secret hideaway fit for a king and queen in a place called Heart Key. Who knew he'd end up being the man who owned it and a bunch of gyms around the world? Not me.

"Babe, are you nearly ready? You're going to be late for work." Arlie's light blue eyes find mine in the mirror. Toothpaste foams over my lips. My hair status is currently unruly. "God, you're sexy as fuck in those scrubs," he growls, stalking me from behind. "How do all those doctors and patients keep their hands off you?"

Arlie's wide, naked chest takes my vision as I dip my eyes downwards while looking at his reflection.

"The things I want to do to you right now are not PG-rated; they're so R-rated it would make even the most sexually prolific person blush."

I squeeze my thighs together to tame the sudden pulsing I experience, then spit toothpaste into the basin, running water over my mouth.

"Come here," Arlie says, all deep-voiced and sexy. I squeal the moment he snakes his arms around my waist and lifts me with ease, carrying me to the bedroom. "Me, Tarzan. You, Jane, and I will mate with you. No doctoring for you today."

My body bounces against the mattress when he throws me against it like he's the king of the jungle and I'm his woman to do what he wants with. He stands tall, wearing only a pair of hot pink boxer briefs, and puffs out his chest, beating his fists against it until I groan in complete discomfort.

"Oh, shit. Are you okay?" He drops to the bed.

I sit half upright, grabbing my waist.

"Did I hurt you?"

"Foot. His foot is in my ribs again." I clutch my side.

"I've got you." Arlie stacks some pillows behind my head and moves me until I rest against them. "This little fellow is going to be a kickboxer, I think."

"Agreed." I wince.

Arlie lifts my green scrub top under my breasts and places his big, strong hand high up on my ever-growing baby bump. "Dude, shove over—you're hurting Mummy, and you're kind of messing with playtime for Daddy right now."

I laugh, then wince, scrunching my face.

Small circular movements—it's how Arlie normally convinces our little rib kicker to move. "Any better?" he asks.

I shake my head. "It doesn't seem to be doing the trick."

Arlie shifts to his plan B and dips his head until his lips brush over my skin. "Maybe he wants some love and attention." He speaks against my belly before leaving small kisses in place of his words.

"He's so needy already."

"Maybe you shouldn't go to work today, babe. You should probably stay here so I can care for the both of you. You don't even have to work."

"I'm pregnant, not dying, and the little gem has just

moved so I'm good to go now."

"He's moved? Excellent." Arlie wiggles his eyebrows.

I giggle.

"Well, in that case, before you take off and save lives with outstanding medical diagnosis genius powers, I have a parting gift for you."

"You have already parted a gift inside me." I point at my rounded tummy.

Arlie throws back his head and laughs. "I have more gifts where that came from," he says, standing upright. "Now, let me take these off. I'm going to rock your world before you have to go out into the real world and kick sickness's arse."

I twist my neck and eye my watch. "I've twenty minutes until I have to leave, and I've not even brushed my hair. Can you work with that?"

"Oh, I can. I'll take fifteen minutes of your time and we'll get you in shipshape and out the door in the remaining five. Deal?"

"Bring it." I cup my palm in the air and signal for him to take what's his—*me*.

I'm his, and he's mine, and we're madly, deeply, and insanely in love. Arlie gets me and all my little quirks. He cherishes me for the crazy woman I am. Every weakness and strength I possess Arlie accepts, and no matter what happens around our happy little life bubble, it doesn't matter because we're strong enough to rise to any challenge. We have each other, and a new little baby on the way. And although we're not married and we're not exactly taking all our steps in order, we're content. Life's not about rushing things, it's about living in the moment, and I'm doing just that. Living every single moment.

"Goddamn, you're fine." Arlie runs his hands over my small bump and cups my boobs. "Yep, they're bigger than yesterday. I'm so happy."

I giggle.

"Hello, sugar dumplings, Daddy's home." It's Chris, calling out with the most feminine tone a male can possess.

Bang!

The door slams shut.

"You know you don't live here," I yell from the bedroom.

"Where are you two?" he shouts.

"Why did you give Chris a key?" Arlie lays his head to my chest. "He's the biggest kid interrupting our Mummy/Daddy playtime, I'm telling you. It's like he has a radar for when we're about to get busy."

"We'll be out in a moment," I yell, attempting to rein in my humour.

"Hurry, hurry. I have a gift for you two."

"Of course, he does." Arlie groans, causing laughter to explode through my lips.

"Get dressed," I say, trying to roll out from under Arlie.

"Can't we pretend we're not home?"

"He knows we're home."

"I'm getting the key back today."

"And what if we get locked out?"

"A locksmith, I'll call a locksmith. It's not like I can't afford it."

"Play nice. He's my best friend," I tut.

"And he's great and all, but he seriously has no boundaries."

"Are you two naked in there?" Chris's voice grows closer.

"We are. Go away." Arlie takes my hands and holds them above my head. "Fifteen minutes. Those fifteen minutes were mine," he whispers against my lips.

"I know, baby, but we have company."

"Unwelcome, gift-bearing company."

"Exactly. Now unhand me and get dressed."

"Fine," he groans, climbing to his feet and adjusting himself while sporting a pout.

Pulling down my scrub top, I straighten my pants before running my hands over my locks. "I'll meet you out there. Don't be long," I warn.

"Okay." Arlie sulks.

I stalk my way over to him, running my finger along his jawline until I pistol grip his chin. "You're my one and only," I whisper against his lips.

"I know."

"Now get some clothes on and play nice."

"Play nice. I can play nice for you."

"I love you."

"Love you, too."

I press my lips to his, and he takes my mouth in a way which speaks volumes of his frustration and hunger. For a split moment, I think maybe if we don't come out, Chris will disappear, but then I remember it's Chris, and he'd not hesitate to barge into the bedroom whether we were naked or not.

When our lips part, I twist on my heel. Arlie taps my bottom, causing me to gallop a few steps. "Tonight. We're going to resume this when you get home."

I peek over my shoulder and blow him a kiss before finding the door handle and exiting the bedroom.

"There you are." Chris's teeth are exposed in a wide smile.

"Hello, bestie. You look very chipper today. I don't have long. I need to get to the hospital." I glance at my watch. "In ten minutes."

"Sex hair," Chris blurts.

"Totally sex hair," Matthew chimes in, stepping into my view.

"Oh, you're both here. This will make Arlie extra happy." I pinch my lips together to rein in my laughter.

"Girl, have I got a big surprise for you."

"It's the best thing ever," Matt adds.

"Okay, what is it?"

"Ta-da." Chris whips out a pink bag with no store label attached from behind his back. "You're going to love it."

"Chris, is it a ..."

He giggles. "No!"

"Oh, thank God." Another vibrator is not on today's agenda for me.

"Take it." He holds it out, and I accept.

Matthew steps forward, snaking his arms around Chris's waist. "I'm so proud of you, sugar bug."

"I know you are, sugar daddy."

They kiss the moment Arlie appears.

"Get a room, you two," he snaps, annoyed.

"One seed inside my bestie wasn't enough for you? You're still violating her, I see," Chris tuts.

"Do you have any boundaries?" Arlie counters.

Chris shakes his head.

I laugh.

"Mindy, open, open it already. The suspense is killing me."

"You're killing him. Hurry up," Matthew chimes in.

"Alright already." I open the bag. I can clearly see a book inside.

"A baby-naming book?"

"Nope. So much better than a baby book."

I drop the bag to the floor and turn it over until I'm looking at the front cover. *Perfect Catch* is the title. *Even crazy girls can find love* is the tagline. C.J. Grandy takes up the bottom of the cover.

"You published a book?" There's excitement in my tone.

"Not any book. Turn it over and read the blurb."

"Okay."

Dr Belinda Trant is hopeless in love. Her life is far from where she thought it would be by her thirtieth birthday. She's broke, single, and living with her cat, Letcher. The only shining star to brighten her days is her best friend, Chris.

I burst into laughter.
"Keep reading," Chris encourages me.

But Belinda's life is about to change in the most explosive way when she meets a smoking-hot, god-like man on a game show called Perfect Catch.

Charlie Right is strong, determined, wealthy, and dominate. He's eye candy and cocky, and he knows it.

What happens when the paths of Belinda and Charlie cross?

Fireworks. A bunch of love-making fireworks.

"Is this serious?" I say.
"It is. I wrote a sexier, heat-filled story about you two."
"Is he shitting us?" Arlie doesn't look impressed. His nostrils are flaring, his eyes thin slits.
"I think it's great." I laugh.
"I told you she'd love it, sugar bug." Matthew beams with pride.
"This is the best day of my life," Chris cheers.
"Is he seriously having us on, or is this real? He just changed the beginning letters of our names." Arlie's

distress only causes me further laughter.

I guess not every love story closes with a happily ever after. Sometimes, it ends with a happily ever after and an erotica book of fiction based on your life, written by your gay best friend …

That's how this story ends.

Also by Belle

Thirty Days Trilogy

Thirty days: Part One
Thirty days: Part Two
Finding the Magician

The Game Of Life Series

One Fear
Two Footsteps
Three Breaths
Four Hearts
Five Fights

Standalones

Always You
Winner

Acknowledgements

A massive thank you from the bottom of my heart to: Kylee Harris, Liz Lovelock, Kirsty Roworth, Caroline Dayas, Jakarra Adams, Natalya Bryan, Shaelene Adams, Donna Martin, Tracey Wilson-Vuolo, Tracey Davis Zelukovic, Serena Worker, Sarah Pilcher and Robin Yatsko. I love you guys.

A massive thank you to my wonderful ARC team. I couldn't do any of this without you. You all know who you are.

To the Tinkerbelles—you're an amazing bunch of people who light up my life and keep me smiling. I love ya faces.

To my husband, Michael, whom I love dearly. It's always been you, baby.

To my beautiful children, the keepers of my soul. I love you to the moon and back.

To my wonderful team of talented and creative people, Lauren Clarke, Jaye Cox, Jenny Sims and Emma Wicker. You ladies have a talent beyond belief, and I'm so grateful to share this journey with you.

Lastly, I'd like to thank everybody who has helped to promote my work—all the bloggers, Enticing Journey Book Promotions for a wonderful promotional campaign, and all the readers. Without the readers, there'd be no purpose for these stories.

My dreams are coming true, and it's all because of you.

Thank you.

Belle Brooks xx

About the Author

Belle Brooks is a former business manager, wife, and mother of three, living in Queensland, Australia. For as long as she can remember, writing has been a major part of her life, bringing her peace and comfort in the arms of her fictional characters. Never planning to have her work published, she focused her attention on her career and family. That is until she finally found the courage to allow her words to become public for others to enjoy, due mainly to the encouragement and support of those who love her. That Guy, is her Eleventh publication.

Stay Connected with Belle Brooks

Website:
www.bellebrooksauthor.com

Facebook Page:
Belle Brooks Tinkerbells

Instagram:
@bbrooksauthor

Twitter
@Bellebrooks16

15085141R00217

Printed in Great Britain
by Amazon